HAVEN Falls

- SHERIDAN ANNE -

SHERIDAN ANNE

Unstoppable

- SHERIDAN ANNE -

Cover Design by: Sheridan Anne
Photograph: Arturkurjan
Editing and Formatting by: Sheridan Anne

CHAPTER 1

RIVERS

I stand before the house that I grew up in, staring up at it and hoping that what I'm about to do isn't going to cause any problems.

Shit. Who am I kidding? Of course it's going to cause problems. Big fucking problems.

It's Noah and Henley's wedding day, and me showing up out of the blue after four years of radio silence is bound to cause a stir. I just hope it's going to be the good kind. Noah is going to have something to say, Henley will be more shocked than anything, and Tully...fuck. I'm in for a world of hurt.

Tully is a fucking mystery. I don't know how she's going to react. It's been four long years since I saw her, and not one minute of that time has passed without me thinking about her. Thinking about what she's doing with her life, if she ended up going to college and opening that flower store that she always wanted, or if she met someone and moved on.

Fuck, why am I so sweaty?

I wouldn't be surprised if she's with someone else. She's the kind of girl who would have guys lining up for her attention, and in high school, I loved being the one who had hers. She was always mine, and not knowing if she still is has weighed on me every single day.

I'd be a fool to assume she sat back and waited for me, and she'd be a fool if she actually did. I was the idiot who told her to move on, I was the one who told her that I wouldn't be coming back, and I was the one who told her goodbye.

I never came home, and that decision haunts me every moment of every fucking day.

That wasn't part of the deal, and I know that must have cut her, but Haven Falls…this place is full of darkness, a darkness that I've worked my ass off over the past four years to forget about.

But how could I not come home for this? It's Noah and Henley's wedding day, for fuck's sake.

I knew this day would come right from the very start. My best friend fell for her hard and welcomed her into our lives with open arms, but not me. I made her work for it and prove to me that she deserved my loyalty. Naturally, it didn't take long. Henley Bronx is a force to be reckoned with. She was a fucking machine, and I don't doubt that she still is.

But what was better was finding out that the little she-devil is my sister. And not just my half-sister like we had thought or my pack sister, but my full on, blood-sharing, irritating little sister. Well…OK, maybe she's not irritating, but she's had some shining moments.

I walk toward the house. I can't put this off any longer.

Man the fuck up, Rivers. You've got this.

I don't know what I was thinking coming here, but I've got nowhere else to go. I don't know what to expect or who's inside the house. It could be Noah and his boys or Henley with the girls. All I know is that there's a shiny black limousine waiting out front telling me that no matter what, there's going to be someone on the other side of that door that's been dreaming about kicking my ass.

As desperately as I need it to be the girls in there, I'm kind of hoping it's Noah. I need to handle shit with him before anything else, but the black limo has a sinking feeling settling in my gut. I should be running for the fucking hills. I'm not ready to face her, not yet at least.

What the fuck am I supposed to say? "Hey, Babe. Sorry for leaving you high and dry for the past four years, but I'm here now. Want to be my date?"

There are no words that I could say to her that would make any of this OK. She's going to need time, and unfortunately for her, I'm not a very patient man.

Shit. Tully's going to tear me a new asshole, and she's going to enjoy doing it. Maybe I'm lucky and she's already at the wedding. Yeah…that's wishful thinking.

With Noah, he'd knock me out, wait until I regain consciousness, and then repeat it over and over again until he gets it all out of his system, but Tully…she's a mystery. You never know what you're going to get. All I know is that the outcome of this one is not going to be good. I deserve the fucking worst from her, and that's if I'm lucky. There's a good chance she won't even give me the time of day.

Why the fuck am I being such a pussy? *Knock on the door already. It's not that fucking hard.*

I let out a tortured sigh and drop my bag beside me. I got off the plane and came straight here. If I had gone back to my place, that would have just brought up a shitload of memories that I'm not ready to begin dealing with, and besides, it's not as though I had the time. I'm cutting it pretty fucking close. I'm surprised the limo is even still here. They must be late themselves.

The thought has a grin spreading across my face. I guess some things never change.

I step forward and raise my hand to the door, sucking it up and realizing that putting this off is pointless. The sooner

I get in there, the sooner I can make things right.

I hear people rushing around on the other side, and I cringe. Now probably isn't the best time to spring a visit on them. After all, there's a wedding that needs to be had. My knuckles barely brush the door before it's ripped open from the inside and a fucking angel appears before me.

My heart stops.

She's radiant.

Tully stands before me, and as her eyes rise and lock on mine, everything stands still. Tully Cage. My beautiful Tully. Over the past four years there have been many times where I thought I'd never see her again, and the fact that she's standing right here before me, tells me there really is a God up there because right now, all my prayers have been answered.

My heart kicks into overdrive. I've been in the middle of a war zone, and my heart has never beat this damn fast. I'm desperate to take her in, have my eyes travel up and down her body, but I'm locked in the moment with her wide jade eyes on mine, neither of us physically able to break the hold.

Her breathing picks up, her chest rising and falling with erratic movements and it's then I can no longer go on without taking her in.

I roam my eyes over her face and take in every little line, every little curve, every tiny detail that sets her apart from the girl I used to know. She's not the same nineteen-year-old girl I left; she's a fucking woman, and damn, it looks good on her.

Her long brunette hair is swept to the side with beautiful thick curls cascading down her back. I follow the curve of her face, down past her jaw and neck and over her body. She wears a strapless gold dress, and I'm fucking breathless.

How is it possible for one person to have such pure beauty?

The door has been open for less than ten seconds, but that time is enough to tell me exactly what I need to know:

she's not happy to see me.

I don't doubt she's been waiting for this moment and in her head, she probably has a speech already rehearsed. Seeing as though not a word has come from her mouth, I'd bet that she's kicking herself right about now. Though I'm one to talk. I've been so caught up that I haven't even said hello.

A gasp sounds behind her, and my eyes flick back. I hadn't even realized someone else was there.

I take in the silk white gown that sits perfectly over the bride's frame and the soft vale that covers her face and I can't help the smile that rips across my own. I've never seen such a beautiful bride. Henley is stunning. This is exactly what Noah's dreams are made of.

A voice to the left has my gaze shooting across the room to take in two guys, both dressed to impress in their best suits. I don't think I've met these guys before, or maybe I have. I don't know, it's been a while.

A strange familiarity pulls at me. One of them looks oddly like a dude I used to go to school with, though too much is going on inside my brain to try and work out who I'm actually referring to. Say, the piercing stare coming from the goddess standing right in front of me, the heat of her intense gaze making me want nothing more than to drown in her eyes.

"Who's this tall drink of water?" the guy on the right questions, looking me up and down as though I'm his next meal.

His question is ignored as my sister's crumbled voice cuts through the room in a pained whisper, filled with all sorts of desperation. "What are you doing here?"

I put my need to drop to my knees before Tully aside and focus on my sister. It's her big day, and I don't want to ruin it, so if she asks me to leave right now, then that's exactly what I'm going to do.

I give her a warm smile. "You didn't think I was going to miss my best friend and little sister's wedding, did you?"

At the sound of my voice, Violet's head whips up from

the mountain of dress she's been focused on in her hands and a gasp comes flying out. The need to throw myself into her arms sails through me, especially as a softness creeps into her features and tears spring to her eyes.

At least someone is happy to see me. I'd give anything for Tully to find her nineteen-year-old self and slap that hand of hers across my face. At least that way I'd have her burning touch on my skin once again.

Tully's brows furrow as Henley watches me, speechless. How is it possible that only a few seconds have passed?

I don't know how it happened, but one minute I'm focused on Tully and the next, Henley has a phone to her ear, still gaping at me as though she can hardly believe what she's seeing.

"Noah, it's me," she says into the phone in a strange tone. She pauses for the slightest moment. "I think you should get over here. He's here. Rivers has come home."

Home.

There's that word that has traveled through my mind over and over again until it started feeling like a place that no longer existed, but standing in this very doorway, I couldn't have been more wrong. Now that I'm here, I don't want to leave.

But seeing as Noah's now on his way over here, I guess I won't be going anywhere as I'll be spending the rest of my day unconscious. Crap. I knew I should have just shown up to the ceremony and watched from the back. Now their wedding is going to be delayed because of me. That's the last thing I wanted.

Tully's gaze drops to the ground before traveling in a wide arc as it makes its way back up to Henley. "I um…" Shit. That voice of an angel has me dying a million deaths. I had nearly forgotten what she sounded like, but it's pure heaven. Always has been and always will be. "I should get to the wedding and let them know things are going to be running a little late."

No, no, no, no, no, baby. Don't you dare go.

Henley nods as a sympathetic, broken sigh pulls from Violet, and before I know it, Tully reaches for the hallway table, grabs a set of keys, and hurries through the door. She gives me a wide berth and absolutely refuses to look back up at me.

The smell of her perfume lingers in the air and I just about die. That's the smell I've been missing, the smell that reminds me of having her in my arms and burying my face into her neck. It reminds me of what could have been and what I fucked up and lost.

I can't help but follow her movements as she drops down into a black car and takes off like a bat out of hell. My brows pull down. What happened to her Jeep? Though that reminds me; my Firebird is no longer sitting out on the lawn. It used to sit right outside Tully's bedroom window, but all that's there is the greenest grass Haven Falls has ever seen.

A longing instantly settles into my chest. She was so close but so far away and just the sight of me had her running.

Barely a moment has passed before Violet is dropping the train of Henley's dress and is flying into me. Her arms are thrown wide and she collects me as though she was welcoming home her son. "Oh, Rivers," she cries. "You have no idea how happy I am to see you."

"And you have no idea how happy I am to be home."

Henley catches my attention over Violet's shoulder and I watch as she demands one of the boys to lift the vale over her head so she can focus a little better. They snap to it, basically fighting over who gets to do it and I have to laugh at the way that she's still capable of ruling the people around her.

Henley was the queen of Haven Falls Private and I don't doubt that she's still the queen now.

Violet pulls back and steps out of my way. "How rude of me. Come in."

I step over the threshold and get two steps past Violet

when Henley crashes into me like a freight train. The wind is knocked out of me, but I suck it up and take it like a man because the sister I've hardly had the time to get to know is here with her arms wrapped around me and I couldn't be happier.

"Why didn't you tell me you were coming?" she demands, pulling back to look up at me.

"Because I had no idea," I tell her. "I was on a mission until two days ago…and well, shit never really goes how you think it will. I thought we were going to be out there for another month, but the second I knew we were done; I was on the first flight home. The rest of my unit are waiting at our base until tomorrow to fly home, but I knew if I left then and there, I could make it. I didn't want to miss this, Henley. Not for the world."

Her features soften and she smacks me across the chest. "Don't make me cry. I don't want to ruin my makeup."

A voice clears in the room and we all look across to the two guys who I still can't seem to place. "We're going to head down to the ceremony and give you guys a little privacy."

"Thanks," Henley says with a grateful smile. "We'll try not to be too long, but if you need to, start handing out glasses of champagne to keep everyone happy then do it."

The two boys walk out, each of them giving me a quick nod before disappearing out the door. The second it closes behind them, I look to Violet before focusing my gaze on Henley. "I hope it's alright that I came. I know I was invited but…"

"Tully," Violet sighs.

"I'm not going to lie," Henley says, giving me a warm smile. "It was definitely a shock seeing you standing at the door, but I'm happy you're here. I wouldn't have had it any other way. And you're right; Tully is most likely going to be a mess today and I have no doubt that this is screwing with her head and is going to be hard on her, but she's strong. She'll make it through to the end of the night with a smile on her face, but don't get me wrong, just because she's smiling doesn't mean things are ok. You hurt her, Rivers."

I nod my head. Everything she just said are the thoughts that have worked their way through my head time and time again. "I promise, I'm going to make this ok."

"I think you're underestimating just how impossible that task is going to be."

"Whatever it takes," I tell her, letting her know just how damn serious I am.

"Ok, but don't think you're off the hook with me. You're just lucky you caught me on a good day. I still plan on reigning down hell on you, but it's going to have to wait until tomorrow because today I'm getting married and not even you can ruin it."

"Are you sure? I'd happily stand here and let you give it everything you've got if it will make you feel better."

Henley considers me a moment before shaking her head and smiling once again. "I'm really glad you're back, Rivers, but now I have to go and check that my makeup is still in place. So no, no ass-kicking for you today, but you better come prepared tomorrow."

With that, Henley heads off down towards Tully's bedroom and I'm left with Violet asking every question under the sun about life in the military and checking up that I've been doing ok. It takes all of two seconds for her to pull me down onto the couch and dive into all the heavy stuff which has me cringing. I love Violet, but I look to her as a mother and there are some things a mother shouldn't know about a son's endless days in the military.

We're hardly two minutes into the conversation when the front door flies open and my best friend comes storming in. "Where the hell is he?" he demands.

Noah's eyes scan the room as I fly up off the couch and face him, standing tall and ready to accept any punishment he deems fit. He strides towards me with a firm set of his jaw, looking more intimidating than I've ever seen before.

Either he's perfected it over the past four years or he's just grown into a man who's had to face down things no man should ever have to face.

His hands ball into fists at his side and it's clear that some things don't change because one thing is for sure; Noah Cage is still run by his emotions.

A vision in white appears in the hallway and Noah's eye flick her way as though he physically can't help it and within the blink of an eye, everything changes.

Noah comes to a startling stop in the middle of the living room. His fists relax and he sucks in a long, deep breath, allowing the anger to fade as he takes in his bride for the very first time. "Fuck," he murmurs as she walks slowly towards him, beaming up at him as though she's never been happier.

Henley comes to a stop right in front of Noah. "Hi," she whispers as her eyes roam all over his face.

Noah glides the back of his knuckles down her bare arm and goosebumps rise on her skin. "You're beautiful," he tells her, making her smile reach right up into her eyes until they're glistening with love.

I can't help but feel as though I'm intruding on this moment but I don't dare move a muscle. Noah is a fucking bomb and despite the moment he's having with his future wife, he could detonate in the blink of an eye.

Henley takes his hands in hers and raises her chin before gently brushing her lips over his and making violet sigh with joy. "Ok," Violet says, stepping forward to physically break them apart. "Break it up. I'm not about to let you kiss the bride before the ceremony. You need to save it for later."

Noah smiles and reluctantly releases her hands which is when he turns on me.

We stand in a silent stare off for what feels like the longest moment and all I can think about is how much I've missed my best friend. I'll never admit it to him, but he's been my rock since the day I met him at just eleven years old. He was there for me without even knowing and opened his world to me, and because of that, I was able to see what being part of a family truly meant. I was able to feel love for the first time, acceptance, and happiness.

Everything positive in my life has come because of Noah, and I owe him more than he could ever know, so whatever he needs right now to make himself feel better, I'm prepared to give even if it means one hell of a beating.

He makes his move and my whole body tenses in preparation, only the hand that I expect to come flying towards my face never quite makes it. It detours and comes around my back until Noah's arms are around me, clapping my back with pride. "It's so fucking good to see you, man."

Joy like I've never known tears through me and my arms fly up around him, pulling him in tight as he welcomes me home. My hand comes down on his back just as he does the same to mine. "I've missed you, brother."

"You know," Noah says, pulling back and looking at me with his heart on his sleeve. "It wouldn't be right if you weren't standing up there beside me today. What do you say? Will you be my best man?"

I can't stop the grin that tears across my face. "I thought you'd never fucking ask."

Henley steps into our sides, taking both our hands as she looks up at us with pride. "Well, now that your cycles are back in sync, can we go and get married?"

"Do I even want to know what that means?"

"Trust me, you don't," Noah grins before looking down at his bride. He pauses a moment and that love-sick, starry-eyed look comes over him once again. He reaches around her and slowly sets the vale back over her face. "Yeah," he murmurs. "Let's make you my wife."

CHAPTER 2

TULLY

I choked.

Four long years. 1,567 days to be exact, which adds up to four years, three months and fifteen days, but who's counting?

I still can't believe it. Every day for the past 1,567 days I've thought of what I would say to Rivers if he was to ever show up on my doorstep. I was going to give him a piece of my mind and I was going to make it count. I was going to let him know exactly what kind of hell he has put me through and I was going to put him right in his place. The way he hurt me, the way I suffered, it's something I'm never going to forget and he was going to know it. I've pictured making him hurt just as he did to me, but when it came down to it; I choked.

Four long years of waiting for him and I choked.

Fuck. What the hell is wrong with me?

Why did I allow him to affect me like that? I stood there like a fool, gaping at the man before me, wondering why I was struggling to breathe. My heart took off at inhuman speeds to the point where I was terrified it was about to beat right out of my chest.

I had to get out of there, and like the little bitch that I am, I ran.

I should have stayed and laid his ass out just like he deserves. I mean, four fucking years of nothing? Not one letter. Not one text. No phone calls? I thought I meant more than that. I thought that we shared something special that was worth fighting for and I know that he had his demons, but I always figured he'd work through them and come around.

How wrong was I? I got nothing for four fucking years.

And now this? How could he just show up like that without any warning? If he intended to destroy me, then he's doing a pretty good job so far. I don't know how much more of that I could handle. I wonder how long he's staying or if he's staying at all. Maybe he was just here to say congratulations and then left straight away. Maybe I just screwed up my one and only chance to let him know what he did to me.

If that's true and he is gone…shit. I don't even want to think about that.

What am I going to do? I'm a fucking mess.

Out of all the days for this to happen, why did he have to come back today? My brother is marrying my best friend and it's supposed to be one of the happiest days of my life. Yet here I am, sitting in my car willing myself to hold it together as I stare out at all the people gathered here at the Haven Falls parklands where an incredible wedding ceremony has been set up.

I should be out there, welcoming everyone and double checking that the flowers are exactly where they need to be. If anything, I should be back with Henley, making sure she's having the time of her life and not about to bail on the best thing to ever happen to her. Though, she wouldn't. If anyone was going to bail today, it'd be me.

If everything had gone to plan, we'd be halfway through the ceremony by now, but instead, people are standing around, sipping on champagne while the bride and groom are...who the hell knows, and I'm here freaking out in my car.

Real nice, Tully. Very mature.

I guess it's time to pull it together. Spencer and Jared have been out there holding down the fort for the past twenty minutes when I should have been out there helping.

I pull the sun visor down and check my reflection only to find a crazed stranger staring back at me.

Disappointment fires through me. I looked so nice before. I had my makeup done by a makeup artist and now I look like I've just come off a three day bender with Aiden.

I try my best to fix up my makeup, but it's a lost cause. There's not a lot I can do about it now.

I double check my dress, take a few slow, deep breaths, and prepare myself to put on the show of a lifetime. I can do this. I just need to smile until the early hours of the morning and then I can go home and try to forget.

I step out of my car and start making my way towards the guests when I decide that a glass of champagne would be in my best interest. Maybe two. Hell, I better make it three just for good measure.

The rim of the champagne flute is only just brushing my lips when Spencer appears at my side, sliding his arm around my waist and drawing me into his strong body. "You look gorgeous," he murmurs, dipping his head and pressing a kiss to my shoulder.

I give him a tight smile, feeling like absolute shit for being this messed up over a guy who hasn't been in my life for over four years. Especially when Spencer was so patient with me, giving me the time I needed to be at peace and allow me to move on at my own pace. He's been incredible, despite the four rejected proposals and the moving box which has remained in my apartment for six months. At some point, that box will turn into boxes and I'll move out, but something keeps holding me back.

I swallow back the lump in my throat and give him my full attention. "Thanks. Henley picked well," I tell him, running a hand down my dress before checking him out. "You don't look too bad yourself."

Spencer grins down at me but it quickly fades from his face. "What's wrong? You look upset."

"No, no. I'm fine. Just emotional, I guess. You know, it's going to be a big day and these are two of my favorite people," I explain, feeling even worse. I mean, am I a liar now? Am I really not going to tell him what's up? That the one person who could change it all showed up on my doorstep not twenty minutes ago and has been messing with my head ever since?

Spencer holds me a little tighter. "Don't start being a girl on me now."

I roll my eyes and let out a sigh. "You're right. I'm just being silly. I'm fine,"

Spencer gives me an encouraging smile before looking up at the parking lot and quickly scanning the cars and people. "Where's Henley? I thought you were supposed to be coming with her?"

"I was, but there was a slight...change of plans. She'll be here soon and then it can get started," I explain, desperately needing to remember that this day is about Henley and Noah, not me and my crazed emotions. "But, I um...I should go mingle and say hi to the guests. You know, apologize for the delay and let them know that everything is on track."

He slowly nods his head as I step out of his arms and I do my best to put it all to the back of my mind.

I make my way around the guests. Aria is here with her dad, who has his new wife, Jackie, on his arm and her other son hovering close by her side. They're so sweet together to the point that I'm actually kind of jealous. All my extended family are here, family friends, all of the guys Noah works with at the fire department, and of course, all of our friends from Broken Hill. So, despite how I'm currently feeling, I'm sure it's still going to be an incredible day.

The black limo pulls up and Spencer, Jared, and I jump into action, gathering the guests to take their seats and make sure everything is as it's supposed to be.

Harrison starts making his way up the aisle so he can walk his baby girl back up it and I follow behind, ignoring the gasps of the guests as they no doubt take in the guy who they never expected to see.

Noah starts making his way down to stand by the alter and shakes hands with Harrison as he passes before stepping in front of me and forcing me to a stop. "Are you ok?" he murmurs low, searching my eyes and already seeing my truth.

I give him a bright smile despite the hollowness inside that's eating away at my happiness. "It's your day, Noah. Don't worry about me."

He shakes his head, not accepting that for one second. "I don't want you hurting, especially not today."

I push up onto my tippy toes and press a kiss to his cheek. "I love you," I tell him before stepping around him and continuing up the aisle.

I feel his heavy gaze on my back, but it's nothing compared to the other intense stare I feel resting on my face. I don't know where he is, nor do I want to, but Rivers is here somewhere and I don't doubt that the next hour is going to be the hardest one of my life.

I shake it off and join Harrison at the back of the limo just in time to watch him offering Henley his hand and helping her out. She's simply stunning. I know I've been with her all morning and watched her transform from Rockstar into a blushing bride, but it doesn't change the fact that she's easily the most beautiful woman I know. Noah is one hell of a lucky guy.

I'm about to remind her of this when Aria comes racing up and crashes into her sister, giving her the warmest hug and holding on with everything she's got.

Henley's eyes come to mine over Aria's shoulder and I see the question on her lips and groan to myself. "Are you ok?" she asks, eying me with concern.

"You know, you and Noah really were made for each other." Henley grins back at me, instantly catching on to my meaning. "Come on," I tell her, looping my arm through hers once Aria releases her from her death grip "Let's get you married."

We stay hidden behind the limo until it's time to go and I have to admit, not having Rivers eyes on me for this brief moment is refreshing and gives me the time I need to catch my breath.

The music starts and the guest all turn in their seats to watch the show and I suck it up. All I have to do is walk down there and keep my eyes on Noah and Henley. It's really not that hard.

We grab our bouquets and a second later, Aria takes off down the aisle looking radiant, and before I know it, I have to get my ass moving. My feet don't want to take me, but I'm not about to ruin this for Henley and make it all about me. This is her big day and as far as she's concerned, I'm absolutely fine.

I start walking and it's not long before I'm walking down the aisle and under the canopy of flowers and fairy lights that I've spent the last week busting my ass on. It's beautiful, but it was hard work. It covers the whole wedding and is hung from the surrounding trees. It's by far my best work and it pisses me off that I'm having a really hard time enjoying it, especially when I look up at Rivers standing right between the two men in my life; Noah and Spencer.

Damn it. What's he doing there?

I should have known. Why didn't I prepare myself for this? Of course, Noah was going to ask him to be his best man.

Stupid. Stupid. Stupid.

I'd always imagined that one day I'd be walking down the aisle to him. Who would have known that it'd be like this?

Rivers' eyes bore into mine and my heart races. I shouldn't be feeling like this. I should be hating on him and cursing him out yet all I want to do is run to him and throw myself into his arms while he tells me that it's all going to be ok. I've missed him so fucking much.

My soul has cried out for him every day for the past 1,567 days and I want nothing more than to be completely consumed by him.

My eyes have a hard time moving from his as my chest rises and falls with my wild emotions. He stands before me in his formal military dress suit just as he was wearing earlier and my heart screams for him.

He's not the teenage boy that I once knew. He's a man now and despite him being larger than life at nineteen, he seems to be so much more now. He's just as much a mystery, but something tells me he's a completely different mystery than the one he was before.

He looks taller, bigger, and broader, and damn, does it look good on him. My knees are weak and I'm struggling to make it down the aisle.

Just a few more steps to go.

Those wicked eyes of his remain on mine, silently begging for forgiveness and it's too much. Way too much. I tear my eyes away, unable to cope with the emotional trauma. My eyes come to a stop on Noah, hoping he'll be able to offer me something to help me down the rest of this aisle, but when they get to him, all I see is pity.

It's then I glance across at Spencer. In fact, it's then I remember Spencer.

Shit. I must be an awful person. Here we are at this moment and all Spencer would ever want is to watch me watching him as I walk down the aisle, instead, he's just watched me with my eyes glued to another man, that man being Rivers of all people.

Spencer's whole body is tense, his jaw clenched, and his hands balled into fits. As my eyes meet his, I see accusation after accusation. He had assumed something was wrong earlier and instead of being open and honest about Rivers being back, I kept it quiet. I should have told him, but instead he was most likely blindsided just as I was. I was too busy thinking about myself and the hurt in his eye tells me that he's not too impressed with me right now.

My heart breaks for him and I send a silent apology his way. The look on my face has Rivers whipping his gaze around to Spencer. He looks between us both for a brief moment and it takes him all of three seconds to figure out that I didn't spend the past four years waiting for him. I moved on and I swear, I have never seen another human look so crushed in my life.

Great. Now they're both hurt, but only one of them has the right to be. Rivers told me to move on so he can't be pissed off that I did.

Having Rivers know that I've been with someone else all this time is almost like having your boyfriend discover you've been cheating. The thought of him being hurt over this cuts me, but it shouldn't. I've done absolutely nothing wrong and it's not like Rivers was ever mine in the first place.

This freaking sucks. I can't wait for the reception. I'm going to clean the bar out and drown in my sorrows, hopefully avoiding anyone with a penis, including Noah.

How fucking long is this aisle? It's only a handful of steps from the top to the bottom, but it feels like it's been a lifetime.

I tune all three boys out and keep my gaze on Ari. She looks gorgeous. She's ten years old and is quickly turning into a beautiful young woman with amazing qualities and morals. She's going to be nothing like Henley and I were. She's going places much further than we are and I'm so glad she's been able to learn from our mistakes.

I take my place beside her and turn my gaze to the end of

the aisle as the guests stand for the bride.

Henley walks down with her arm looped through her father's and tears in her eyes. My heart swells, finally for all the right reasons. I couldn't be happier for the two of them. They're so crazy in love that it's nauseating.

Noah was heading down a bad road dating girls like bitchy high school cheerleaders. He nearly learned that lesson in a life-changing way which is when Henley came along and changed the game, setting the bar for the rest of us.

I hope one day that I can have something like that. Well really, I've been with Spencer for three years and I'm doing my best but sometimes the feelings aren't quite there. Don't get me wrong, I really like the guy and I certainly have love for him. He's sweet and caring and always puts my needs first. He's the perfect boyfriend and every day I fall for him just a little bit more, but it's been a long road and given enough time, maybe another few years, we might just make it over the finish line

Henley takes Noah's hands at the end of the aisle and the rest is history. I forget about Rivers and I forget about Spencer despite both their eyes remaining solely on me.

I watch the ceremony and tear up as they say their vows. I don't think I have ever witnessed anything quite so beautiful, but then it all comes to an end and they start making their way back up the aisle as husband and wife, making my world come crashing down around me once again.

I hesitantly walk forward. If Rivers is Noah's best man, then that means…shit. I am not ready for this.

Rivers offers me his arm and I look down at it knowing that this one touch is going to destroy me. I let out a breath. It's just walking up to the end of the aisle and then that's it, I can hurry away after that.

I can do this.

Wait. I'm going to have to dance with him at the reception.

Fuck me, this shit is too much.

My hand curls around his elbow and I ignore the way my skin burns against his strong arm. He's wearing his suit jacket so it's not as though my skin is even against his, but it's more than enough.

We start making our way up the aisle and it doesn't go unnoticed that Spencer walks behind us, accompanying one of Henley's college friends while his eyes shoot daggers into our backs.

Poor Spencer. He doesn't deserve this.

We get halfway up the aisle when River's low, murmured voice cuts right through to my soul. "Can we talk?"

I shake my head ever so slightly while still trying my hardest to maintain my fake smile for the guests. "We have nothing to talk about. You left four years ago and never came back. You and me…whatever we had is long gone," I tell him as I pull my hand free from his arm while taking the final step up the aisle. "I've moved on and you should too."

With that, I walk away, willing the tears to stay at bay.

CHAPTER 3

RIVERS

The music sounds around us, drinks are flowing, and the guest are having an incredible time. All but one. The maid of honor has spent more time at the bar than any other guest, drowning herself in alcohol.

I watch her time and time again, get up from the bridal table, head across the room, and order herself another drink. I can't take it anymore, but just as she pointed out, I left years ago and now she's moved on.

Yeah fucking right. I've never heard a bigger lie in my life.

If she had moved on, she'd be sitting right here next to me with a smile, asking all about my time in the military and catching up. Instead, she's fucking miserable and it's absolutely killing me.

I should have just stayed away, I should have watched from afar and given her the night to enjoy herself, then maybe tomorrow have let her know I was back and given her space before showing up on her doorstep. But then, standing up there beside my best friend as he married his girl meant the fucking world to me and despite my very presence making things hard for Tully, I wouldn't have changed it for anything.

She's strong. She'll get past the ceremony. She needs to as I have a feeling things are only going to get harder from here on out as now that I've seen her again, I'll never be taking my eyes off her.

I did it all ass up and now she's a mess and not only has she got me to worry about, but it's clear that my being here is causing some sort of issues between her and Spencer.

But seriously? What the fuck is she doing with that guy? Spencer fucking Jones. He was nothing but a fuckwit in high school, constantly running his mouth and seeing how much pussy he could get. She's so much better than him, but then, I guess I'm not that much better.

Tully returns to her seat with a drink in hand and I scowl across at Spencer. If he's her man then he should be doing something about this. He should be taking care of her, keeping her from this reckless behavior, and treating her like his queen, but he's too fucking busy thinking about himself. The need to knock the fucker out has never been so strong.

Don't fucking tell me this is the bullshit she's been dealing with since I've been gone. Thank fuck for Noah and Henley keeping her grounded. I don't even want to begin to think where she'd be without them.

Noah and Henley are pulled away by the photographer who want to take a million pictures of them doing the same boring shit over and over again and it leaves me, Tully, and Spencer at the table, each one of us looking down at our hands. I mean, this is awkward as fuck. If Spencer would just piss off, I could move in beside Tully and try to talk things through, but something tells me the bastard isn't letting her out of his sight for the rest of the night.

Fuck this. The second I saw her, the decision was made. I'm moving back home. There's no way in hell that I'll be going back to live at the base, especially while things are so fucked up here. I don't need to be there all the time, besides I'm on reserve now. I've just come home from a mission and have a feeling it will be a while before I'm deployed again, it ever over the next four years. At least I fucking hope so.

I'm twenty-three years old and fell in love with Tully cage at eleven and that feeling didn't go anywhere while being away and if that kind of time doesn't do anything to fade what's in my heart, then nothing will.

I'm getting my fucking girl back if it's the last thing I do.

Tonight isn't the night though. I need to give her space to wrap her head around this and figure out what's going on inside her. She's always been so fiery. Noah calls Henley 'Spitfire' but I always thought the name was more appropriate for Tully, but the fucker stole that one and locked it up. Don't get me wrong; the name definitely suits Henley as well.

I get up from the table and head across the room. There are a lot of people here who I haven't seen in a very long time and catching up with them should be a good distraction from the drunken, emotional wreck across the room.

I start with Eddison and Violet, they've both been a massive part of my life since I was a kid. They took me in when they didn't even realize they were doing it and I'll be forever grateful for their hospitality.

I spend a good hour going from table to table, saying 'hey' to all the guys I used to hang out with at school. It's funny how whenever you see someone from another time in your life, stories from the past are always brought up and laughed about, especially when everyone has had a few drinks and are slightly buzzed. Next up, the Broken Hill crew.

Before I know it, the emcee is calling everyone back to their seats and main meals are served. I let out a sigh of relief. At least now Tully will have some food in her stomach to soak up all that alcohol, though, that's assuming she actually has an appetite and eats it. A lot could have changed in four years, but something tells me she's still just as stubborn when it comes to looking out for herself.

Speeches are had and I even get myself up there, telling as many embarrassing stories about my best friend as I can think of on short notice. Though, it's not hard. When you're deployed and all alone with your unit, sometimes your stories are all you have.

The boys I was out there with know all about my pack. They know them just as close as I do just as I know their families and loved ones without having ever met them.

As I talk about my fond memories growing up with the kid addicted to ink, I can't help but mention Tully over and over again as for a long time, it was just the three of us. As her name slips from between my lips, I look over at her, loving how her eyes are glued on me with a fond smile playing on her lips as she listens to what I have to say. It's clear she's fallen into the past, reliving those incredible moments right along with me.

I finish my speech and move my ass along. I could stand up here and talk for hours about Noah and Henley which I guess is a stark contrast from the dark, silent type that I used to be.

Desserts are served and then Noah and Henley are finally invited to the dancefloor for their first official dance as husband and wife. This usually isn't my favorite part of weddings, I'm usually the one in Tully's position; silently drinking in a dark corner, but this dance means one step closer to the bridal party being asked to join them.

I'm no dancer, but as Noah's best man I have to dance with the maid of honor and I've never been so fucking thrilled to be able to put my hands on her.

Their first dance seems to go on forever, but when the emcee announces the rest of the bridal party to join them, I get up from my seat like a smug asshole.

There's nothing better than seeing the scowl on Spencer's face as he walks across to offer his hand to Henley's friend from college and I place myself before his girl and offer her my hand.

Tully gets up, ignoring my hand while also avoiding looking at me. We walk out onto the dancefloor side by side and the fire burns within me as I place my hand at her lower back and she flinches from the touch. I ignore it as best as I can and hate how it fucking cut as I lead her around to stand before me.

She reluctantly places her hands around my neck and I curl mine around her, pulling her in close, but not being as much of a dick to crush her body against mine despite how badly I want to.

Tully keeps her eyes locked over my shoulder, still refusing to look at me, but for now, I'm content just to stay here in her arms. That is until her body tenses and she looks as though she's going to bolt.

I can't resist it any longer. "Hey," I murmur as I release a hand from around her waist and run my thumb over the heated skin of her wrist. "It's me."

Her eyes rise to come to mine and I break at the devastation within them. "I...I don't know what to say to you."

"You don't need to say anything. There's plenty of time for that. Just be here with me and enjoy your night."

She shakes her head ever so slightly, trying not to draw attention to us, but she's overthinking it. She needs to relax and if I was to ask, she'd tell me no, so I make my move, not giving her the option.

My arms curl tighter around her waist and I pull her in, sliding one hand up her back and holding her close to me by the back of her neck. She resists for a second, but it doesn't take long before she's sinking into me and resting her head against my chest right where it fucking belongs.

Home.

Tully's hand comes down and sits over my heart as the other remains around my neck. I don't even know if she realizes that she's doing it, but her fingers curl into the back of my hair, just like they used to.

The music wraps around us as our bodies sway from side to side, neither one of us giving a shit about actually putting effort into our dance. At this moment, all that exists is us. My mind tunes out Henley and Noah who both continue looking over here, making sure Tully hasn't broken down into tears, and I sure as hell tune out Spencer whose sharp glare hasn't left my back since I rose from the table.

The way she melts into me and the way she seems to relax for the first time all day tells me that she's still mine. The way she looked at me while walking down the aisle and the way she can't seem to catch her breath around me. She's affected by my very presence and I fucking love it.

Tully might be with Spencer, and I'll do my fucking best to respect that, but she doesn't love him, not like the way she loves me. She doesn't even need to say it for me to know it. It's in her actions, but more than that, it's in those beautiful eyes.

The question is; how do I go about making it up to her for all the shit I've put her through and earning her trust back to the point that she'd even consider being with me?

The announcement is made for the rest of the wedding guests to join the dancefloor and if only now just realizing what's happening, Tully pulls back from me and looks up in horror.

Wordlessly, she pulls out of my arms and walks away, snatching her drink off the table in the process before walking straight out the back door.

I want nothing more than to go after her, but from the corner of my eye, I notice Spencer already on his way, and the tense hold of his shoulders tells me they're about to have it out. Maybe I should be backing off and giving them a little privacy to sort out whatever the fuck they've got going on.

I go and order myself a beer before heading out the front exit for some air. Tully and Spencer went out the back so they should have plenty of space to sort themselves out. I walk around the gardens of the nicest manor house in Broken Hill. This place is huge and is the top-rated venue for wedding receptions and big events in the area, and it shows by how incredible the night has been.

I sit down on a stone bench and sip my beer. It's been a long fucking day and even longer since I slept last. In fact, I haven't slept since the moment I realized I was coming home.

It was a long flight in shitty weather and all I could think about was what I was going to say to her and what I could possibly do to make this all ok. I didn't have the intention of staying, but now that I've seen her and felt her in my arms again, I won't be letting go. I was a fool at nineteen and wasn't ready to let someone into my life, but all that darkness is in the past and I'm home, ready and willing to make it happen.

My beer runs dry and I decide that I've wasted enough time out here. I should be inside enjoying this night that will never come around again.

I'm just about to push my way inside when yelling from somewhere on this huge property is carried over the night. There's loud music coming from inside, but it doesn't mask the sound that's so damn familiar to me. After all, I've been on the receiving end of that particular tone many, many times and it's not somewhere anyone wants to be.

I try to ignore it. All I have to do is push open the door and head back inside.

She's not a teenager who needs me to come and rescue her anymore. She's a grown-ass woman who, hopefully, has her shit together. I've been dying to know what happened with her business degree and if she ended up with that store, but I didn't want to ask. I think if I found out that it didn't happen for her, I would have been searching for a way to come home and make it happen despite it being important that she achieve it on her own.

Tully's voice tears through the serenity of the gardens and

has my hand falling off the door handle. I'll just check on her real quick, make sure she's safe, and then back off. I know Spencer had followed her out, but you never know what's going on. Perhaps she shooed him away and she's yelling at someone else, now in need of help.

I start heading around to the back of the property. They have lights all around, but being nearly midnight, it's not particularly easy to see. Though, navigating this shit is like a walk in the park compared to the things I've been through over the past four years.

The back part of the manor has endless manicured lawns with one of those ridiculous hedge mazes that you only ever see in movies or when people have way too much money to figure out what to do with it.

I find Tully almost immediately. The lights from the manor glisten against her golden dress, showcasing exactly where she is on the property. She sits on a bench, similar to the one I'd been on earlier with Spencer standing before her. Though, maybe pacing is a better word for it.

I stand in the shadows and I make my way towards them, ready to jump in and help her out if she needs it, but something tells me that she can handle herself pretty damn well. I know she could in high school and now she's had a few extra years to perfect it.

"Just…FUCK!" Spencer roars, instantly putting me on edge as he stops pacing to stare down at her. "Did you know he was coming? Have you been hiding this from me?"

Tully throws herself to her feet while crossing her arms over her chest and trying to keep warm on this chilly night. "Are you kidding me? How would I have known that? He literally just showed up out of nowhere this morning. Trust me, I'm just as surprised as you were. But what does it matter anyway? I'm with you now."

"Really? You could have fooled me," Spencer scoffs, only managing to piss me off a little more with the way he neglects to realize his woman is shivering. I mean, is it that fucking hard to offer the girl standing two feet in front of you your jacket? "You looked like you had no idea who you were with on that dance floor and you've been a mess since you arrived at the ceremony."

"Seriously?" she yells, throwing her hands up. "What were you expecting? Rivers was a huge part of my life for a very long time and he just showed up after four years. Please, tell me how I'm supposed to be feeling right now and I'll magically make it happen for you."

"There's no need for the sarcasm."

"Give me a break, Spence. It's not like this is easy for me."

"Yeah...nothing ever is with you."

"What's that supposed to mean?"

"It means that I just proposed for the fourth fucking time and I still haven't gotten your answer, though I guess I won't be fooled, it's always 'no' when it comes to you."

The fuck?

"That's not fair," Tully shoots back at him. "I'm twenty-fucking-three. I don't want to be married yet and I told you that when you asked me six months ago and again last year. It's like you're not even listening to what I want."

"What about what I want?" he demands. "There are two people in this relationship, you know? I'm tired of constantly waiting for you to figure out what you want, though to be honest, I don't think you have a fucking clue what you want. Or maybe you do and you're just too scared to say it."

Tully shakes her head. "Don't. This has nothing to do with him. I agreed to move in with you, didn't I?"

"Come on, babe," Spencer groans in frustration. "That was six months ago and you've only managed to pack one box, and now that box has dust on it. You and I both know that you only agreed to move in with me because you felt bad for rejecting my third proposal."

"Spencer," she sighs as the emotional turmoil of the day gets too much. "I just...I don't...I'm not ready."

"Yeah…you're never fucking ready." I go to step in as that was a low fucking blow and after the day she's had, that's the last thing she needs, but his next question has me stopping and anxiously waiting. "You still love him, don't you? After everything that he's put you through, he's still the one you want."

"This again? Really, Spence? Are you that insecure that you need me to tell you over and over?" She steps into him, grasping his forearms as she looks up at him. "I love you and you know that."

Well, well, well. It seems we have a liar on our hands.

I've been on the receiving end of one of her 'I love you's' and that's certainly not the way she looks at a man she loves. That was forced. That was something you say out of habit to make a situation go away. That was Tully desperately trying to cling onto the guy who's been by her side since the day I went away.

This woman standing before me isn't the one that I knew. This one holds back her feelings and hides her truths. She's not open and forcing her thoughts, hopes, and dreams on him. The Tully I knew was always wanting to talk 'feelings,' always wanting me to be open, and above anything else, she loved hard. She wasn't fake with me. Never fake.

This woman before me is the picture of someone who's already given up. She might love him, but it's not in the all-consuming way it was with me. She has everyone fooled, even Spencer, and that line of 'I'm not ready' is absolute bullshit. Tully has no intention of ever being ready with him because she already knows what it's like to feel a love so strong that you can hardly breathe. She had that with me and she's not the kind of girl to settle for less.

Any other time, I'd be thrilled to be overhearing this conversation. Watching her walk down the aisle and realizing that she was with someone else was shattering, but I should have expected it. She's fucking beautiful and everyone can see it. But discovering that she's been settling for less and suffering through a relationship just to have a companion by her side breaks my heart. Who knows, maybe she thrives on feeling his love in return. After all, I starved her of that and it's damn clear that Spencer has been giving it to her in spades.

I kind of feel sorry for the bastard. It wouldn't have been easy trying to fill my shoes and failing at every turn. She would have constantly been comparing him to me, and now that I'm here…well, I couldn't imagine being in his position. He'd be terrified of losing her.

Spencer breaks free from her hold on his forearms and steps back. "Don't you ever notice how you never actually answer the question? Maybe I wouldn't be so insecure about it if you were straight up with me for once," he tells her. "So, what is it, Tully? Do you love him or not?"

Tully shakes her head and I don't doubt there are tears in her eyes that makes me want to knock him the fuck out. "Don't do this," she begs. "You're going to ruin us."

"Answer the question, Tully."

She lets out a barely audible sigh and I find myself inching closer while trying to remember to stay hidden in the shadows. "No," she finally whispers. "I don't."

Spencer nods slowly, watching her through narrowed eyes as disappointment spreads across his face. He backs up another few steps. "I never took you for a liar, Tully." And with that, he walks away, leaving my girl shivering in the cold and dropping down onto the bench with her head buried in her hands.

CHAPTER 4

RIVERS

Seeing Tully like this tears me apart and I have no option but to step in. I can't have her feeling like this. I need to help her forget and something tells me that today, there's only one way to do it.

I duck back inside the party and head straight for the bar, leaning against it as I wait for the bartender to finish up his previous order. He looks to me with a nod. "What can I get you?"

"Bottle of Vodka, thanks." The bartender gets to work and reaches for a shot glass and I shake my head. "Nah, man. I'm going to need the whole bottle."

His brows crease and he watches me for a prolonged moment, trying to work out if I'm crazy or just a little unsure how this works. "I'm sorry, Sir?"

"The bottle."

He shakes his head. "I can't do that."

"Yeah, you can," I tell him. "Look, I'm not trying to be a pain, but I wouldn't be asking if I didn't need it."

"Need it?"

I let out a frustrated sigh and turn to look through the big glass windows covering the back of the room. "See that girl way out there? The maid of honor," I say, pointing Tully out in the dark of the night. The bartender nods and I continue. "Her boyfriend is a real asshole."

"Boyfriend?" he asks with a sigh. "Shit. She's spent most of her night right here at my bar. I assumed she was just into me."

"Nope. Bottle."

His eyes flash back to her before coming to me. "Fine. But if anyone asks, you didn't get it from me." He goes about grabbing the bottle and discreetly passes it across the bar while looking out for his superiors. I roll my eyes. I'm not in the mood for this childish bullshit. I just want to get out there and make sure she's ok.

I grab the bottle around the neck and stalk out the door, ignoring the people calling my name, all wondering where I've been for the past half an hour.

I push my way out the door and this time, I don't dare hesitate. I beeline straight for her, removing my jacket as I go.

She's too caught up in her emotions to notice me approaching which for the first time, I don't want to scold her about as it gives me a chance to get close without her telling me to fuck off in the process.

As I step up behind her, I can't help but breathe her in. She's so fucking beautiful and that smell is the most potent drug to me. So enticing, intoxicating, freeing. It's the smell of everything good and pure in my life and I don't know how I possibly went four years without it.

I drape my jacket over her shoulders and her back stiffens. She doesn't need to turn around to know that it's me. She senses it just as I would had it been her behind me.

A soft sigh slips through her lips as I silently drop down on the bench beside her. I hand her the bottle of Vodka and she doesn't hesitate for a second taking it from me. The idea of her drinking the night away makes me feel sick but there's nothing anyone can say that's going to change her mind about this, so if that's what she needs to do, then I'll be sitting right by her side the whole time, making sure she doesn't do something reckless.

She lets out a broken sigh and I find myself looking across at her. Mascara is smudged under her eyes as tears continue rolling down her face. It kills me. I hate seeing her like this and I hate it more that I'm the reason those tears are there.

I look away knowing that she wouldn't want me watching her like this. She has far too much pride.

Tully breaks the seal on the bottle and within seconds of handing it to her, she's tipping the bottle up and letting it slide down her throat. She cringes and grunts as it burns on the way down, but it doesn't stop her from tipping it up a second time.

She brings the bottle back down and traces her finger over the label. "You heard all of that, didn't you?"

I wince. I don't exactly want to admit that I stood there and listened to their argument, but on the other hand, she knows me well enough to know that I wouldn't have been able to resist. "He's a dick, Tullz. What are you doing with him?"

Tully scoffs as she looks out towards the garden while attempting to dry her eyes on the back of her arm. "You sound jealous."

"I am."

Her brows pull down as she turns to look at me with a desperation in her eyes that has me needing to reach out and pull her into my arms, but I can't. That's the last thing she wants right now. Those green eyes that I've been missing so damn much search mine. looking for some sort of clarification. Her voice is low and broken. "You still...?"

My heart shatters realizing that this question has tortured her just as it has for me. Constantly wondering if I still feel the same and not knowing if I've moved on. Those questions have plagued my mind and coming home to see her in the arms of another man was enough to kill me, but she should know it was her who got me through it all. There were nights I thought I'd never see morning, but knowing she was out there somewhere kept me going. She always kept me going.

She's my sunshine after a thousand storms.

I reach out and run my thumb over her cheek, capturing a tear and wiping it away. She instantly leans into my touch and I hate myself for having put her through all of this. "How could I not?"

Tully's eyes close for a brief moment as she's flooded with relief and as she opens them once again, they seem brighter than I've ever remembered.

Joining the Military was one of the best decisions I've ever made. At the time, it was what I needed and it went so far in pulling me out of the darkness that surrounded me. Without it, I would have ended up in prison right alongside my father. I was heading down a destructive road that I couldn't possibly see a way out of. I had no other options so I did what I had to do.

I've never regretted the decision to leave, not until this very moment.

Tully pulls back from my touch and brings the bottle of Vodka back to her lips. "He's not a dick, by the way. He's just…"

"Clinging onto the one good thing in his life."

She closes her eyes as though my comment wounds her, but she knows it's true. Spencer sees her slipping through his fingers and there's not a lot he can do about it. I've only been home for a few hours and already my presence has reduced her to tears.

"Yeah," she finally says. "You know, he's a good guy…he's," her eyes grow watery. "He's all I had when you left."

Fuck. I'm not even going to pretend that didn't sting.

I put my arm around her waist and pull her into my side. "Don't," she sobs, trying to pull away.

"Tully, please. Just let me be here with you."

"I can't. I'm with Spencer now."

"You're hurting, Tully, and the man who claims to love you just walked away, leaving you alone in tears. I'm not going anywhere, especially while you're hurting so bad."

She watches me for a moment with a strong desire flaring in her eyes, wanting nothing more than to sink into me and allow me to take all her pain away.

Her head finally falls onto my shoulder and I run my hand up to the bare skin of her shoulder and hold her close. She lets out a breath and the next words out of her mouth are like taking a bullet straight to the heart. "Why did you have to come back?"

"Do you want me to leave?"

"I...no. I don't want that."

"What do you want, Tullz?"

She lets out a heavy breath as I feel her tears drop onto my shirt and soak through to my skin. "I want to forget."

"I don't think that's possible."

There a short silence and something tells me that's she's far away right now, lost inside her mind. "It's my brother's wedding day. Today is supposed to be one of the best days of my life. I'm supposed to be in there with Henley celebrating, dancing, and having an incredible time, but instead, I'm out here, an absolute mess, wondering why it hurts so bad." I go to respond but something tells me that she's not quite done yet. "It's been four years. I shouldn't be feeling like this."

"I fucked up, Tully. I spent years hiding away in my father's shadow, doing all sorts of shit for him that I'll never be able to forget. I deserve to be rotting in prison right beside him. All those years I should have listened to you when you told me that I was better than that, but I was covered in darkness and I couldn't see a way out. That's all done now.

I've spent the last few years in my own hell, making up for the shit that I've done. I've grown and finally put it all behind me. Baby, I'm coming home, and it's ok to hate me and be confused. I fucked up. I hurt you and I left without an explanation so I don't expect you to just welcome me back in. I know your life has changed, but you need to know that I'm not going anywhere."

Tully brings the bottle to her lips once more and groans as the Vodka makes its way down her throat. "I'm not letting you back in, Rivers. You destroyed me and I've spent the past four years hating myself for letting you do that. You made me weak, you made me question myself, and you turned me into this person that I don't even recognize anymore. Four years, Rivers. I haven't recognized myself for four years. You left this gaping hole inside my chest and I've done everything I can possibly think of to fix it, but it's still there and it hurts more and more every day."

More tears fall onto my shoulder as she brings up a hand to wipe her face. I have to strain to hear her next words but the second they enter my brain, they're words that will never disappear. "I hate you, Rivers. So fucking much. I hate you."

The sound of her tortured sobs on my shoulder mixed with the words she just spoke will haunt me for as long as I live. "It's ok," I tell her, holding her a little tighter. "I hate me too."

We sit in silence as I promise myself that I'll do whatever the hell it takes to make it up to her. I hate her hurting and I hate her confusion. She used to be so sure of herself, so confident, she always knew exactly what she wanted, but this girl beside me isn't the Tully I used to know and I hate that I'm the person who reduced her to this.

I will make it up to her if it's the last thing I do.

Spencer hasn't helped her to find herself over the past four years. He's allowed her to hide and lose track of who she really is. Where the hell has Noah and Henley been during all of this? Aiden? Either they've all given up on her or Tully puts on one hell of a good act.

Half an hour quickly turns into an hour where not a single word passes between us. The bottle of Vodka is nearly empty and it's not until her breathing evens out and her body goes slack that I realize she's fallen asleep.

Ten minutes pass as I contemplate taking her home. If I do, that means that tonight will be over and I don't think I'm ready for her to wake up in the morning and keep me at a distance, but if I don't do something soon, she'll end up sick and I don't need any more reason to hate myself.

Just as I go to scoop her into my arms, a voice is heard from the backdoor of the party. "Tully? Are you out here?" I look back over my shoulder and spot Henley by the door with Noah standing at her back, his hands resting on her shoulders. They spot me in the same instance that I see them and they start making their way towards me.

I pull Tully into my arms and stand, leaving the bottle of Vodka behind. Tully curls into my chest and my heart races a little faster.

God, I've missed this.

I watch Noah's brow dip down as he takes in his passed out twin sister and he can't even wait until he's standing before me before the question comes flying out. "What the fuck happened to her?"

"She drank too much," I tell him as Henley steps in front of me and takes in her best friend. "I guess it all got too much for her and she passed out."

"Shit," he grumbles. "Where's Spencer?"

I bite my tongue and resist saying what I'm really thinking. "Good fucking question."

Noah lets out a deep sigh as Henley looks back up at him. "We should take her home."

Noah looks just about ready to cave although the very last thing he wants to be doing on his wedding night is dealing with his drunken twin sister. "I've got her," I tell them, instantly making Noah's face fall in relief. "You guys go and enjoy your night."

"Are you sure, man?"

Am I sure if I want to spend more time with my girl in my arms? What a stupid fucking question. Does he not know me at all?

"Yeah," I tell them, holding back my thoughts once again. "Besides, don't you guys have to go and consummate your marriage?"

Noah grins wide as Henley's cheek flush bright pink. "Already have," he laughs, nudging his wife. "Three times."

"The fuck? When the hell did you find time to do that? And where?"

Henley spins around and slaps a hand over Noah's mouth knowing he's more than happy to share all the little details. "You better shut it before you lose your chance at hitting this a fourth time tonight."

Noah's eyes go wide in horror as I shake my head at the two of them. I'd give anything to have what they have with Tully.

I look down at Henley. "Could you grab Tully's purse? Then I'll get her out of here."

"Sure," she smiles. "Though, are you sure you don't want to just lay her down under the bridal table with a pillow and keep partying. I'm sure she'll be fine under there."

"Really?" I laugh, shaking my head. "She already hates me as it is. Can you imagine how she'd react if she found out that I dumped her under the table so I could keep partying?"

"Yeah, you're right. She'll eat you alive."

"Come on, Spitfire," Noah says, grabbing Henley and throwing her over his shoulder. He spanks her ass before spinning around and marching off back towards the party. "The only thing getting eaten alive tonight is you. Now, is the bar still open?"

Henley looks up at me as she dangles off her husband's shoulder. She rolls her eyes and shakes her head but the joy is as clear as day. "I'll be back in two seconds."

"Meet me in the parking lot."

The door falls closed behind them and I start making my way around the building, not wanting to walk her straight through the party for the world to see the mascara all over her face and give them something to talk about.

By the time I get to the parking lot, Henley is busting out the front door with a little purse that matches Tully's golden dress. She hands it over and looks at her best friend with a tight smile. "Is she going to be ok?"

"I fucking hope so," I tell her as she balances the purse on Tully's stomach.

"Just…make sure you put water and pain-killers on her bedside table because she'll need them in the morning, and check the doors are locked, and…and maybe put a bucket beside her bed in case she gets sick."

I grin at my little sister, still unable to actually believe that's what she is to me. "I've got it," I tell her. "This isn't my first rodeo with Tully. I've been dragging her drunken ass home and putting her to bed since we were teenagers."

"I know, but…"

"I'll take good care of her. I'll even be a perfect gentleman."

Henley rolls her eyes and I sense the smartass comment on the tip of her tongue, only Noah's booming voice by the entrance of the manor cuts her off. "Spitfire, get that fine ass back up here."

She grins up at me. "Got to go."

"Use protection," I laugh. "You wouldn't want to pro-create with that thing."

Henley skips away and the sound of her scolding her new husband is the only sound I hear through the darkness. It's got to be close to two in the morning, but I really couldn't be sure. I've been so caught up with Tully that time could have stood still and I wouldn't have known.

I search through the cars for the black one Tully was driving earlier in the day and make my way towards it. It doesn't slip my mind that the last time I was driving with Tully on the passenger's side, she was almost killed.

I try to put it out of my head, but it's hard. It's something that's woken me at least once every week since it happened. With all the shit I've been involved in and the crap I've suffered through while being deployed, that's the moment that has always stuck in my nightmares, always there and ready to come back and haunt me right when I least expect it.

I fish her keys out of her purse before unlocking the car and placing Tully down in it. I can't help but look over the car, once again wondering why the hell she would have gotten rid of her Jeep. But I guess it doesn't really matter. That thing was getting old anyway, though I don't doubt that she misses it. She used to love that thing.

After sliding the driver's seat back as far as it will go, I get myself in and start the engine. This car is way too small for me. I feel like a fucking mammoth in here. My knees are practically squished up against the dash and I have to bend forward to be able to see clearly out the windshield.

I let out a sigh. I guess now that I'm back, it's time to get my Firebird fixed, but then that could take a while. Maybe I should be buying a new car and fixing up the old one on the side.

I back out of the parking spot and get Tully home. With no traffic on the roads, I get us there in less than twenty minutes and scoop Tully out of the car, thankful that Eddison hears me and opens the door.

He gives me a tight smile as I make my way past him while Violet hurries ahead and opens Tully's bedroom door. She bursts in and prepares her bed before slipping her purse off her stomach and leaving me to deal with the rest.

I place her down on her bed and start taking off her heels. It doesn't go unnoticed that her bedroom is exactly the same as it was four years ago. It's still filled with all her things, but there have been no changes. There's nothing here that tells me what her life is like now. There's nothing to give any hints about her life with Spencer and no business degree up on the wall.

Maybe she doesn't live here anymore, but that's a question that can be answered later. For now, I need to get her into bed.

I find an old shirt and pull it over her head before letting it fall around her thighs. I slip my hands under the fabric and pull down the zip for her dress before shimmying it down her body while trying my hardest to keep my word and be a perfect gentleman.

I throw the dress over the desk chair, not wanting it to get ruined from spending the night crumpled on the floor. After all, it's highly likely that Tully will wake up in the middle of the night and hurl chunks over the side of her bed.

After pulling the blanket up over her and making sure she has a bucket, water, and pain-killers, I take a step back, once again wondering where the hell her boyfriend is and why he isn't around to take care of her.

I go to walk out of her room when the voice of an angel pulls me right back in. "Don't go," Tully murmurs.

I look back to find her peering at me through slitted, sleepy eyes.

I walk back towards her and bend down, pressing a kiss to her cheek and wishing I could do so much more. "I'd do anything to be able to stay right here, but I can't," I tell her. "I have to go."

"Just stay tonight," she murmurs. "Please. I don't want you to go."

"I have to, Tullz. You might want this now, but come morning you won't and I don't want you hating me more than you already do."

"Please," she whispers.

Unable to keep myself away, I lay down on her bed beside her, instantly pulling her into my arms while remaining on top of the blanket, knowing that if I slide under the sheets with her, I won't be able to resist. "I'll stay until you sleep."

Tully nods and snuggles into my side, the same way she used to and I hold her a little tighter. She instantly falls back asleep but I find myself laying here much longer than necessary. It's not until I hear Eddison and Violet's murmured conversation in the living room that I decide it time to go.

I get up and make sure she's alright before walking out of her room and making sure to leave the door wide open. I find her parents, both giving me sad smiles from the living room. "How is she?" Violet questions, taking off her heels and rubbing her sore feet.

"She'll be alright," I tell them. "She drank a bit though so maybe keep her door open through the night. You know…just in case."

Violet nods and gets up off the couch before walking forward and placing a hand on my shoulder. "Thank you," she says. "Do you want to stay? You can use Noah's old bed."

"No, thanks," I tell her, shaking my head. "I think I'll head home. I haven't been there in a while and I guess I could use the walk to clear my head."

"Don't be ridiculous," Eddison says, reaching into the bowl by the front door and pulling out a set of keys. "Take my car and bring it back tomorrow. I don't want you walking in the middle of the night. You don't know what kind of people are out there in the middle of the night."

I thank him and take the keys while finding it amusing that it wasn't that long ago that I was the person out in the middle of the night that good parents like Violet and Eddison would have been wary of.

I get out of the house before it all becomes too much and take myself home. By the time I pull up in my drive, I'm staring up at the house in wonder.

"What the fuck is this?" I grumble, taking in all the changes. There are blinds up on the uncracked windows, fresh paint on the door, a new mailbox, and flowers in a garden.

Did someone move into my fucking house?

I was coming home and expecting to find it ransacked. Maybe kids had been using the abandoned house as somewhere to fuck around. I was expecting a broken window, boarded up door, hell maybe even some police tape. But to find it looking better than when mom was the one looking after it was something I wouldn't have expected in a million years.

I get out of the car and as I walk forward, sensor lights spring to life, showcasing the house just that bit more. I notice a blue tarpaulin covering something in the carport and decide to check it out later, for now, I need to make sure no one is living in my home.

I go up to the front door, a little annoyed that I can no longer peek in through the window. My key slides straight into the lock and my brows furrow in confusion. If I was going to squat in someone's house, I'd sure as hell change the locks.

The door creaks open with the same familiar sound and I switch on a light. The place looks fucking good. There are new carpets, new furniture, even a vase in the middle of the dining table with fresh flowers.

I creep through the kitchen and towards the bedrooms. It's only a two-bedroom home and seeing as though my room was filled with my belongings, I check the master room first.

I push the door open and switch on the light, prepared to fight off whoever I need to fight off to get my house back, only there's no one in here.

I take a quick look around and soon find myself gawking. This is just as I remember it when I was a kid. It's not the mess it was after my father's men raided through here, but the beautiful way my mother liked to keep it. There's even that old photo she took of us on my ninth birthday.

What the fuck is going on here?

I back out of the room and dive for the door of my bedroom. I fly through it and stare in wonder. This isn't a little kid's room anymore, but it's still my room. My clothes in the closet, my things on my desk, the photo of me and Tully on my bedside table.

This is my fucking room. but how? I don't understand what the hell is going on.

I pull my phone out of my pocket, not giving a shit that it's well past three in the morning and bring up Lacey's name. I hit call and wait impatiently as it rings five times. She finally answers and it's clear that she was fast asleep. "What the fuck do you want?" she groans, not very happy to be hearing from her favorite cousin at this time of night.

"What the hell did you do to my house?"

"Your house? What do you mean your house? Are you home?"

"Lace. Just answer the question."

There's a slight pause before she lets out a barely audible sigh. "It wasn't me. well, it was sort of me. I helped, but it was Tully. She fixed it up years ago and now goes back every few days to keep it nice in case you come home."

"You know Tully?"

"Yep. A lot has changed since you went away."

I stare at the house in wonder. "Tully did this?"

"Uh-huh," she murmurs. "She wanted you to have somewhere nice to call home so you wouldn't be ashamed. I know she's with Spencer now, but fuck, Sam, Tully is head over heels, crazy in love with you."

Well...shit.

CHAPTER 5

TULLY

"No, no, no, no," I groan, rolling over in my bed and slapping my hand down on my bedside table. I feel around, searching for my phone only to find a photo frame, a pencil, and a bottle of water.

What the hell? I don't remember having this shit on my bedside table. But more importantly...where is my phone? Last night was a disaster and I think it's time for damage control.

I reluctantly peel my eyes open and instantly squint into the bright sun pouring through my bedroom window. Crap, this isn't my bedroom. Well, technically it is, but it's not my current one. The question is, how the hell did I get here?

One minute I was fighting with Spencer over...*him* and the next thing I know, I'm searching for the bottom of a Vodka bottle.

In fact, I think I can still taste it.

I think the mystery of how I got from the manor to how I got here is one that will never be solved. Well, more like one that maybe I'm a little too scared to solve. Scrap that! I know exactly how I got here, but I'm cool with acting as though I don't.

My arm falls over my face, trying to block out the sun and I lay here for at least ten minutes before deciding that it's time to get up and start putting my life back together. Too much was said between me and Spencer last night while not enough was said to Rivers.

I still can't believe he is here. I'm pretty sure we talked at one stage, but truth be told, the details of last night are a little fuzzy. Actually, I better find my phone and start apologizing to Noah and Henley. I can't be sure, but it's possible that I ruined their wedding. Maybe I should double check that one with mom before I go and make a bigger fool of myself.

I push myself up in bed and the movement has the contents of my stomach churning. Shit. This is not good. I throw myself over the side of my bed while slamming my hand over my mouth. If it was in fact Rivers who brought me here, there's bound to be a bucket down here somewhere.

Just as I knew it would, the bucket stares up at me from the floor and I hastily grab it before allowing last night's mistakes to come pouring out of me.

Fuck. Fuck. FUCK! What was I thinking?

Once I've thoroughly thrown up as much as humanly possible, I sit on the edge of my bed, wondering how it all went so wrong. I've pictured the moment Rivers came back a million times. It's like a movie that plays on repeat inside my head. I was supposed to shut him down. I was supposed to kick his ass in a big way. I was supposed to show him that he means absolutely nothing to me. He fucked up and he was going to know it. He was going to lose me and he was going to feel it.

But nooo. Instead, I broke the fuck down and panicked like a little bitch. I fell right into his arms and instead of acting like the warrior queen that I've so clearly pictured, I acted like a lovesick puppy who has been starved of emotion.

Poor Spencer. No wonder he lost it. I would have too if the roles were reversed. The whole night he had to sit back and watch me pine over the guy I never even dated. He's the guy Spencer has tried over and over again to help me forget, but it's as though the task is impossible. Rivers is engraved on my heart. He's there for all eternity and that's something I've had to come to terms with time and time again.

I need to make it right, but first…I need a shower.

Pushing off my bed, I struggle to keep myself on my feet. My body is begging me to fall back into the warm sheets and try again tomorrow, but too much has happened. I need to deal with this today.

I find my purse on the end of my bed and hear the familiar beeping of missed calls and texts from inside it. I grab my purse and struggle to open it before quickly realizing that this is going to be my day.

I eventually get my phone and find three texts from Henley, a missed call from Noah, four missed calls from Spencer, and a voice mail. It's then I check the time. It's after three in the afternoon. No wonder my phone has been blowing up.

I start with the texts.

Henley – Are you ok? You were a bit of a mess last night.

Henley – What's going on? Call me when you're up.

Henley – Don't tell me you're going to sleep the day away? You better not be ignoring me or I'm going to make you pay, bitch!

Damn. I quickly hash out a response.

Tully – I'm fine. Just woke up. I think you and I need to have a chat about last night. Maybe you can fill in all the blanks.

Henley – How many blanks are there?

Tully – Basically the whole reception.

Henley – Shit. Ok, Noah and I will come around for dinner. We can talk before we head out to Italy

tomorrow morning.

Tully – K, but you better bring take out. There's no way that I'm cooking!

Henley – Figured!

Next up; the voicemail.

Not having the energy to hold my phone up at my ear, I hit speakerphone and crash down onto my desk chair. Spencer's voice comes through the line a moment later and the sound crushes me. He's devastatingly broken.

"Babe, it's me. I just…I'm sorry. Look things were said last night and I was drunk, and I…can we talk? Where are you? I went to your apartment, but you weren't there. Just…shit. Just tell me you're not with *him*? Babe, I'm so sorry."

Well, that wasn't exactly fun to listen to.

Anger pulses through me. How dare he assume I just climbed into bed with Rivers? Surely he knows I have a little more class than that. We've been together for three years now and I've never once been unfaithful to him. Just because Rivers is back, that doesn't mean that's going to change.

Well, at least I hope it hasn't already. My night was foggy and I'm sure I said things that I'll regret the second I remember them. But Rivers is a good guy. He would respect the fact that I'm with Spencer, so if I tried something, I'm sure he would have shut it down. Well, I hope he would have shut it down.

Over the past three years, I've respected what Spencer and I have, but last night he was a possessive, jealous ass, and he's right; we do need to talk. But not right now. I can't handle that right now.

I send him off a quick text so he's not worrying and to keep him off my back for a while.

Tully – I slept at mom and dad's place. I'll be home in an hour then we can talk. K?

Spencer – Ok, babe. Glad you're alright. I love you.

Tully – Love you too xx

As I send the last text, something stirs within me. It's never felt right telling Spencer that I love him when I know deep down that there's really only one man I've ever truly loved, but I've had so much pressure from everyone telling me how I should feel about him. Saying that Spencer is the perfect boyfriend and that I'm a fool for not taking things further with him.

I know it's not right and it's not fair to him, but I don't want to hurt him. He has stood by my side for the past four years and I owe him so much. Don't get me wrong, I do love him. When I was seeing the world in black and white, he brought a little color back into my life. He gave me life when I was about ready to give up, but the love I feel for him is nothing compared to what I once felt for Rivers, and I think Spencer knows it.

If mom had her way, we'd be married with kids by now, but it's just not…right, and I think he can feel it. He's been clinging on, hoping for the best and I've been letting him because I've been terrified of being alone. The last guy that left me tore my world apart and it's a feeling I never want to experience again.

If I had to go through the pain of that again, I think it might just kill me. So, I've let him hold on and ignored the feeling inside me telling me that it's wrong.

I should let him go but I can't.

I make my way over to my old closet and begin rifling through it while wondering how I got into this old shirt. It doesn't go unnoticed that this is one of Rivers' old shirts. In fact, it's the shirt I'd stolen from him the night we'd slept together before he went back to complete his training with the military. That was the last time we were physically together and it was everything I'd imagined.

After that night, I'd thought things were going to change between us. When he got in that taxi and drove off, I thought I'd see him again in a few months. If I'd known I was never going to see him again, I would have held on with both hands and never let him go.

The year following that was hard. I would constantly check the door and mailbox, waiting to hear something, anything from him, but nothing ever came and the door never opened.

Until yesterday afternoon. Which has me wondering how the hell he knew about the wedding in the first place. Something screams Noah, but the sneakiness of it has Henley written all over it. I think we're going to have a lot to talk about over dinner tonight.

I don't know how I ever came out of that depression and truth be told; I think I'm still kind of there. Spencer was like a little piece of magic thrust upon me He kept me going. He kept me sane, and he never allowed me to fall. But here I am.

I grab something to wear and search out a towel before heading down to the bathroom and ignoring my parents' piercing voices. I'm just about to step into the shower when I remember the bucket.

Shit. Without a doubt mom will walk in there to deal with it and I don't want her having to clean up after my mistakes, especially after all the mistakes she's already had to clean up when it comes to me and Noah.

I double back to my room, grab the bucket while trying my hardest not to gag. I push my way back into the bathroom and deal with my mess before finally giving myself a few minutes of peace to shower. I clear my head and focus solely on the hot water cascading down over me. At this moment, no one exists. There's no Spencer to deal with, no Rivers to torture myself over, no Henley and Noah to be apologizing to. No one. Just me and the hot water.

I scrub myself, trying to wash away the memory of last night before washing my hair and realizing it smells strongly of my past. When the water begins running cold, sadness seeps into my chest. I'm not ready for this shower to be over. The second I step out of here, I'm going to have to face the real world and right now, the real world terrifies me.

What happened to me? I used to be so strong and so sure of myself. This person that I've become isn't me. I miss the old Tully. I miss the girl who would stand up for what she believed in and was able to tell it like it is. I'm barely even a shell of that girl now and I want her back.

The next hour passes in a blur. At some point, I find some pain-killers that were left on my bedside table and throw them down the hatch while mom shoves something in my face to eat, only that makes me want to hurl all over again. I ask dad to drop me back at my apartment as I don't think it's a good idea to be driving, and before I know it, I'm collapsing down onto my couch, absolutely loving the silence of my empty home.

I've lived here for nearly three years and have enjoyed every moment of my independence. When Noah got his own place with Henley, it left me the sole focus of my mother's attention and while I love her dearly, I was in no state for that constant hovering.

Now living on my own, I feel as free as a bird and I've never looked back. Besides, there's nothing quite like your own private space to throw yourself a pity party and wallow in all of your doubts, hurt, and pain.

My breathing slows and my eyes grow heavy as I toe the line of unconsciousness. I'm just about to fall over the edge when I hear the familiar sound of a key sliding into the lock.

I groan to myself. I knew Spencer was coming over, but I've never regretted giving him a key so much. All I want is to sleep for the next week or so. Candice can handle the store and everyone else can get lost.

The door creaks open and I hear Spencer's voice calling out. "Babe? Are you home?" he says moments before the door clicks shut behind him.

"Over here," I grumble from the couch, not bothering to open my eyes.

Spencer walks across the room and stops before me, looking down at me as a breathy chuckle escapes him. "Shit.

you've had better days, huh?"

I open one eye and glare up at him. "Really? You want to start this by reminding me how shitty I look?"

"Tully," he scoffs. "You could be covered head to toe in crap and still look like a radiant fucking beauty queen."

I groan as I sit myself up on the couch and drop my face into my hands. "You're such a suck-up."

Spencer lets out a heavy breath before dropping down onto the couch beside me. He doesn't touch me and I don't attempt to reach out to him.

We sit in heavy silence, both with way too much on our minds to know where to even begin. It's not until Spencer leans forward and rests his elbows upon his knees that he finally says something. "I fucked up. I drank way too much and talked shit."

I nod, unable to disagree with him. "You did."

He lets out a sigh, staring at the carpet and refusing to look at me. "It's just that I saw you breaking over Rivers and it reminded me that no matter what; I'm always going to be second place to him."

My head whips around to Spencer in shock. "What are you talking about? Why would you say that?"

"Come on, Tully. You know it's true. It's always been him when it comes to you. How am I supposed to be with you knowing that just the sight of another man can tear you to shreds?"

I shake my head as tears begin to fill my eyes. "Don't do this, Spencer. I need you more than you know."

Regret shines brightly in his eyes as he reaches out and places his hand on my thigh. He gives it a gentle squeeze. "I don't want to. I love you so goddamn much, but what does that say about me? Am I a fool because I'm holding onto someone who can never fully commit to me because she can't get over her ex? I've loved you with everything I have. I've given you everything you could possibly need, but it's never enough for you. I can't keep being shut down by you.

You're slowly killing me, Tully."

I fly into him, climbing up onto his lap and looking into the eyes of the man that has been my rock for the past four years. "Spencer, no. Please don't. I don't want him. I want to be with you. I know that you've given me the world. This is just one setback. We'll get through it. I promise you, we will."

His arms curl around me and he pulls me into his chest, holding me just the way he knows that I need. "I don't know what to do," he murmurs. "Rivers sent your whole world spiraling last night and seeing you unable to even function tore me apart. It should be me who has the ability to affect you like that, not him."

"I'm sorry," I say, burying my face into his neck and breathing him in as my tears soak into his shirt. "I was just in shock and all the hurt that he caused me since I was eleven years old came back to haunt me, and I just…I couldn't breathe. It was too much, but I swear, Spence, it's over. I'm through with him. I don't want anything to do with Rivers. I want you. I want to make this work."

Spencer pulls me back to look into my eyes and the hurt on his face is nearly enough to tear me to shreds. I hate that I've put it there, but I need him to fight for this. I can't have my heart broken again, I just can't. I won't survive it.

"Please," I whisper when the silence grows too loud.

He looks absolutely shattered and I see him breaking as dread fills me. His head finally falls and he rests it against mine as he holds me a little tighter. "Ok," he murmurs making my heart finally stop racing. "But I need you to do one thing for me."

"Anything," I tell him, searching out his hands so I can lace my fingers through his.

"I need you not to see him. I can't have him in your life."

My brows dip down as I pull back to look at him. "What? I…I can't do that."

"Please, babe. Look what happened to you last night. I can't have you breaking down like this every time he's near.

You'll never move on like that."

I continue staring at him, wondering what's possibly going through his head. "Rivers is my family," I remind him on a whisper. "I can't just not see him. I need to…"

"Need to what? Make sure he's doing alright? Sit by his side when he's having a shit time? You've already put Anton away and made sure he had a home to come back to. Haven't you already done enough?"

I shake my head. "It's not like that."

"Then what's it like?" he snaps at me, making me lean back on his lap. "I'm having a real fucking tough time trying to work it out. You tell me that you don't love him anymore, you tell me you want to make it work between us, you tell me that it's over with him, yet the second you see him you turn into a mess, and now this?"

"What's that supposed to mean? Do you not trust me when I tell you that I want to be with you? He hurt me, Spence. I don't want to be with him. I can't risk it."

"But you still love him."

"I don't."

"And I don't fucking believe you."

He pushes me off his lap and gets up from the couch before storming to the door, leaving me gaping behind him. "Spencer, don't go."

He stops by the door and lets out a heavy breath as he turns to look back at me. "Are you going to stop seeing him or not?"

I stare at him as I think it over. Spencer is right, for my own health and wellbeing, I should probably be avoiding spending any time with the guy, but something tells me that Spencer's request comes from a place of jealousy rather than wanting to look out for me. If this was any other guy, I'd probably be able to deal with it, but it's not. It's Rivers and the thought of not seeing him kills me. I only just got him back. How could I possibly lose that again?

No matter what happened in our past, Rivers is my

family. He may not be blood, but he's so much more. He's my pack. He's the person I gave my heart to when I was eleven and he's the one who still holds it in his hands, refusing to ever give it back.

I shake my head as I look up at Spencer. "I'm sorry," I whisper across the room. "I can't do that."

"Right," he says, looking at me with regret. "Then I can't do this."

With that, he walks out the door, leaving me gasping for breath.

CHAPTER 6

RIVERS

Hot water cascades down over my back as I stand in the shower. All I've been able to think about over the past two days is that wedding. The way she looked, the way she felt, the way she cried. It's always Tully and forever will be. Hell, I haven't even spared a thought for the fact that my sister and best friend just got married.

I spent all of yesterday pacing around my home, convincing myself not to go and find her. I woke up way too early and worked out, just trying to give myself a reason to stay put. A visit from me is really not what she needs right now.

After how much she drank at the wedding, she would have spent the majority of the day in bed and then I'd assume that she spent what was left of her day trying to work things out with Spencer. They didn't exactly end things that night on a good note, and I'd dare say that I might have had a little something to do with that.

I feel for the guy. Kind of. I stand by my claim that he's

a douche. At least he was in high school and he certainly hasn't done anything to prove otherwise, but having a woman like Tully hating on you is not easy, especially when your heart is caught up in it. So yeah, I feel for him…just a bit

I spent what was left of my day catching up with Noah and Henley, that was until Henley tugged on Noah's arm and told him that they had dinner plans. She never clarified what dinner plans they had, but something tells me they were heading to see Tully and make sure she was alright.

Noah and Henley will be heading out for their honeymoon this morning. In fact, I wouldn't be surprised if they're already at the airport waiting to board their flight to Italy. I don't doubt that they've been looking forward to this trip, but when they were here talking about it yesterday, they couldn't seem less interested.

They never admitted it but they're hesitant to go. They're worried about Tully and how she's going to handle me being home, but they shouldn't worry themselves. I know I'm the problem, but I'm also the solution. I'm not going to hurt her and they should know that no matter what, I'm going to be there for her, even if it's so she has someone to use as a punching bag.

As much as I want Noah and Henley to go and enjoy their honeymoon, I can't help but want them to stay. They hold all the answers to Tully's last four years and I want nothing more than to get every last bit of information out of them. I want to know it all. I feel as though I've missed so much of their lives and I need it to survive. They're my pack and I've been missing too much.

There was a time when it was just the four of us. Whatever was happening in our lives, we all knew. That dynamic has shifted and I don't like it.

I fucked it all up when I left. I don't regret leaving, but I regret leaving her behind.

I turn off the taps and step out of the shower. It's only

ten in the morning and after spending yesterday fucking around, I'm quickly running out of things to keep me busy. I could always go and pay both of my parents a visit, but...fuck that.

Henley sent me a few letters over the past four years keeping me updated with our parents and I have to say, when that first one came that explained how she was going to attempt to get my mother out of prison, I was in shock, but as the letter went on and Henley detailed her innocence, I started to believe it. That's when the guilt hit.

I was only a kid when I went to the cops and told them about the dirty little business my mother was running. I had Anton in my ear and I've felt nothing but disgust in myself since the second it happened.

What kind of twelve-year-old kid puts their mother behind bars?

I felt sick. I hardly knew what prostitution was and allowed my father to cloud my mind with his judgment. I let him control me. I was a pawn used in his twisted games. I was never a son, but a soldier.

Breaking away from that shit was the best thing I ever did. Well, I never really broke away until I joined the Military, but finding Noah and Tully went a long way to help heal something inside of me.

Being my father's son wasn't easy. It was a life filled with darkness and at that time, Noah and Tully were the only good I had in my world. I didn't want to risk losing them or allowing them to discover who I really was. I was the broken kid and what parents would want their child to hang out with me? I couldn't risk losing them, not for one second.

I never once told them what I'd done and I refused to tell them about my family. Who I was or where I lived. Hell, for a few years, I didn't even know where I lived. I was part-time between staying at Anton's place and running back home to an empty house. Half the time, I'd crash on Violet's couch and I've always been grateful for the fact that she never asked questions.

Well, that's not entirely true. She did at first and I can't blame her for her curiosity, it's only natural, but there came a point where Violet gave up asking. They all did and when that finally happened, I felt a wave of relief rush over me.

Though, I've never felt more relieved than when I heard Tully tell Spencer that she loved him and realized that she didn't wholeheartedly mean it. Nothing will ever compare to the moment that I realized that she was still mine.

I get myself dressed and ready for the day while doing my best to stop thinking about my girl. I've just come back from a war zone. I should be concentrating on the shit I saw over there and checking on my boys instead of endlessly thinking about a girl who wants nothing to do with me.

I doubt that I'll be deployed for a while so that leaves me with way too much time to myself. I need to find something to do, something to keep me busy and keep me from bugging Tully, and I guess for now, that means rebuilding the Firebird.

I step outside and make my way over to the massive blue tarpaulin covering the old car and with one quick pull, I rip it off and expose the mess beneath.

Damn. It looks worse every time I see it.

I remember the day I got it, I was so damn proud of myself. It was such a big fucking deal. To everyone else, it was just a car, but to me, it was my first step towards freedom. It wasn't long until some fucker ran a red light, took out the car, and almost fucking killed Tully in the process.

I've never forgotten that moment. It was my turning point. I had always said that she was better off without me and seeing her fighting for life was when I realized that I had to get out. She needed better. They all did. I was only going to bring them down into my darkness and the only way to escape it was for me to disappear.

With a sigh, I begin looking over the Firebird and working out what the hell I'm going to need to make this thing look brand fucking new. It's not going to be a small job and it's not going to be cheap, but I've got nothing but time. Though I should really look into getting a car to drive in the meantime, otherwise there will be a lot of taxis and walking in my future, and how am I supposed to get my girl back like that?

I get the hood open and look over the engine, but my mind keeps taking me back to her. Noah and Henley are gone and I know they were with her just last night, but what if she needs something? Has anyone checked in on her today?

She's probably having a shit time and who knows what happened with Spencer. Though, if anything, he's got her wrapped around his litter finger and is with her right now.

Before I realize what's happening, my phone is in my hand and I find myself hashing out a text, not knowing how this is going to go.

Rivers – Dude, where's your sister's place?

Noah – Fuck no!

I grin to myself. I should have known it wasn't going to be that easy, but if he's using his phone, he's not on the plane yet which means I still have time to twist his arm.

Rivers – You and Henley are gone for three weeks. Spencer fucked off during the wedding so who knows where he is now. What if she needs something or there's an emergency?

Noah – If there's an emergency, she can call mom and dad.

Rivers – That's bullshit and you know it. That girl doesn't rely on anyone.

Noah – She's not the same girl you used to know.

Rivers – Come on, man. I just need to go and check on her.

There's a short pause and I wonder if he's going to reply at all or if maybe their flight has been called, but a moment later, my phone lights up and I find myself scrambling to open the text.

Noah – She's in that apartment complex down behind the new mall. Apartment 308. If you so much as make her shed one fucking tear, I'll end you. Got it? She's fragile now. You can't come at her like you used to. She won't be able to handle it.

My heart shatters. Just from looking at her and listening to the way she speaks makes it clear that she's not the same girl I once knew but having Noah confirm it is a whole new thing.

He's even more protective of her than he used to be. At the wedding, he was chill, but something tells me that was a front so he didn't ruin things for Henley, but now the wedding's over and the real Noah has come out to play.

It probably kills him that he's not here to warn me face to face. Either way, I hear him loud and clear. I'm not here to hurt her. I'm here to earn her forgiveness and give her everything she ever wanted.

I want to make her happy and I'll do whatever it takes to prove it to her.

Rivers – I got it. I just want to check on her and make sure she's doing ok. If she tells me to fuck off, I'll fuck off, but just know, I'm not going anywhere. I'm not going to hurt her.

Noah – You're not that fucked up kid you used to be, are you?

Rivers – Nope. I've put all that shit behind me.

Noah – You're going to try and win back your girl, aren't you?

Rivers – Only if that's what she wants. I told you, if she tells me to fuck off, I'll go.

Noah – Shit.

Noah – You're going to have a hard time getting her to admit anything. She's a closed book now.

Rivers – She's a closed book to you maybe. Took me three seconds to work her out. She's not happy with Spencer, she's terrified of getting hurt, and she still fucking loves me. Besides, I have a lifetime of getting her to admit to shit that she'd prefer to keep hidden. Trust me, I've got this.

Noah – Do you still love her?

Rivers – More than you're prepared to know.

Noah – And you're here for good?

Rivers – Yeah, man. I'm on reserve now. I'm fucking home.

Noah – Fuck.

Noah – I know she's with Spencer, but fuck it! Go get her back. I'm sick of seeing her hurting.

A grin rips across my face. I was going to get her back with or without Noah's consent, but knowing that I have his approval to be with his sister just makes it that much better.

Now knowing where she lives, I find myself moving, I don't even think that I locked up my house in my need to get to her. Hell, the door could be left wide fucking open for all I know, but I can't find it within myself to care. I just need to check on her. I need to start working on this plan to win her back because fucking around doing nothing is only going to drive me insane.

I had the smallest taste of having her in my arms again and I need more. She's my addiction and I've gone far too long without it.

I get to the entrance of her building before realizing that I don't have a game plan. What am I going to say to her that isn't going to have her kicking me out within seconds? She's no doubt still pissed off. Out of all the chicks I've ever met, Tully Cage takes the prize for grudge-holding.

I pull open the door and look around in wonder. Tully lives on the outskirts of Haven Falls and it's nicer than I could have possibly imagined. It's not quite Broken Hill standards but for a kid from Haven Falls, it's pretty fucking impressive. She must be doing really well for herself.

Pride surges through me as I hit the call button on the elevator. I always knew that she was going to succeed with whatever it is that she's doing, but being able to afford a place like this at twenty-three is astounding. It's an accomplishment that hardly any other people in Haven Falls would be able to achieve and seeing that she has it well within her grasp tells me that whatever she's doing with her life, she's kicking ass at it.

I make my way up to level three and over to apartment 308.

This is it.

This is either going to go really well or really bad. There's never any middle ground when it comes to getting inside Tully's head, but maybe I should be taking Noah's warning. She's not the same girl I once knew.

I come to a stop before her door and let out a breath as I clutch the frame with both hands and rest my head against the door. My future is on the other side of this door.

I pull my shit together. Tully needs a man, not a fucking pussy.

I knock on the door and wait patiently for her to answer. I wait a little longer and then some more before wondering if she's even home. After all, it's Monday. She's probably at work.

I'm about to give up when the softest sigh comes from the opposite side of the door and I'd bet anything that she's been watching me through the damn peephole.

Placing my hand on the door, I lean into it, knowing that only a piece of wood stands between me and my girl. "Baby, let me in."

There's a short pause, but I don't dare move. I'm not here to pussy around. I'm here to check on her and win her back. The softest murmur comes through the door and despite her voice being muffled through the door, I know the sound of heartbreak, especially when it comes from her. "You need to leave, Rivers."

"I can't do that, Tullz. I'll stand out here all day and night if that's what it takes."

71

A frustrated groan comes through the door and I don't doubt she's contemplating all the different ways to torture me, but she should know that just having this door closed between us is more torture than I've ever endured.

I'm just about to get down on my knees and start begging when I hear the little piece of metal siding along the lock before the sound of the deadbolt being released. The handle turns and the door begins to fall open and not a second later, my breath is taken away by the woman standing before me.

Four years really has changed her. The night of the wedding, she looked spectacular. She was radiant and looked like a fucking angel, but that's not the woman I fell in love with. This is. The one who wears sweats and has her long hair a mess. There's no makeup, no gown, no attitude, just her, all-natural just the way she was intended. It's raw and those green eyes shimmering with years of memories is enough to draw me forward.

I don't even realize that I've moved until she's taking a hasty step back. "Don't touch me," she whispers. "You can't be here."

"There's no place else I'd rather be," I tell her.

Her eyes drop away and it nearly kills me. She takes another step away from me and before I know it, she's crossing the room and dropping down onto her couch. "What are you doing here?" she questions, watching me warily.

I close the door behind me before stepping around a big fucking box and walking deeper into her apartment. I can't help but take it all in while looking around the huge room. "I just needed to check you were alright."

"Well, you shouldn't have bothered," she says with a slow nod. "I'm fine."

My eyes return to hers with a smirk playing on my lips loving that not everything about this little she devil has changed. "You've always been a great liar, Tully, but you forget that I can read you like a book."

She lets out a slight huff and looks away. She's never been able to handle being called out and I absolutely love it. Getting that reaction out of her makes teasing her that much better. "How'd you know where to find me?"

My smirk turns into a full-blown grin. "How do you think?"

"Fucking Noah," she mutters under her breath. "Absolutely no respect for my privacy."

"Chill out," I say, making my way around her living room and checking out the life she's built for herself. "He's just worried about you."

"He was here until two in the morning. I doubt he's got himself all worked up about me over the past nine hours," she explains, keeping her eyes on me as I start to wonder if winning her back isn't going to be as hard as I thought.

"You know better than anyone just how quickly Noah can be worked up," I say, taking in her bookshelf and admiring how she seems to have organized it by color. It looks fucking awesome, but wouldn't it make more sense to arrange it by series or author? I could fix it for her, but that would probably get me killed. Tully's books have always been precious to her and since the last time I saw her, the collection seems to have multiplied.

Tully doesn't respond, but I don't expect her to. She's trying to show me that my presence doesn't affect her and if I were anyone else, I would have bought the act, but I'm not and she can't fool me.

I look back over my shoulder to her and watch as her eyes slowly meet mine. "You fixed up my house."

She shrugs her shoulders. "Yeah, that was years ago when I assumed you were coming home. It wasn't just me, everyone chipped in. It's no big deal just forget about it. I have."

"Uh-huh. The fresh flowers on the dining table really show how you've forgotten about it."

"I don't know what you're talking about," she murmurs

as I start walking down the hallway towards her bedroom and hear her flying up from the couch. "Where do you think you're going?"

"I want to see your place," I throw back, not relenting in my way down the hall. "Why is there a moving box at the front door?"

"I uh…didn't think you noticed that."

"I've spent the past four years in the military, I notice everything. Besides, it's not like it's right in the doorway or anything. I had to step around the big fucker just to get in."

I can practically hear her cringe already knowing the answer to my question. After all, I was listening in to her and Spencer arguing about it during the wedding. "Not that it's any of your business, but I was going to move out."

"Past tense or present tense?"

"Seriously?" I don't respond and she knows me well enough to know that I'll keep asking until I get the answer I'm looking for. She lets out a sigh. "I told Spencer I'd move in with him, but I don't want to leave my apartment. Not yet. This is my home and I worked hard for it. I'm not ready to give it up."

I nod. Finally, a straight answer, though there might be a little more to it.

I walk into her bedroom and take a look around. It's exactly how I pictured her to live. An empty ice-cream tub on her bedside table, cookie and cream flavored, of course. There are books everywhere with her Kindle at the end of her bed, clean washing piled high in a chair, and not to mention an old photo of our pack framed up on her wall right where it should be, right where she can see it, see me. Every fucking night.

I wipe the grin from my face before noticing a little black velvet box on her dresser. I make my way across her bedroom, unable to resist looking inside. "Rivers," Tully whispers from the door of her bedroom, trying to save me from myself. "Don't."

I take the little box in my hand and open it up. A diamond ring shines up at me and I don't doubt this is the one that Spencer has proposed with four times now. I feel Tully's eye burning into the back of my head and I can't help but wonder what things would be like if I never went away.

Maybe my ring would be on her finger and maybe that heaviness inside her heart would never have existed. But then, maybe that darkness would still be inside me and I would have ended up hurting her anyway.

The only blessing I can find in all of this is that Spencer's ring is not taking up residence on her finger. For now, it lives discarded in this little box and that's exactly where it's going to stay until Spencer can find someone else to give it to.

I take the ring from the box before turning and walking towards Tully. Her eyes widen and she sinks away as I stalk her. I toss the empty box onto the bed as I pass before situating myself right before her and staring down into those beautiful, mesmerizing eyes.

I reach over and take her hand before placing the ring in the center of her palm and curling her fingers around it. "If you were truly his, if you'd have given your heart to him, then I'd let you go. But you haven't. You're mine, Tully. You always will be just as I'll always be yours. I'm not going anywhere. I'm going to make this right."

Tully steps into me, raising her chin and looking up into my eyes just as she used to. Her hand presses against my chest and she melts into me as I take her waist. "You see that's where you're wrong," she whispers. "I don't know if I'm his but what I do know is that I'm sure as hell not yours. I'll never go back to you, Rivers."

Her words are supposed to cut, but the fight within her has a smile ripping across my face. I pull her in closer to my chest as confusion has her brows dipping low. "God, I fucking missed you."

She fights against me for a moment before realizing she has no hope of me letting her go and then finally wraps her arms around me. I tilt my face into her hair and breathe her in as she finds comfort in my hold. "I was serious," she murmurs into my chest. "I'm making it work with Spence."

"You don't really believe that, Tully. You've had three years to make it work with him. He's been down on one knee four times and asked you to move in with him. If you wanted to make it work, you'd be married with a kid on the way. If you were in love with him, you would have thrown yourself into it just like you did with me, but you haven't. You've been waiting, biding your time in case I was to come back to you."

"You're setting yourself up for disappointment."

I shake my head as I pull back and look down at her. "No," I tell her, pausing to know she's truly hearing every damn word that I'm saying. "I'm setting myself up for the most important fight of my life. So, understand this, baby. I'm all in."

Her eyes widen just a fraction and before she can fight me on it, I lean back in and press a kiss to her cheek.

A breath escapes her and before I push her too far, I walk away.

Noah might think she's a fragile little butterfly and at the wedding, I might have thought the same thing, but that fierce look in her eye that tells me she wants nothing more than to castrate me, says that tiger still lives within her and it's getting ready to break free.

CHAPTER 7

TULLY

Stupid, stupid, stupid, stupid.

What was I thinking letting him through the door? I stood on the other side of it, listening to the way his head fell against the hard wood. I could hear a rapid heartbeat and I'm still not sure if it was mine or his. All I know is that it's been three days and I still can't get him out of my head.

The words he was saying...they were the ones I've heard every single night in my dreams when I should be dreaming of someone else.

I'm in big fucking trouble here.

I tried to be strong. I tried to hold him off and throw as much attitude as I could find at his face and it seemed the harder I tried, the more he liked it. It was almost as though, for the shortest moment, that I had found my old fire. The one I lost when I lost him.

Rivers says he wants me back and the fire in his eyes tells me he means it and that scares the shit out of me. It's one thing dealing with the loss of Spencer from my life, but fearing that Rivers could play with my heart all over again, well, that's something that I couldn't possibly bear.

I haven't told a soul about Spencer leaving me and I have no idea why. It could be guilt over the fact that I've spent the past three days thinking about a guy from my past rather than the incredible man I just lost.

But what's worse is that heartache I've been fearing for the past three years and the terror I would feel over the thought of him breaking up with me simply isn't there. I'm not hurting and that must make me some kind of monster. I've just spent years with Spencer and after crying for about twenty minutes, I put the pain away and filed it for another day and have since forgotten about it.

Three years of my life with him and I didn't turn into a mess. Surely, he meant more than that to me.

God, I'm such a bitch. He was right to end it with me. I turned into more of a mess when I watched *'The Notebook'* for the first time.

I should be sent straight to hell for this. Though maybe I shouldn't because I'm positive that I'll live out eternity with Rivers right there by my side and then I'll be as happy as a fat fucking pig in mud. I can't win. I don't deserve to be happy.

When Rivers was at my place on Monday, I failed to tell him that Spencer had left me and I sat there wondering why I didn't tell him. In fact, I haven't told anyone. I've spoken to Henley at least four times since she left for her honeymoon and each time, the topic fails to get mentioned. She'd hate it and would constantly be worrying when she should be enjoying her honeymoon, so at least I have somewhat of a good reason.

Mom and dad? They'd just hover. Noah? He'd come storming back here with a vengeance and demand answers out of Spencer which would probably make things awkward. Then there's Aiden…I don't know what to do there. Spencer is his cousin and there's no doubt that he'll hear about it eventually and then comes that accusing conversation where he demands to know why I never said anything.

This shit sucks.

All I want is to forget. I wish things were simpler but they haven't been that way in four years and now that Rivers is back, it's all that much more complicated.

I just wish I knew how to understand what I'm feeling. I love him so damn much, but I hate him for what he put me through. There's no getting past that. He's my family and my pack and I'll always be there for him, but when it comes to an 'us' it's just not possible. My heart is still too broken and because of that, I've managed to hurt everyone else.

I'm such a fucking bitch.

A sigh pulls from deep within me and I sink onto my workbench. I'm supposed to be arranging a dozen roses for a delivery tonight, but every time I look down at the flowers on my table, the will leaves me.

Why does everyone else get to find their happiness and I'm stuck with this awful hatred?

"What's wrong with you?" Candice asks me as she makes her way around my store, checking over the arrangements she'd put together this morning and making sure that they're still just as wickedly stunning as they were when she first arranged them.

"Nothing," I grumble, wanting nothing more than to close my eyes and pretend today isn't happening. Hell, I might pretend the last few days haven't happened as well.

Candice scoffs. "You're so full of shit."

I resist throwing the pile of thorns I've collected at her. She came to me two years ago asking for a job and at first, I was reluctant to give her one, but the business was booming and I was going crazy keeping up with all the orders on my own. After I 'ummed' and 'ahhed' over whether to hire her or not, I finally gave in and she's been here ever since.

I had to teach her the ropes and I quickly realized that she's done a hell of a lot of growing up since high school. I even consider her one of my friends now, though I'm not pushing it. It's not like we're BFFs and tell each other our darkest secrets. So, when she says shit like that to me, I don't fly off the handle like I would have had we still been in high school.

"Shut up," I tell her. "Remember, I'm still your boss."

"Uh-huh," she grins, focusing on tidying up a tulip arrangement that looks a little tired. "What are you going to do about it?"

"Dock your pay and spend my savings on finding your replacement."

"You can't do that and you know it."

"I know," I groan, pushing myself up from the table and trying to look alive. "But I can think about it and picture just how nice this place would be without your endless ramblings. Trust me, it's going to bring me all sorts of joy."

Candice chuckles to herself and shakes her head. "You're such a dork. But seriously, what's this mood about? Is it because Spencer was hanging out with Lacey last night?"

My head whips around to her. "What? What are you talking about?"

Her brows dip down in confusion as she watches me for a silence beat. "Yeah, I saw them at dinner last night. I didn't think much of it because you guys are all friends, but it was kind of strange that it was just the two of them. Looked like more of a date if you asked me, but I know how much he's into you so it's probably nothing."

My head drops straight back down to the table and I instantly wonder how bad it would be for business if I just closed up for the next year or so and drowned my sorrows in bed. I could come back from it...I think.

I don't know why it should bother me so much. We ended it as I was clearly a pretty shit girlfriend. Spencer deserves someone who will love him in that same intense way that he loves and it's not fair for me to hold onto him knowing I'll never love him like that, but still...if that was a date with Lacey last night then that kind of sucks. I mean, we've only been apart a few days.

My face squishes into the table and I glare at the wall. "He broke up with me."

The tulip drops from her hand and she turns and looks at me in shock. "What?" she shrieks. "Just...what? Are you shitting me?"

"Nope."

"He broke up with you?"

"Yup."

"Are you sure it wasn't the other way around?"

"Seriously?"

Candice's eyes narrow on me and I groan as I can practically see the light bulb flashing above her head. A sly grin slowly creeps across her face. "It's because of Rivers, isn't it? Because he's back. You know, I heard he's done some growing over the past four years."

She's damn right, he has. He looks mighty fine with those strong arms and intense eyes, but I'm not about to dive into that sinkhole. "It's not because of Rivers."

"You know, in high school, you were a much better liar."

Why do people keep saying that?

I roll my eyes. I could probably do without this conversation. I'm just about to tell her where to go when a mountain of a man walks across the front window of my store and stops at the door. "Showtime," Candice says, collecting the tulip from the ground.

I zip my lips and peel my head off the table while pretending to have a shred of professionalism about myself. I slap on a smile and act as though I'm happy to be here as the giant pushes his way through the door.

The bell above the door jingles and both Candice and I give him a welcoming smile. Candice takes the reins and makes her way across the store. "Is there anything I can help you with?"

The big man cringes and looks at the array of flowers, chocolates, gift baskets, and balloons surrounding him. "I, uh…I'll let you know."

Not being one to hover, Candice gives the guy some room to browse and comes to join me behind the workbench. Knowing I'm in a bit of a mood, she takes over the rose arrangement for tonight's delivery while I head over to the counter and start tidying things up.

The big man towers over everything in the store and even has to duck his head to avoid crashing into my ceiling fan. I can't help but check him out because well, I'm a woman and he's a fine piece of man meat. He has muscles upon muscles, a sharp jawline covered in stubble that has me wanting to run my fingers over it, and not to mention tattoos covering both of his strong arms.

I glance across at Candice who's practically drooling but she knows better than to say anything. The guys who come in here are generally already taken and are only here to find something nice for their girl, or girls as it seems a lot of guys in Haven Falls seems to have.

I swear, Valentine's day is the holiday for finding out the dirt in this town. Every fucker comes in here and puts in an order, but it's the guys who put in two orders, claiming one is for their mom, are the guys you need to watch out for. I mean, what guy is sending his mother a dozen roses on Valentine's day? Clearly, there are a few side chicks running around Haven Falls.

I look back at the beast of a man and can't help but notice how lost he looks. It makes me smile every time this happens. Guys never know what they're after when they come in here. Most just come straight up to the counter and start explaining their situation, but the fact that this guy is giving it a good try and having a look tells me he's actually interested in what he's looking for.

By his second walk around the store, I start feeling sorry for the guy despite how amused I am. I lean forward on my counter. "Is there anything specific I can help you find?"

His head snaps up and there's that same cringe marring

his handsome face. The need to decline my offer shows on his face but his desperation for help shines through. He lets out a heavy sigh and starts making his way towards my counter. "Look," he finally says in the deepest voice I've ever heard. "I'm going to lay it all out for you."

Candice makes her way over as though it's storytime and he's about to give us the juiciest gossip. "By all means," I tell him, raising a curious brow. "Hit me with your situation."

"I, ah…shit. I hope you ladies don't get offended easily."

"No, Sir. We don't," Candice purrs.

I roll my eyes but I can't help that slight thrill that pulses through me. Maybe Candice was right to settle in for storytime. Something tells me the next few minutes are going to be quite entertaining.

"Well, look," he starts, gesturing down his body. "I'm not exactly a small guy."

"That you are not," I agree. "What are you? 6'6? 6'7?"

"6'8 actually," he grins proudly. "And before you ask, yes, I play basketball."

"Damn," Candice sighs. "Are you single?"

"Well, that's just the thing. I met a girl last weekend and she finally agreed to go out with me last night, and well, one thing led to another and…"

"You took her home?"

"Yep."

"Ok…" Candice says slowly. "Am I missing something here? This doesn't seem quite so out of the ordinary."

The guy grins. "She's 4 foot 11."

My eyes bulge out of my head as Candice's jaw drops. I can't help but scan my eyes down his body towards his junk. Judging by the size of him, I'm assuming he's the kind of guy you'd need both hands for, and if he was with a girl who can barely even reach the kitchen sink…well, damn.

"Fuck'" Candice gasps. "Is she alright? You sent her to hospital, didn't you? Oh, the poor girl. You probably tore her pussy apart and not in the good way."

"No," he laughs with a mischievous sparkle in his brown eyes. "Actually, that's a story for a another time, but what I was getting at is that she took it like a fucking pro, and well, it's not often I find a girl who can handle what I've got."

Candice leans over the counter, showing off her cleavage. "Fuck it. I'll climb on top and give it the good college try."

"You'll fucking rein it in and finish off the rose arrangement," I tell her before turning back to the guy and noticing that Candice hasn't moved an inch, though I'm not surprised. I wouldn't want to miss this either. "I'm assuming that you want to see her again?"

"Fuck, yeah."

"So, what you're looking for is something that says 'Thanks for leaving your gag reflex at the door and swallowing my cock like a fucking porn-star?'"

He grins wide. "You see, I was standing out there wondering if you chicks would even understand my issue and you just get it."

I laugh as I walk out from around the counter and start making my way through the store, plucking out bits and pieces from all different arrangements, not giving a crap that I'm going to have to fix them all up later. This is a special case and this girl deserves the best. After all, the poor girl probably can't even walk today and if this guy has a shot at hitting it again, then he needs to give her the best fucking flowers in Haven Falls. Hell, maybe I'll throw in a 'congratulatory' balloon from me just to let her know the female population is bowing down.

I bring all the flowers back to my workbench and get busy doing my thing as the big guy leans over my counter and chats with Candice. I laugh along with their ridiculous conversation and shake my head as Candice somehow manages to convince the guy to set her up with his best friend who's just as big and athletic as he is.

I finish off the arrangement and am just working out the card to go with it when Candice looks up and stares out the front window. "Well, damn. There's a blast from the past."

Oh no.

My eyes instantly snap up to take in Rivers across the road talking with one of the few mechanics in town. I don't doubt they're discussing his Firebird, or hell, maybe he's looking for a job or something to keep himself busy until the Military drags him away again.

"He really has grown," Candice murmurs, definitely approving of the new stronger, buffer, and overall intimidating version of the man I've been in love with since I was eleven years old.

I slam my elbow into her ribs. "Keep your eyes to yourself."

"Why?" she questions, raising a brow. "Is he spoken for?"

"No."

"Then what's the problem?"

I clench down on my jaw. It seems this is just the way things are going to go around here now that Rivers is back. Everybody wants to know my business and everybody thinks they're entitled to know what's going on inside my heart. "Why don't you put this order through," I suggest.

She does what she's told like a good little employee and I finish off the arrangement before handing it over and sending the big guy on his way.

The bell jingles as he exits the store and I curse the little fucker as the sound has Rivers' head whipping around. He scans over the store with disinterest as he chats to the mechanic, but it takes all of two seconds for him to realize what he's looking at and even less time for me to realize that no one has told him about this.

His jaw drops just a touch and he turns directly to face my store while he looks it over. I don't doubt he's currently taking in the store name which is flashing in lights reading 'Read My Tulips' and is quickly coming to the realization that this is my store.

Rivers waves off the mechanic and starts walking across

the road and I swallow back fear. I'm not ready for this.

He left the ball in my court on Monday and there's no way in hell I'm prepared to face him again, not after he told me everything that I've been needing to hear. I'm not strong enough to push him away again.

He walks right up to the front of my store while I stare on with bated breath. I watch as his eyes scan over the flowers and takes in the way I've done up the entrance of my store. He looks over the decorations in the front window and then finally his eyes find mine. They shine with unbelievable pride and for the first time since he's been back, I feel absolutely elated.

Electricity pulses through me just as it does every time he's near.

Please don't come in here. Please don't come in here.

His fingers brush over the bucket of lilies I keep at the very front of my store for my little sister and he scoops one up, letting the stem dangle low. I doubt he knows what kind of flower he's holding, but the meaning isn't lost on me.

His eyes bore into mine and I see the desperation within him to run in here and pull me into his arms and I don't doubt that he sees that reflected in my eyes. But if he can see that, then he can also see that I'm not ready, that now's not the time, and it's certainly not the place.

Being the silent brooding hero that I've always known him to be, he lowers his chin and takes a step back. That one tiny movement allows me to catch a breath and a wave of relief crashes down over me. As if reading my mind, a sexy as fuck smirk cuts across his face and he sends me a wink before walking away with my lily.

I'm left panting and it takes me way too long to remember that Candice has been standing right beside me the whole time, witness to the effect Samuel Rivers has on me.

My eyes slowly scan across to her to find her smirking and shaking her head. She grabs the finished arrangement of roses and begins wrapping them as a chuckle pulls from within her. "Tell yourself whatever helps you sleep at night, but just know, that no matter how much you lie to yourself; you're fucked."

CHAPTER 8

RIVERS

I gather all the papers that I've been preparing with my lawyer over the past week. I don't know what convinced me to do this but I had to keep myself busy while Henley and Noah are away otherwise, I would have been barging down Tully's door day in and day out.

I haven't bothered her since I saw her a few days ago and knowing that she's so damn close and not being able to be near her is killing me. I hate being away from her, but I need to respect the fact that she needs space to sort through her emotions.

Everyone keeps telling me how much she's changed since I went away, but when I look at her, I still see a fighter and that means that she can still deliver one hell of an ass whopping if need be. I'm not here to barge into her life and screw it all around, despite the fact that I sort of am. I want to make her happy, but I want to do it respectfully.

Besides, she's still with Spencer and I need to let her work that shit out before I go and steal her away. Tully is not a cheater. She hates people like that and I refuse to make her feel as though she has a decision to make. I know in my gut that she's never going to accept Spencer's proposal. So, for now, it's a waiting game.

She's going to end things with Spencer eventually because her hearts not in it, but it also has me wondering why she's allowed it to go on so long.

Tully looked so fucking beautiful when I saw her in her store. I've never been so damn proud. She's managed to build everything that she's ever wanted for herself and done it with her own two hands. She's so unbelievably strong.

Despite not wanting to bother her, I haven't exactly been able to keep away. I've had an excuse to walk by her store every fucking day this week. I ran out of milk so I went an extra twenty minutes out of my way just to go to the grocery store near 'Read My Tulips' and check in on her. Every day it's getting harder to stay away.

I'm pathetically and hopelessly in love with her and I need to make things right.

A loud buzzing draws my attention away from the papers and I look up to see the woman I haven't seen in over ten years.

Gina Rivers. My mother.

How did I ever allow Henley to talk me into this shit? This woman is where my issues as a kid started. I never knew the real reasons behind what my mother was doing and why. That's all shit Henley, Noah, and Tully were able to discover in my absence and now, I guess it's time for me to face my demons.

I find my mother almost instantly, but not because she looks like the woman I once knew. I recognize her because she looks just like my sister, only a little older. The woman I used to know would have her hair died so dark that it would match the black makeup she used to circle around her eyes.

This woman is all natural just like Henley. She has golden hair and beaming blue eyes, nothing at all how I remember, but she looks a million times better than the horrible images stored in my memory.

As she walks my way, her eyes roam over me, taking in the man that I've become compared to the boy that she once knew. As she gets closer and her eyes fill with warmth and excitement, guilt pours through me. All these years she's been rotting away in prison because of a decision that I made. If I had known the truth and known that it was my father behind it all, I never would have done it.

I have so much to make up for.

I always knew my father was a snake. He recruited me into his ranks when I was just eight years old. I saw things that no kid should ever see, but he would tell me that it makes me stronger, makes me a soldier, but never would I have thought that he'd do something like that to my mother.

Anton was always telling me how important blood is, yet that's how he treats my blood, how he made me treat my own blood.

By the age of twelve when I'd done the unthinkable, it was water off a duck's back. I barely had a second thought for what I'd done to my mother. I was dark. I wasn't the kid that she once knew. She needed to be punished for her crimes and I thought it was my duty to make it happen.

I was Anton's soldier.

I didn't learn what it truly meant to be a soldier until I joined the Military and I was able to find some sort of peace within myself. I took my time at war as a punishment for what I'd done, and fuck, it was certainly a brutal punishment, but it's what I needed.

I forgave myself and the second that happened, the darkness lifted off my shoulders and I was finally free. It's the exact feeling I'm getting from my mother right now.

I expected her to come at me with anger and fury for doing this to her, but it's as though that doesn't exist.

As she steps up to the table, I rise from my seat and watch as she tilts her head up when I tower over her. Pride surges in her eyes and I'm oddly struck by just how similar she looks to Henley. We really are related. I never doubted it before but seeing and hearing are two very different things.

"Samuel," mom whispers, holding back tears.

"You look good, mom."

We both stand face to face, staring at the other for a silent moment before emotions take over and I throw my arms around her, crushing her into my chest and holding her close for all the years we missed out on.

Mom's arms wrap around me and she cries silent tears. "You're so big now," she murmurs against my chest. "Nothing at all like the little boy I remember."

"I'm so sorry, mom," I tell her, hating the gut-wrenching grief that comes over me knowing I was the one who did this to her. How could she ever forgive me? How can she bear to have my arms wrapped around her? Surely, she must hate me.

"You have nothing to be sorry for, son," she tells me, pulling back and roaming her eyes over me. "Now let me get a good look at you. I've missed you like you could never know."

I look at her in shock, ignoring the second half of what she just said. We can come back to that later. "How can you say that? I did this to you. I went to the police and told them what you were involved with when I had no business talking about something I didn't understand. How could you ever forgive me?"

Her lips press into a tight line and she indicates down to the seat I'd just vacated as she gets herself comfortable in the one opposite mine. "Sit down, Samuel. Clearly, we have a lot to discuss."

I couldn't agree more.

I get myself comfortable before her and prepare myself for the ultimate smackdown. Whatever she's got for me, I'm ready to take it. I deserve whatever's coming for me after the shit I've put her through.

"Henley told me you joined the Military. You were deployed?"

I gape at her. "Really? It's been eleven years and you want to talk about the Military? How about the fact that I have a sister who just happens to be my best friend's wife?"

"Oh, the wedding," she gushes. "Henley was telling me all about it. I can't wait to see the pictures. I bet she would have been a beautiful bride. I'm so sorry I couldn't be there. We thought I'd be out by now. That Noah though, he sure is a lot to handle."

I gape at her again. Is she for real?

"Mom," I say, not wanting to set her off. "Henley's my sister. Why did you never tell me that?"

A seriousness comes over her. "I wish I could have," she tells me with a sigh. "You would have been an incredible big brother to her. You would have been protective and adored her just as a brother should."

"I am protective of her and I do adore her. She was family to me before any of this came out."

Mom nods with pride shining through her eyes. "You're a good kid, Samuel. I'm glad to see that after all the suffering you went through that you turned out so well."

My heart swells, but I don't want to dwell on it. "Why didn't you say anything about Henley being my sister?"

"I don't know how much Henley has told you, but I had to protect my little girl. Your fate was sealed with Anton as I gave birth to you, but Henley had a chance of escaping it. I had no choice, I had to give her up. Not a day went by that I hated myself for that decision, but she had a much better life than the one she would have had with us. Surely, you must know that."

"I do," I tell her. "As much of a shock that it was to find out she was my baby sister, I wouldn't change it. It feels right and I'm glad that she had a happy upbringing. I wouldn't be able to bear the thought of her having to go through the same kind of shit that I did."

Mom reaches out and takes my hand. "I'm so sorry, Samuel. I tried to get you away from it, but he found us. Every move I made, he would counter and I would be condemned for it."

"If I knew how evil he was, I never would have gone with him."

"You were just a child and you had no reason to doubt him. He loved you fiercely and the second you were born, he had stars in his eyes and when he looked at you, he saw an heir, not a son. Anton is a very charming man and he could convince even the purest of men to do something despicable. You cannot blame yourself. Do you hear me? He corrupted your poor soul before you even knew the difference between right and wrong and I should have tried harder to save you from that."

"You did. You moved us away. He's Anton Mathers. No one can escape him."

She lets out a sigh and gives a slight shrug. "It's all in the past now. He's been put away where he belongs and now we can all move forward. I'll be out soon and I can close the book on all of this."

I rub my thumbs over her knuckles. "I thought about coming and visiting you every fucking day, but I was too ashamed with what I'd done and by the time I realized that I was wrong, I was already deployed. I failed you, mom."

"No, Samuel. I failed you. You did the right thing going to the police. Despite your father's involvement, I still did the crime and I needed to be punished for that."

"But you didn't deserve to be punished. He made you. He gave you no other choice."

She squeezes my hand. "I wasn't around to teach you any life lessons, but if I can teach you just one thing, then know this; in life, there's always another choice. Anton backed me into a corner and where it came to protecting you, I would have done anything. I chose to agree to his terms when I could have found help. I could have spoken to the police. I could have run. There are hundreds of choices I could have made, but I was terrified and chose the easy way out. I ran that prostitution ring and I broke the law. I deserved to be in here, and while it was the hardest thing I've ever been through, it was also a blessing because it freed me from his hold. But don't you think for even one second that I didn't think about what that meant for you. Every damn day I panicked over what kind of hell he was putting you through and not a moment went by that I didn't wonder if I'd lost you to that life."

My eyes drop to the table as a whisper comes slipping from between my lips. "There was a moment where I think you did."

Mom slowly nods her head. "I know, but you're unbelievably strong. You're my son and if I was able to fight to get out of there and had the strength to give up my child, then I knew that you'd be able to do anything you put your mind to. You just needed to want it bad enough."

"I did."

"I knew you would," she smiles proudly. "When Henley showed up here that very first time and told me how you'd left for the Military, I knew you were fighting and I knew that it'd be hard, but you'd get yourself to exactly where you needed to be and seeing as though you're sitting here right in front of me, something tells me that you made it. You've let go of all the horrors of your past and now you're ready to build yourself a life."

"I am."

"With Tully?"

A smile cuts across my face and mom smiles right back. "I've missed that smile," she tells me. "No matter what kind of horrors your father put you through, there's still that mischievous little boy hiding inside of you."

"I've really missed you, mom."

"We have a lot of missed time to make up for."

"And we will. As soon as you get out, I promise you, I'll

make it right. I'm going to be the son you've always deserved."

"You already are. You and Henley, you're both everything to me and I'm so grateful to have you both back in my life."

I release her hands and grab the bundle of papers sitting beside me. "I actually wanted to talk to you about you getting out."

"Oh?" she questions, furrowing her brows.

"Yeah, I, uh…I wanted to sign the house back into your name."

"What?" she gasps, flicking her eyes down to the papers before bringing them back to mine. I slide the papers across the table and she hesitantly takes them before scanning over them. "No. I won't allow you to do this. That is your home and it has been for the past twenty years."

"No. To me it was never a home, just a house to keep me warm at night. It's always reminded me of the bad times, especially seeing your empty bedroom at the end of the hall. Henley told me just how much you loved that place and when I got back from deployment and saw how Tully had fixed it up and made it look like a home again, I knew that's where you belonged. I've always felt more peace with Tully. Wherever she is, is where I call home. I know Anton bullied you into signing it to me and now I want to give it back."

Mom's eyes grow watery before she looks up from the papers. "Are you sure about this? There's no money owing on the property. Having this home sets you up with a future where you will never have to struggle."

"I don't struggle. I've made plenty of money over the years from my father and I have plenty of savings from the Military. You don't need to worry about that. I want you to have it and I want you to have somewhere to call home when you get out. Though," I add with a smile cutting across my face, "I might have to share with you until I can find a place of my own."

"Oh, of course," she laughs, throwing herself across the

table to pull me into another tight hug which results in a guard barking sharp orders for her to sit her ass back down. "You really have turned into an incredible man. I'm so proud of the person you've become, Samuel. I always knew you'd be able to overcome all the hurdles in your life."

"Yeah," I say. "I still have one big hurdle to go and then I'll have it all."

"You'll get her back," mom says, knowing exactly what I'm referring to. "I've met her a handful of times over the past few years and that girl is deeply in love with you. No matter what's going on in her life, she'll come home to you."

"I hope so."

"Have faith."

I nod. "There's a lot I need to make up for."

"I don't doubt that. There's a fire within that girl and she's going to make you work for it."

"Trust me it's going to be the hardest thing I ever do," I laugh before indicating down to the papers. "I've already had the papers drawn up by my lawyer so all you need to do is sign them and the house is yours."

"What about the fees? Surely there must be a few."

"They're all taken care of. All you need to do is sign."

She nods and I slide a pen across the table before watching as she reclaims her home with tears of joy in her eyes. I don't doubt that today, as well as the day that Henley came back into her life, is one of the best days she's had in a while. I can't imagine much good happens for inmates, but knowing that she's going to be set up for a bright future after she gets out is important. I'll have to organize a job for her and make sure she has everything she needs before I move out.

Though, that brings the question of where the hell I'm going to go, but I'm sure my new wedded best friend and sister wouldn't mind giving up their couch for a little while.

Mom finishes with the papers before sliding them back across the table. "While you're mending bridges, are you going to visit your father? He's only down the road from here."

I shake my head. "No. I don't think I could walk in there and see his face without getting myself locked up too. I've got too much to live for. Besides, I don't want to give him the satisfaction of ever seeing me again. He tore me down and turned me into a monster that was clouded with darkness. I did terrible things under his thumb that's going to haunt me for as long as I live and I'm ready to put it behind me. It's taken me four years and finding Tully to be able to move on and I'm not prepared to take any steps back. I'm only looking forward from here."

Pride shines through her eyes. "That's a great answer, Samuel. But just remember, one day you're going to be ready to face him and when that day comes, you'll have my full support."

"And if that day never comes?"

"Then nothing. Either way, he dies knowing he lost the most important people in his life and there's not a damn thing he can do to get them back."

"Well, that sounds fucking perfect to me."

"I might be incarcerated, but I'll still curse you out for your language."

I can't help but grin at the fire that burns brightly within her. "I'm going to enjoy having you home again."

A sparkle lights up her eyes. "Yeah, well something tells me dealing with you on the regular is going to be one of the most frustrating things I'll ever suffered through."

"Prepare yourself, mom. This is going to be fun."

CHAPTER 9

TULLY

I lean over my kitchen counter staring at the little silver ring that could have changed it all. I was right to never have married Spencer, but it doesn't make it suck any less. If things were different, I could have had it all. I could have had the white picket fence surrounding a beautiful home that housed two little mini-me's. I would have liked a little boy first and then a girl so she would always have her big brother to look out for her and protect her from the ugliness of the world.

Instead, I'm standing in my empty apartment wondering where it all went wrong. This ring held the promise of a future and my heart just wasn't there. I shouldn't be holding this. Especially now that I've seen this ring in Rivers' hands and could see just how wrong it was.

I need to return it. In fact, I've been thinking about returning it for the past week, but I simply haven't been able to find the strength to go over to Spencer's place and give it back.

It's been two weeks since the shocking break up and I call it shocking because it hit me out of left field. One second I thought he wanted to make it work and the next, he'd given up on everything and let go of the three years we shared.

Since then, I've heard that he's taken Lacey out three times. Now, it could just be a budding friendship that's growing over some kind of mutual respect, but something tells me it's something much more. While I shouldn't let it bother me, I can't help but wonder how much he actually loved me if he's able to be moving on so soon.

He used to tell me that I was his world and that I was the only woman he could ever see his life with. I guess words are just words and they don't mean anything unless it comes with action.

Crap, Tully. Don't get yourself worked up over this bullshit again.

Two weeks this shit has been circling my head and when it's not, it's Rivers. He's been doing me a favor by keeping away, but he's stupid if he doesn't think that I notice him walking by the store every damn day. My soul burns for him, my body craves him, and my heart belongs to him. When he walks by, it's as though something pulls from within me and instantly has my eyes snapping up to the window.

I had a day where there weren't too many orders to fill so didn't go in until after lunch. Candice took charge for the morning and kept everything running smoothly, but when I got there, I'd found Rivers sitting across the road on a bench with a mountain of a hamburger between his fingers. When he looked up and noticed I was there, his eyes instantly scanned over me and I realized that he was making sure I was ok. His face smoothed out with relief and I walked on through to my store.

I don't know how long he'd been sitting there, but something tells me he would have waited all day just to make sure I was doing alright. The second the door closed behind me, he got up off the bench and walked away, still focused on throwing the hamburger down the hatch.

I know I shouldn't, but I'm starting to believe him when he says that he's going to make it right. He's never wanted to openly be there for me before. He's always loved me in secret. It was always something that was hidden from my brother and when that finally came out, it was something we never acted on…well sort of. We certainly had a few dirty nights between the sheets, but for the most part, we could never cross that line to finally be together.

But now…things seem different with him. He seems open, willing…wanting. And I'm terrified of letting him because when it comes down to it, nothing has really changed. While he seems different, he's still that stranger I fell in love with at eleven.

Everything I know about him, I've discovered through other people. I don't know the real him, the him that he's kept hidden from us for so long. How does he expect anyone to be ok with that? When it comes to me, he knows every tiny little detail about my life. He knows what makes me tick, what I like, and how I love. With him, there have been many things that I've been able to learn over the years, but yet he's still a closed book.

I don't know if I could even consider moving forward with a friendship with him without knowing who he really is, but then, I'm also terrified of learning all the dark things that he's worked so hard to keep hidden from me.

It won't change my perspective of him though. He was dealt a shitty hand in life and judging by the way he walks with his head held so high, I'd dare say he's come right out the other end, stronger and braver than ever before. He's making a life for himself and I don't doubt that he's going to be just fine. Perfect in fact.

Shit. Why do I have to love him like this?

All I've wanted for the past four years was to forget him, but it's impossible. I'll never be able to move on until he finally gives my heart back and I have a feeling he'll be holding onto it as hard as he can. My heart is never coming back to me and one of these days, I'm going to learn how to function without it.

I pull myself out of my turmoil. I've spent every night over the past two weeks falling into this endless cycle of thinking about boys who I should be trying to put behind me, but every night I fail. Not even Netflix and ice cream can save me.

Glancing up at the clock, I realize that Spencer should be home from work. He spent four years of college dominating the football team, but when it came to signing a contract afterward, the luck just wasn't there. That was a major downfall for him, but nobody can deny that what he'd achieved in his short football career was incredible. Not many others could say that they've done what he's done.

That was only five months ago and I'd dare say the pain from that is still living strong within him.

And now this…

Great! Another reason that points out how much of a bitch I am. I should get the words 'Pathetic bitch' tattooed across my forehead so people know to keep away.

I scoop the ring up off the counter and close the lid. If I don't do this now, then I may never do it. Spencer is the kind of guy who likes to worry. If something was said or done, he likes it resolved so I don't doubt that over the past two weeks he's been concerned about me. He always has been, even during that year before we actually got together.

Things really suck on my end, but I need to show him that I'm doing ok and that I don't hold it against him, otherwise he's never going to let it go. He's constantly going to worry about me, despite the fact that he shouldn't. I don't deserve his concern.

I drop the ring into my handbag and double check my reflection in the mirror. There have been way too many times that I've caught my reflection over the last two weeks only to find mascara smudged all over my face. If I'm going to show Spencer that I'm doing ok and tell him that he made the right decision, then I need to act the part.

He doesn't need to know that I've been a mess. No one does, though there is one person who will know even if I don't say a word. He just...he always knows.

After getting myself cleaned up and out the door, I pull up in front of Spencer's home and look up at it. Spencer and I shared a lot of memories here, even though he bought the place when he probably shouldn't have.

He bought it with the inheritance that he'd received from his grandmother who had passed when he was twenty-one, right before he proposed for the second time. He had this big vision of us living here and starting a family together which was his big dream. But he dropped this news on me only six months after I purchased my dream apartment and at that time, I felt as though he wasn't listening to anything that I wanted. Actually, I don't think he ever did.

It was always about the big dream of getting married and having a family, but not once did I say that's what I wanted. In fact, I went out of my way to make sure he understood that, but the proposals kept coming with the assumption that I just wasn't ready.

He needs to find a girl who's willing to fall at his feet and give him the world he wants.

Don't get me wrong, marriage and babies have always been the dream for me, but I just couldn't see it happening with him. I don't know. Maybe there's someone out there somewhere who's going to fall at my feet and make my heart explode with love...or maybe I should start buying cats.

I grab my handbag and get out of my car before taking my sweet time walking to the door. Do I knock or just walk straight in like I used to?

Shit. Why do I feel so nervous?

I let out a shaky breath and pull on my big girl panties. It's just Spencer.

I knock on the door and stand there awkwardly, just now realizing that I have no idea what I'm going to say to him. I start to search every deep corner of my brain for the right thing, but nothing comes up and before I know it, it's too late.

The door swings open and Spencer stands before me with a welcoming smile that quickly drops into a frown marred with concern. "Um…hi," I say like a dork, giving him a stupid as fuck little wave.

He stands there gaping at me for a moment and it's clear he doesn't know what to say either when a softness creeps into his features and he reaches out for me. "Come here," he murmurs, pulling me into his arms and crushing me into his chest.

My arms instinctively fly up around him and I find comfort in his familiarity. "I'm sorry," I tell him as I try to hold back tears. "I just…"

"It's ok. You don't need to say anything."

We stand in each other's arms for a short moment as we each find ourselves and it's not long before I hear the sound of the door closing behind me and find myself in the middle of the small living room.

Spencer's hands come up and he takes hold of my upper arms, but doesn't step away. His thumbs rub back and forth over my skin. "Are you ok?"

"I think so," I murmur into his chest. "You?"

"I will be."

I nod and take a deep breath, breathing him in one last time before stepping back.

"Did you want to come in?"

I look up at him with a slight cringe. "No, I, ah…shouldn't." I dig through my bag and pull out the ring which only makes him cringe. I hand it over and his fingers linger on mine for a moment too long. "I wanted to give you this back."

He takes the ring from me as he presses his lips into a

tight line and stares down at it. "Thanks," he says slowly before looking back up at me. "Listen, Tully. I'm sorry about how I ended it. I didn't mean for it to be...you kno, so quick."

I shrug my shoulders. "Just like ripping off a band-aid. Sometimes things are better done quickly."

He shakes his head. "Not this. I was insensitive and only thinking about what I was feeling and I think that meant hurting you more than what was necessary."

"No," I tell him. "I've been doing a lot of thinking and I've realized that you were right. I should have ended it with you when I first realized that it wasn't right. I strung you along for so long because I was terrified of getting hurt and in doing that, I hurt you. I treated you unfairly and you deserve so much better than that."

"I can't disagree with that, but you're not the only one at fault," he says with a slight smile before reaching out and tucking a lock of hair behind my ear. "I knew from the very start that you'd already given your heart away, but I wanted to make you happy and I think for a while that maybe I did. After the second proposal was when I realized that I could be fighting a losing battle, but I saw how much you needed me in your life and I wasn't ready to let you go. In hindsight, maybe it would have been healthier for you had I left back then. Maybe you would have had a chance to heal on your own, but I liked the idea that you depended on me. I liked that I was your constant and even though I shouldn't have, I gave you all of me because I held onto hope that maybe one day you'd be able to do the same."

"I'm so sorry, Spencer."

"Don't be sorry, Tully. That was my mistake and it was a risk that I was willing to take. But don't think for one second that I regret any of it. I loved you so much and every day with you was an adventure. I was happy to share the spotlight with the memory of a man that I was certain was never coming back..."

"But now he is," I finish for him.

"Now he is and I don't think there's enough spotlight for the two of us."

I step back into him and raise my chin so I look up into his pained eyes. "I don't think you deserve to ever have to share the spotlight with anyone."

Spencer's arm curls around me and his lips gently brush over mine. "You're right," he whispers. "I don't and I won't ever do that to myself again."

I nod until he drops his forehead to mine and holds me in silence once again, just the sound of our breathing between us. It's almost the perfect goodbye, that is until he goes and ruins the moment. "Are you going to get back together with him?"

I shake my head. "No. I'd be a fool to allow him back in just as you'd be a fool to do the same with me."

"You say that now, but when it comes down to it, I don't know if you'll have the strength to tell him no."

"I have to," I whisper. "I can't go through that with him again."

"As much as it kills me to say it, but maybe you should. Your heart has always belonged to him, Tully. Maybe you're not going to find your happiness until you go back home."

"No."

"At least do yourself a favor and think it over," he tells me before releasing me once again. "Has he come and made his intentions known?"

I look down at the floor, feeling a little uncomfortable talking to my very recent ex about another man. "He has."

"And?"

"And nothing. I'm not prepared to go back there," I tell him. "Are you just pushing this because you feel bad about your date with Lacey?"

Spencer's eyes fly open and guilt instantly begins coming over him. "How'd you hear about that?"

I mask my pain. Ever since I first heard about it, I've

been holding onto the hope that maybe they'd been hanging out as friends, but the look on his face tells me that maybe there's a little more to the story, and I think it's a story that I'm not ready to be listening to. "Candice has a big mouth," I remind him.

"Shit. I should have known," he winces. "Are you ok with this? It was more of a friend thing, but there could be something more. I just…I didn't want you getting hurt because of it."

"No, it's fine. It was a bit of a shock that you'd been out with a girl so soon, but you deserve to find someone who'll treat you right. Just don't go parading it around, at least, not just yet, you know. It's still a bit fresh."

"I promise."

I nod as I take a step back towards the door and grab the handle behind my back. "I think maybe I should get going," I tell him, feeling the emotions beginning to creep up on me.

"Are you sure? Have you eaten? I could get you dinner."

"Bad idea, Spence. Besides, I was going to grab take out on the way home. You know how I feel about Chinese food."

His eyes narrow suspiciously. "Really? So, you're telling me you're not lying and you're not actually planning on stopping by the gas station to get endless tubs of ice cream?"

A smile spreads across my face. "So, what if I am?"

"Well, then remember not to get the caramel one. You never seem to like it as much."

"I won't," I whisper as I pull the door open. I step out into the night before looking back through the door and taking in the man who helped me through so very much. "You know I really do love you, right?"

"I know," he smiles, walking forward and pressing a kiss to my forehead. "I love you too, Tully, but get your fine ass out of here before I drop to my knees and start begging for you to come back."

I do as I'm told and get my ass out the door because seeing him on his knees, begging for me back might just have me doing something stupid like agreeing.

Knowing that he doesn't hate me has something settling in my heart and I realize that I'm going to be ok. I can put it all behind me and start working on moving past Rivers.

Maybe Spencer will end up with Lacey or maybe not, all I know is that at the end of the day, I'm going to be doing everything I can to make sure he somehow remains in my life.

Spencer was an incredible friend before he became more than that and I hate myself for hurting him. I know things might be a bit rough as both our hearts are healing, but I'm happy knowing that one day, it's going to get better.

I get myself home and crash down into bed with my tub of ice cream while scanning through Netflix for something to watch. It's been two long weeks of agony and confusion, but for the first time in those long weeks, I'm finally starting to feel at peace.

CHAPTER 10

RIVERS

Fuck me. I'm so lame.

If this was any other girl, I'd be arrested for stalking her, but Tully knows better. She knows that I need to be close to her and seeing as though she hasn't told me to fuck off yet, I'm assuming she's cool with my random walk-bys. Though, it's getting harder not to walk my ass in there and tell her enough is enough.

I've let her mope for the past two weeks. The first few days were hard because she looked so damn broken. There was a look in her eye that told me to back the hell off and give her some time to think and I've been doing just that, but how long is this going to go on for?

I haven't spoken a word to her since I barged through her apartment, but something has changed. For two weeks she's looked pained, confused, and hurt. Some of the days she even looked downright pissed off, but today…she looks like the old Tully.

I've been working on my Firebird and working out to

pass the time because there's really not a lot to do around here when my best friend is in Italy with my sister and the love of my life is too busy re-perfecting her glare in case she needs to start using it again. She used to give me the filthiest glare every time I managed to piss her off. It was sexy as hell and since leaving for the military, I haven't seen it, but something tells me it's going to make a come back one of these days. Though there are a lot of things she used to do that I'm noticing she doesn't do anymore, me being one of them.

I spent most of last week pulling the Firebird apart and working out what parts need to be scrapped and what can be saved, and so far, it's actually looking better than I thought. Most of the damage was to the body of the car, but the engine still has a shot at being brought back from the dead. So, this week has been all about searching for the parts that I need to make it happen.

I can't wait to see Noah's face when I fire it up. The fucker is convinced that I can't do it, and just because he thinks that, I've got all the more motivation to prove him wrong. Fuck, nothing feels better than proving Noah Cage wrong. Henley can vouch for me on that one. I'd bet anything that she'd get the same thill out of it that I do.

When I'm not working on the Firebird or obsessing over Tully, I've been working out, which is exactly what I've been doing this afternoon. I spent a good hour doing weights and the past thirty minutes running through Haven Falls which is how I ended up here. I always end up here, but today, I think I might hang around for a bit.

I find myself dropping down onto the bench to watch her. Tully clocked me the second I came into view and hasn't taken her eyes off me since. This has been our routine for the past two weeks. I come past, check that she's doing ok, and then I keep going. Sometimes I stay for a moment and sometimes she gives me a smile that puts everything at ease and has me happy to leave her be.

Today though, I ain't going anywhere.

She's so goddamn beautiful. She has a black shirt with her 'Read My Tulips' logo across the back that hugs her frame just beautifully. She was wearing this shirt the day I'd come across her store and she may have a million pairs of the same shirt, but this particular one seems just a little bigger on her.

I highly doubt that she ordered a shirt a size too big which could only mean that she's lost weight over the past two weeks. Though I don't know how it's possible. She's most likely been curled up on her couch watching Netflix and eating ice cream. Not exactly healthy but it's not as though her body isn't used to that kind of torture. Eating endless tubs of ice cream has been her go to thing since before I met her. That and chicken nuggets of course.

The realization has my jaw clenching and I have to remind myself of all the reasons why I should be staying put right now. Why the hell hasn't Spencer been picking her up on it? Someone needs to be shoving hamburgers down her throat.

My fingers start to twitch. There's a takeout store just down the road. I could go down there, get her something to eat, put it down in front of her and back away, but with that fire in her eyes today, she'd most likely throw it back at me. But fuck, I wouldn't even care because I love that fire.

My phone rings and I welcome the distraction. I dig it out of my pocket and grin down at Noah's name. "Well, if it isn't the biggest fuckhead in all of Haven Falls," I grin.

"What the fuck did you do to Tully? She hasn't answered my calls in two weeks."

"What are you talking about? I didn't do anything. She's fine. I'm looking at her right now."

"Really?" he grumbles in surprise. "Then put her on the fucking phone. I have a few things to get off my chest. No body gets away with ignoring my calls."

"Um…" Shit. How do I tell my best friend that when I say 'looking at her' I mean in more of a stalking kind of way?

"I'm at her store and she's busy with a customer. I'll get her to call you later on."

"Fine."

"How's it going over there? Are you enjoying Italy?"

"Yeah," he grumbles under his breath.

A grin rips across my face at his tone as I watch Tully chatting with Candice. "What's the problem?"

"Nothing," he sighs. "Henley wants to keep exploring while I'd rather keep her locked up in our hotel room. You wouldn't believe how many fucking times she's made me visit Juliet's Balcony and rub her right tit."

I stop staring at his sister and focus on my best friend in case he's just gone insane. "What the fuck are you talking about?"

He lets out a frustrated sigh. "We're in Verona and there's a building here which is said to have inspired *Shakespeare's 'Romeo and Juliet.'*"

"Ok…" I say slowly. "Go back to the rubbing her tits thing."

"There's a statue of Juliet in the courtyard. You're supposed to rub her right tit for good luck or some shit like that."

"It's for luck in love," Henley's voice comes shooting through the line.

I shake my head. "Don't you two already have enough luck in love? Bring that tit home for me to rub."

"What do you mean?" Noah questions in a too cheery tone. "Shit ain't going well with Tully?"

Has he lost his fucking mind? "You remember she's with Spencer, right? You know, the dickhead who all but abandoned her at your wedding and has let her lose weight over the past two weeks."

"The fuck? What do you mean she's lost weight?"

Henley's voice comes through the line again and I realize I must be on speakerphone. "You know, Spencer isn't as bad as you think he is. I would have abandoned Noah too had he been all caught up on his ex."

"She's not my ex," I throw back at her.

"Not officially," she chimes. "But you were hers and she was yours. Tomato/tomato."

"Why hasn't anyone answered me about my fucking sister losing weight? Put her the fuck on the phone."

I ignore his last demand. "I don't know man. Her shirt was tight around her body last week and now...it's not."

"Shit," Henley says, sounding a lot closer to the phone. "Something must have happened."

"What do you mean? Nothing's happened. I've been keeping an eye on her."

"Right," Henley scoffs. "Because she's really going to tell you all about it. Do you forget who we're talking about here?" I roll my eyes. The girl has a point. "The only things that could cause such a big reaction out of her is either her store or Spencer, and I seriously doubt it's the store. She must have ended it with Spencer."

I raise a brow as my eyes flick back up to my girl to find her eyes still on me. "Nah, there's no way," I say, but it might actually explain why she's looking a little more alive.

"I don't know," Henley mutters. "With you back...I guess anything could be possible."

Well shit. In that case, I don't have time for listening to these two bullshit about a statue's tits. I should be in there figuring out this Spencer stuff. "Alright, I'm going to get to the bottom of this," I tell them.

"Yeah, alright," Noah grumbles. "Just...if she did end it, take it easy on her. She'll be hurting."

"I know how to handle my girl."

"Maybe. But she wasn't your girl for four years. She's changed."

"That's where you're wrong, brother," I tell him. "And Henley? Stop making my boy touch the tits of random statues."

"She's not random. She's *Juliet*."

"So? The pussy only wants to touch yours."

With that, I leave them to their honeymoon and get on with it. Apparently, I have a bit of a mystery to solve.

I get up from the bench and slide my phone back into my pocket and as I cross the road towards 'Read My Tulips' Tully hasn't stopped watching me and the second she realizes what I'm doing, her eyes practically bug out of her head.

'No, no, no, no, no,' she mouths to herself as she starts shaking her head, making a smirk cut across my lips. She doesn't look terrified like she had last time, but she certainly doesn't look as though she's about to welcome me in with open arms, but I don't care. The time for waiting is over. If she's through with Spencer, then I'm not sitting back and wasting any more time. I've got a girl to win back.

The closer I get, the more her head shakes, but there's a flare of excitement hidden within her eyes. I've always been unpredictable and hell, so has she, but this is the kind of bullshit she fell in love with. She'd never admitted it but back in high school, she used to love it when I'd storm in and take control and from the way she's looking at me now, I'm sure she's busy looking deep within herself and searching out that old attitude she used to reserve just for me.

I push my way through the door and without taking my eyes from hers, I storm right up to her, hating that I have to resist touching her. I miss the old days where she'd just naturally fall in beside me or I could just throw her over my shoulder and go, but it won't be long and we'll be right back there again.

Tully sets her jaw and raises her chin before crossing her arms over her chest, unintentionally pushing her tits up and drawing my attention away from her fiery eyes. "What the hell do you think you're doing?"

My eyes rake back up her body before stopping on her eyes to find them shining with a strange mix of pissed off excitement. "Get your shit. You're coming with me."

She raises a brow before letting out a sharp laugh.

SHERIDAN ANNE

"Excuse me? Who do you think you are coming in here after four years of radio silence and pulling this alpha bullshit on me? I don't think so, Rivers. That shit ain't going to fly with me, not anymore."

"Tully," I say slowly, narrowing my eyes on hers. "I'm not asking. Get your shit. Let's go."

She leans forward onto her counter and smirks at me as though I haven't said a word, but the fire in her eyes tells me she loves every moment of this, and fuck it, I do too. "I'm not sure if you've realized," she says, sweeping her arm around and gesturing to her store. "I've got a store to run now. I can't just grab my shit and go because some douche comes storming in here demanding my attention. Besides, did you consider that I don't want to go anywhere with you?"

Fuck me. My dick practically jumps out of my jeans. What is it about Tully Cage and her attitude that gets me so fucking hot?

My eyes snap across to Candice and I find myself still wondering why Tully would hire her. "Have you got a key?"

Candice's mouth drops open as she gapes at me. "Uhh...yeah."

"Good. You're doing close. Tully won't be coming back."

"Umm...ok."

I look back to Tully and raise a cocky eyebrow. "Sorted. Let's go."

"No."

"Baby, don't make me come back there because you know I fucking will." And if I do, I'm going to end up fucking her right there on her workbench. Hell, I don't even care if Candice wants to hang and watch, I'm that fucking desperate for her.

Tully steps around her counter and walks towards me, raising her chin in defiance as she faces me. "I'm not your 'baby.'"

My hands slide to her waist and she sucks in a breath while I beg myself to find some sort of self-control. "Try and

114

stop me calling you that," I dare her, only managing to make her eyes dance.

I watch as her jaw clenches and not two seconds later, she caves, though I have a feeling it's because she doesn't want to have this out in front of Candice. "Fine, but you put one foot wrong and I'll take you the fuck down. Now please remove your hands from my waist before I castrate you."

I wink. "My pleasure, baby."

Tully groans as she moves away from me and goes about finding her things, but puts an extra, overdramatic attitude with every move she makes. "That was a risky little game," Candice warns me as Tully ducks out the back.

A soft chuckle escapes me. "Really? Because that wasn't even my warm-up."

Candice shakes her head. "Shit. I'm going to be hearing about this tomorrow."

All I can do is grin.

Tully walks out a second later with her handbag thrown over her shoulder and storms straight past me, making sure to nail her other shoulder right into the soft spot of my arm, giving me an instant dead arm. I groan and slap my hand over it, trying to rub a little bit of life back into it while spinning on my heel and following her out the door. She used to do this to me all the time, only today she hit it much harder than ever before. Clearly, she's trying to make a point, but so am I.

She's set herself a good pace and I have to hurry to catch up to her. She steps up before her car and pulls out her keys and I get there just in time to catch her elbow and pull the keys from between her fingers. I turn her down the street and start pulling her along. "What are you doing?"

I revert to my silent, brooding days and keep my mouth shut. If I tell her that I'm about to buy her dinner and shove it down her throat, she'll probably have a few things to say about it and I'd rather prolong the inevitable.

My hand remains at her elbow for too long before I finally

pull it away, not wanting to push her over the edge. I lead her to the little café down by her store and the second I step through the door, Tully puts on the brakes. "What the hell is this?" she demands. "Tell me you did not just bombard me at work and force me to leave just to take me on some cheap ass date?"

I ignore her whining and step up to the counter to order us each a juicy burger and when I turn back to Tully and take in the shirt that looks too big, I add some fries to the order.

Tully clears her throat once I've finished paying and makes sure to raise an unimpressed brow at me. "Feel free to explain yourself at any time."

"We need to talk."

"No, we don't."

"Why didn't you tell me you broke up with Spencer?"

Her mouth drops for a moment before she regains herself. "Why didn't you tell me that you joined the Military? Come on, throw another question at me, Rivers. I bet I have a million more to throw right back."

I stare at her for a moment. "Are we really not capable of having a civilized conversation?"

"Says the guy who was two seconds away from man-handling me out of my own store," Tully scoffs as her hands find her hips. She waves her hand behind me, gesturing to the chef in the back putting our order together. "Why are you doing this?"

I snap.

My arm snakes around her waist and I pull her tightly into me. Tully sucks in a deep breath, making her chest rise and press firmly against mine. "Because you're my fucking queen and you deserve to get what you need. For the past four years you've been allowing people to give you what they think you want, never getting what you actually need. I've only been here for two fucking weeks and I can't stand back and watch it happen anymore. You have people thinking you're this fragile little butterfly, that you'll fly away with even the

116

slightest breeze, and you know what? I think sometimes you might even believe it yourself, but I know you, Tully, right down to your core and that's not who you are. You're a fucking tiger always ready to roar."

Tully raises her chin, putting her lips just before mine, but never touching. "You don't know me, Rivers. Not anymore."

"Baby, right now, I'm the only fucking person who knows you. I don't even think you know yourself."

"It's funny. After all we've been through, I don't think I even know you."

My brows pull down. "What the fuck are you talking about?"

"You," she says, pulling out of my arms. "How is it possible to fall in love with someone you don't know? You were just some kid who'd fall asleep on my couch every now and then. I never knew a damn thing about you."

"Of course, you did."

"I'm not talking about your birthday or your favorite fucking position, Rivers. I mean you. I don't know you," she demands, poking me in the chest. "I don't know where you grew up, I don't know what your life was like and why you are the way you are. I don't know your reasons for leaving or for staying away. I don't know why or how you thought busting Gina was a good move. I don't know what awful things your father made you do. And I don't fucking know if I'm ever going to have answers for all of these damn questions. They've plagued me for years. How can somebody fall in love with a complete stranger?"

"I was never a stranger to you and you know it. You may never have known the details of my past, but that doesn't mean that you didn't know me. You're the only person I ever allowed in. You're the only person who actually knew me, Tully. Not even your brother."

She shakes her head. "It's not enough, Rivers."

I watch her in silence as I try to work out what exactly it is that she needs from me and whether I'm willing to go

117

there. I sealed my past up and did my best to never think about it again. The things I had to do for my father were awful and the little boy who was quickly corrupted and destroyed is all in the past.

If all it is, is telling her a story, I would have done it years ago, but it's not. The story comes with a darkness that seeps into your soul and feeds off it. Knowing the real me is like cancer. But sharing that with her…is it a risk I'm willing to take? How badly does she need to know this to be able to move on and find peace within herself? I couldn't bear knowing how she'd look at me after hearing the things that I'd done.

It was a miracle that I've been able to pull myself out of that world and even more of a miracle that my pack had the strength to put Anton away and make Haven Falls a place that I could proudly call home.

The girl behind the counter interrupts my thoughts and I reluctantly peel my eyes off Tully. My head swarms with her questions and I don't doubt that there's many more where they came from.

I walk out of the café with our dinner and Tully silently walks beside me. We head for her car and I take her keys that I'd stolen from her earlier and open the passenger's side door for her before helping her in.

Once she's in, I close the door and let out a heavy breath. This really isn't how I was expecting the night to go. After sliding the seat back as far as it will go, I drop down and push the key into the ignition, only my wrist never turns and we sit in an uncomfortable silence, both with thoughts heavier than we can handle.

My head drops as my past comes back to haunt me. One awful thing after another. I'm never going to be able to escape it.

Tully turns to me after we've sat for a few pain-staking long minutes. "I'm sorry…I shouldn't have bought it up. I think once we found out that Anton was your father, I kind of filled in a lot of those blanks, or at least, I tried to."

I nod my head. I can only imagine how she has answered those questions, but I can guarantee that whatever she thinks happened, it was much worse. But what it comes down to is that she isn't going to stop asking until she gets what she's looking for and she's never going to be able to put it behind her until every last riddle is solved.

I blow out a breath. This is going to be harder than I ever thought. Plaguing her pure mind with the horror of my past is unforgivable but something tells me that she needs to hear it just as badly as I need to release it.

I reach across the car and take her hand in mine, forever grateful when she doesn't pull away. Her fingers lace through mine and the electricity pulses between our hands. I could die right now and be satisfied with the life I have because I would have died with her hand held tightly in mine.

"My dad wasn't a good man. Even right from the start when I was first born. In fact, I think it started long before that. He was a monster and he treated everyone and everything as property. I don't remember mom leaving him, I was too young, but all I know is that Anton took it as the deepest betrayal. Family to him is everything. Family is blood, and blood is power. I never knew this at the time, but Anton had agreed to let mom raise me away from him and in return-"

"She would run the prostitution ring," Tully finishes for me.

"Yeah. And of course, she agreed." I look to Tully. "You have to know that if I knew that, that if I knew he had blackmailed her and tried to take me away, I never would have turned her in. I loved her. She was all I had."

Tully's hand squeezes in mine. "I know, Rivers. I don't blame you."

I watch her for a moment and see the compassion in her eyes and it urges me to finish the story. "On my eighth birthday, I was going to school with you guys, but we hadn't actually met. There was one day, I had just walked into class when Anton showed up at the door. All the other kids were scared. Even at eight, they knew to fear him even the fucking teacher looked like he was going to be sick." I shake my head, recalling the memory. "Anton took me out of school that day, telling me it was time to become a man and start training for my future. I remember being excited because my father went to the effort to pick me up from school so we could spend the day together on my birthday. It was a kid's dream come true."

Tully starts shaking her head, but I don't dare stop in fear of not being able to start again. "He took me to a home a few hours from here. There was a family inside and I was confused because they were all tied up, but we weren't helping. I thought he was taking me to the fucking arcade. But instead, there was a mother and father sitting on the floor back to back and two children. I remember the girl was maybe four or five and she had a younger brother. They were both in binds yet somehow the girl was still able to hold the younger brother. She was protective and did what she could to block his vision."

"It felt wrong. When you see someone struggling for freedom in binds your natural reaction is to help them and I couldn't understand why we weren't doing anything. Anton was talking at the father while the mother screamed for her children. Anton's men were all around us and things started to blur. I went to the little girl to free her and was hit for moving. That was when I first realized that we were the bad guys and we weren't there to help."

"Still to this day I don't know what their crimes were against Anton. Whether it was the mother or the father who'd wronged him or even both. All I'm able to remember from that day was when Anton told me that to become a man and have power over others, I'd have to have the strength to do God's work."

Tully gasps and her eyes go wide. "No, no. Please tell me

you didn't," she begs. "Please, Rivers. No."

My eyes close as I remember the moment that's haunted me since my eighth birthday. "I told him no. I didn't want to do it, but he gave me a knife anyway. When I cried, I was yelled at. When I begged, I was hit. When I pissed my fucking pants out of pure terror, I was kicked in the back. I was beaten until I had nothing left to give. That was the moment I realized my father would have killed his own son and out of desperation, I stood, bloodied and bruised, before the woman with a knife in my hand and tears streaming down my face."

Tully squeezes my hand and I fight to keep control. "I was shaking and there was disgust in her eyes and it took me a very long time to realize that disgust was for my father and not for me. She pleaded with me, she would have preferred to see my father beat me to death than to lose her life and not be with her children. But in a situation where Anton is involved, he will always get his way, even if it meant killing his own son."

"He told me what to do and eventually, I did it. I killed that woman in front of her children. I stood back and watched how the life drained from her body, I watched Anton's men take the children, I watched the father realize he was never going to see his children again, and then I watched Anton put a bullet between his eyes."

Tears stream down her face. "You were only eight."

I nod. "Afterward, he took me out for pizza as though I was being congratulated for making my first kill, the bastard even had the nerve to give me a birthday cake. I never knew what happened to those children, but from what kind of businesses Anton was involved in, I'd dare say they were sold to the highest bidder. I remember Anton had said now I was a man. I'd seen and dealt death and no one could touch me. I was powerful. I was a Mathers'. His blood and his heir. He kept me hidden at his home until my bruises had faded and I'd finally stopped screaming in my sleep. He told me to never speak of it again and if I did, he would come for my mom. From then on, my real 'training' started."

"No," she whispers.

I give her a sad smile, trying to remind her that this is all in the past. "It's ok, I didn't have to do something as horrifying as that until a was a bit older. One day he had explained it as getting the worst over and done with so I'd never have to fear anything ever again. He's never been so wrong."

Her voice breaks as she looks across to me with her tear strained cheeks. "How many innocent lives were there?"

My heart breaks and something inside of me is tears into pieces. "I've taken three lives. Each just as horrifying as the last and each for a reason unknown to me."

"All with your father standing over you?"

I nod my head. "The second one, I had a gun at the back of my head, and the last..." I let the sentence fall flat between us as the memory of what I did tears me apart.

"The last?" she prompts.

"The last he was holding up a photo of you."

Tully climbs across the seat and places herself in my lap before threading her arms around my neck. Her face buries into my shoulder and she holds on with tears streaming down her face. "I'm so sorry," she cries as I do my best to try and forget the images coursing through my mind. "I never should have asked."

"No," I tell her. "You need to know. This is the man that I am. This is the darkness that I've always told you about. It's the reason I didn't want to drag you down into my life. It's not pretty. The shit I've had to suffer through is uglier than anything you've ever had to know. You're pure, Tully. You're the best damn thing that's ever happened to me and your light is always what brings me back. I was terrified of letting you in and learning about all the things that I'd done. I'm a monster."

"No," she cries. "You're absolutely everything. You've

always been everything to me. You were his pawn. He was a monster and you were a child who should have had a parent's love, but instead you were given someone like Anton Mathers."

"I don't think you understand just how grateful I am that your parents allowed me to crash at your home. You have no idea what that meant to me. Your place was my salvation and your smile is what healed me each time I was forced to do something that went against everything that I believed in."

Tully pulls back until she's looking at me and presses her lips against mine before closing her eyes and resting her forehead against mine. "You're a good man, Samuel Rivers. I hope you know that."

"You know I love you, right?"

She pulls into me a little tighter. "I do," she whispers. "Now take me home. I think I just want to curl up on my bed and forget the world."

"I've never heard anything so damn good."

CHAPTER 11

RIVERS

The drive back to Tully's apartment is silent. The weight and horror that I've held onto over the past fifteen years have lifted off my shoulders, but I fear that it's come down on hers. What I shared with her was only the beginning of the horrendous things that I've done, but for some fucked up reason, she needed to hear it. Truth be told, I think I needed it too.

I can't help but feel as though sharing this part of myself somehow brings us closer together. It's as though she can finally begin to understand who I am and what made me so damn closed off to the world. It's as though I'm completely open to her now. No secrets between us.

I just hope she doesn't think any less of me.

What I told her was heavy and I know she was expecting something bad but I doubt her pure mind has ever considered that it was the kind of stuff nightmares were made out of.

My father turned me into a monster and now she knows

exactly what kind of monster I am.

I didn't realize just how desperately I needed to get that off my chest. All this time I thought I was protecting her when in reality, she was the one protecting me by knowing exactly what I needed. She's always known and I wasted years of my life not letting her in.

I've been such a fucking fool. I've always listened to every word she's said, but when it came to my past, I never actually heard her. Her questions fell on deaf ears and I was determined to avoid it at all costs. Sometimes, I went as far as being an ass about it, but she always stood right by my side, always standing tall.

We make our way up to her apartment and it seems as though it takes forever for Tully to get the door unlocked. The bag of take out is dropped on the coffee table as Tully walks straight through to her kitchen and digs the tub of ice cream out of her freezer.

Without another word, she slinks down the hallway to her bedroom and I follow behind, leaving the already cold food to sit on the coffee table, completely forgotten and disregarded.

We must have been sitting in the car longer than I had thought because the massive clock up on her wall is telling me that it's nearly seven in the evening. There's still daylight coming in through the windows, but over the next hour or so, it's going to drain away and something tells me that she wants nothing more than to close the book on today.

Tully pushes into her room and walks straight over to her bed before pulling off her work clothes replacing them with a pair of tiny sleep shorts and a tank. She's never been uncomfortable stripping off before me and I can't help but roam my eyes over her body. It's still the perfection it was four years ago, only now she's grown into more of a woman, and fuck me, it's the sexiest thing I've ever seen.

She slips under the blankets and sits up against the headboard and without hesitation, I step out of my shoes and climb in right beside her, just as we've done a million times before.

I pull her into my arms and scoot down in her bed getting comfortable. Her body relaxes against mine and her head falls against my shoulder as she works on opening the tub of ice cream. The second it's opened; she can't resist scooping a mouthful into her mouth and holding the spoon between her lips as she reaches for her Netflix remote. Clearly, she has this all down to a fine art.

The TV is put on, but it's as though she doesn't have it within her to go searching for what to watch as her hand falls back to the bed with the screen remaining on the Netflix home page.

She stares at it as a deep sigh pulls from within her and I squeeze her waist. "Are you ok?"

She shrugs her shoulders and it's clear her mind is still plagued by what I told her. "Can you just…stay until I fall asleep?"

My head dips and I press a kiss to her temple. "There isn't anywhere I'd rather be."

Tully relaxes just that bit more and we fall into silence, her still staring at the television screen while I stare down at her, re-learning all the lines of her face and taking in all the subtle changes.

She has a few more freckles over her shoulders and a hint of a tattoo peeking out from behind her tank on her back that has me desperate to peel back the material and see what she's got going on back there. But now's really not the time…

Fuck it.

My curiosity gets the best of me and I can't stop myself from reaching across and brushing my fingers down her skin until they're pushing back the fabric of her tank to expose the words tattooed on her skin.

Tully sucks in a sharp gasp as I read over the words and it's almost as though she'd forgotten all about the ink on her back.

This isn't goodbye.

My heart races as my fingers still on her skin. They're the final words in the letter I sent to Tully four years ago, forever on her skin, tattooed in my shitty handwriting. I did everything that I could to make her feel better about our situation. I told her to move on, I told her to find someone else and to be happy. But then I went and told her 'this isn't goodbye' in my selfish need for her to hold onto me. Hold onto us.

I gave her hope when I knew I wasn't coming home and that's something I've always regretted. Maybe if I let her know straight up that I wasn't coming home, she would have found happiness without me. I can't even begin to imagine the amount of pain and confusion that letter must have caused and I hate myself for doing that to her.

I brush my fingers over the ink before leaning into her and pressing my lips over her tattoo. "I'm sorry," I murmur against her soft skin.

Tully nods while discreetly wiping away a stray tear before snuggling back into my side and pretending as though it never happened.

The daylight quickly fades from the room and before I know it, the only light is coming from the moonlight filtering through the window and the television screen which I'm sure will turn itself off eventually.

When she finishes off the tub of ice cream, she reaches across and puts the empty tub on her bedside table before grabbing the remote off her lap. She turns off the TV and dumps the remote at the end of the bed and instantly curls back into me while scooting down the bed a little further.

Tully's leg slides up over my hip and I can't resist sliding my hand up over her thigh as her head falls into my chest, right where it belongs. Her hand slides under my shirt until it's resting against my chest and my eyes involuntarily close in pure satisfaction. Nothing has ever felt so right.

Right here and now…I'm fucking home.

The room is dead silent until her murmurs have my head snapping down to check on her. "I think Spencer is already moving on with Lacey."

"What? Lacey? As in my cousin, Lacey?"

"Yep."

"No. That's not…no. She wouldn't be interested in a douche like that. Besides, it's a bit soon, isn't it? They're probably just hanging out."

She shakes her head against my chest. "He's not the douche you keep thinking he is. He's sweet and charming. He was great to me for four years and I treated him like shit. He deserved so much better than that."

"There is nothing better than you, Tully."

"Maybe to you, but to him…it's a different story."

"How so?"

"Can you imagine being in love with someone who could never feel the same, no matter how hard you try and what kind of life you promise them? Every move he made was for nothing. No matter what he did, I couldn't give myself to him and he should hate me for that. I wasted three years of his life knowing I'd never be able to give him what he needs when he should have been out there looking for the girl who will."

I hate seeing her so down about this especially after everything we've already talked about this evening. I pull her in a little tighter and splay my fingers over her skin. "You can't be so hard on yourself for not being in love with someone. It's either there or it's not, and with Spencer, it wasn't. You at least did the right thing by letting him go."

"But that's just the thing; I didn't let him go."

"What?" I grunt. "Don't fucking tell me I'm lying in bed with another man's woman."

"No," she says. "I mean that I wasn't the one to let him go. He ended it with me the day after the wedding."

"Shit, babe," I say as a deep regret sinks into my soul. I kiss her temple again, realizing that over the past two weeks she's been dealing with a different kind of heartbreak than I had been picturing. I thought she would have been the one to end it and Spencer was the one wallowing in a pit of self-doubt, but it's not. It's been her all this time and I've sat back and left her alone when I should have been right there beside her, holding her up. "You should have said something."

"Couldn't," she grumbles. "I just...I wasn't ready and besides, I didn't want you assuming I was single and trying to take advantage of that."

"I wouldn't have done that," I tell her. "I'm more than willing to force you to admit what you're too scared to think about, but you know I would never make a move until I knew you were ready."

"I'm not ready."

"I know, that's why I haven't kissed you when every single piece of me is screaming to do it."

Her head tilts up and her eyes instantly find mine before dropping to my lips. The desire is strong in her eyes and I know she wants this just as badly as I do, but the fear overtakes her. She doesn't trust me and as much as she wants to give herself over to me, she's not quite there yet.

Tully looks away and with a guttural sigh, returns her head to my chest. "As long as you need, Tullz. I'll be waiting."

"I don't think I ever apologized for my drunken state at the wedding and thanked you for getting me home safe," she tells me, clearly trying to skip over the whole 'I'll be waiting for you' bullshit. Though, as much as she doesn't want to hear it, she needed to know and I have a feeling I'll be reminding her every chance I get.

"You have nothing to apologize for. You were in shock and clearly, you weren't expecting me to show up on your doorstep like that."

"No, I wasn't, but my behavior was inexcusable. I was nasty and I said things that maybe I shouldn't have."

"You said you hated me."

"At the wedding I did."

"Do you still feel that way?"

I feel her cringe against my chest and my question is followed by a long pause before a short sigh. "I don't hate you, Rivers," she starts. "In fact, I think I love you more than ever. I hate what you did to me, I hate the power I allowed you to have over me, and I hate the way it feels every time I think about it."

Her eyes fill with tears as she slowly shreds me to pieces "I'm not going to lie because I know you can see it all over me. I love you, so freaking much that it hurts. I've always loved you and I fear that I always will, but I don't trust you. Not anymore. I can't trust that you're going to keep your word, I can't trust that you're not going to walk away when it gets too hard, and I can't trust that you're not going to tear me apart all over again. So, no matter how many times you stand before me promising that you're going to love me and make it up to me, it means nothing because when it comes down to it, I can never open myself up to you again. You broke me into tiny little pieces and every single day I suffered."

Her words rocket through me and my heart shatters, but I know this isn't the end. We're only just getting started and for once she's actually sharing what's in her heart, rather than just yelling at me for the shit I've put her through.

In the blink of an eye, I roll us so I hover above her. My hips fall between her open legs and she instinctively wraps her legs around me. "I know you're hurting and I know you want to fight me every step of the way just to put me in my place for what I did, and that's ok. If that's what you need to do, then fuck it, I'll take it like a man with a smile on my face, but hear me when I tell you that I'm not going anywhere. I fucking love you and I don't care what you say; you're my girl. I will make it up to you no matter how long it takes, even if that means fighting you on it for the rest of my goddamn life. I will make it up to you and I will love you every single day of forever. I hope I've made that fucking clear."

She watches me with wide, teary eyes, truly hearing me. "How am I supposed to trust that?"

I dip my face to hers, not quite touching but close enough that if she wanted to, she could crane her neck up and capture my lips in hers. "You won't, but that's what time is for. One of these days you're going to stop looking back and only see what lays ahead, and when you do, it's going to be me that you see. Every time, Tullz."

Those beautiful green eyes of hers search mine as a lone tear falls and runs down the side of her face. Not even two minutes ago, I promised her that I wouldn't make a move until she was ready, yet here I am, just seconds from breaking that.

Only I don't have to. She breaks it for me and raises her chin, closing the distance between us. She captures my lips in hers as her hands slide up my chest and around my neck where she holds on with everything that she's got.

My body crashes down on hers as my arms curl under her body. I roll us back over so the weight of my body doesn't crush her and she straddles my hips while threading her fingers through my hair, not once breaking the kiss.

Tully's lips are gentle and soft against mine, nothing like the fast, needy kisses from our past that felt as though we were both trying to prove ourselves. Don't get me wrong, it was always incredible with her, but this...this is something different. This is two souls crying out for the other, both desperate to find their way back to one another.

All too soon, Tully pulls back, breathing heavy as she looks down at me in confusion. "I can't...I'm sorry."

"It's ok," I soothe her. "Too much. I get it."

A sadness creeps into her eyes and a moment later she drops back down into my chest, snuggling into me and closing herself off to conversation, but it's fine. Enough has been said tonight and I don't doubt there's plenty of shit circling her mind to keep her busy for the next few years.

My arms curl securely around her as I hold her to my

chest. We fall back into a comfortable silence as she listens to the sound of my heart beating. My hand runs up and down her back and all too soon, her breathing slows as she falls into a deep sleep.

I remain right where I am, not for one second wanting to leave. She told me that she wanted me to stay until she fell asleep and that's exactly what I should do. Only, I can't find it within myself to get up and leave.

Staying here is an invasion of her privacy and trust. We've each said what needs to be said and now I should be giving her space until she can work out what her next step is going to be.

But then...I've never really cared for what I should do. I'm more of a grab hold with two hands and hold on while things get fucking wild kind of guy.

I lay here until the moon has shifted out of sight through the window before deciding it's time. She's not one of those girls who would just giggle and tell me exactly what I want to hear when it comes to waking up and finding that I did exactly what I said that I wouldn't do, she's the kind who will fight me tooth and nail just to remind me that I fucked up and went back on my word...again.

After pressing a soft kiss to Tully's head, I lift her off me and place her down on her pillow. I pull the blanket right up around her to make sure she keeps warm and has the best possible sleep.

I slip out of her bed with a weight settling into my gut. I don't want to leave, but it's what she needs. I get my shoes back on and take myself out of her room after double checking that she's ok and closing her door.

I come into the living room and find the bag of take out staring back at me. I grab hold of it and detour through the kitchen to throw it out before heading for the door. Only when I grab hold of it, someone stands on the opposite side, knocking.

My brows furrow. Who the fuck would be coming to her

place now?

Already with the door handle beneath my fingers, I twist it and pull the door wide to find Spencer standing before me with a box of crap in his hands.

"The fuck is this?" I demand as he gapes at me for a moment too long, clearly not having expected to see me standing before him. "What do you think you're doing showing up at her apartment with a box of her old shit this late at night? Don't you think you've already done enough damage?" I grab Tully's leather jacket that sits at the top of the box. "In what world is this a good idea?"

"Excuse me?" Spencer grunts, putting the box down and tearing the leather jacket from between my fingers as he attempts to peer around me into Tully's apartment. "I'm just returning her shit as any decent person would do. What the fuck are you doing here? Sneaking out after taking advantage of her? You know, it took me four fucking years to help her out of the grave you dug for her and now you're hanging around again. What exactly are you trying to achieve?"

"Really?" I laugh. "You think you accomplished something wasting three years being with her? Tell me how did it feel knowing your girlfriend was in love with me? That every time you got down on one knee, that she was wishing it was me, that every time you touched her, she was imagining me, that every time she uttered the words 'I love you' that it was my face in her mind."

"Fuck you. What the hell would you know? You haven't been around."

"One look at her face and I knew exactly what's been going on over the last four years. You see, unlike you, I can read her like a fucking book. Every tiny little thing she does tells me a story. The way she does her hair. If it's up; she can't be fucked. If it's down, she's feeling good about herself. If she braids it; she means fucking business. The same goes for if she wears makeup. The way she holds her body. Which fucking smile she gives. Every move she makes, I read. I bet you couldn't say the same thing, and you know why?"

He raises a pissed off brow and I step into him. "Because you've done nothing but think about yourself. You're right. I dug a fucking grave and left her in it, but instead of helping her out, you threw her down a few things to keep her comfortable. You never once pulled her out of it, because you were fucking scared that if you did, she'd realize that you're not the one that she ever wanted."

"You don't fucking know that. We were great together. She just needed a little more time, but then you had to come back and fuck it all up. We would have been married if it weren't for you. You broke her."

I shake my head. "I'm so fucking sick of everyone saying that I broke her. If you really think that, then you don't know Tully at all. She's a fucking warrior. No one can break her, not even me. Sure, she was hurting, but every fucking day she got up and she built herself an empire and showed the world that she can't be fucked with yet you keep treating her with kiddie gloves. She's a fucking force to be reckoned with and maybe if you'd treated her like a fucking queen rather than a defenseless princess, you could have had her."

"I did have her."

"She might have shared your bed. But you never had her."

Spencer's jaw clenches and I watch as his hands ball into fists at his side. Tully tells me over and over again that he's a good guy, but from what I've seen, he's still the same dickhead from high school and the way he rears back and throws a punch that hurtles towards my face proves it.

I narrowly avoid having my jaw broken and slice my hand out towards him. I catch his wrist as it passes my face and step out of the way as the momentum forces him forward. He slams into the wall and I step in behind him, keeping him pinned. "You don't want to fucking try me, Spencer. I'm giving you the benefit of the doubt because it's still fresh and because I know Tully would want me to take it easy on you.

I'm warning you, back off and bow out."

I lean in closer. "You asked me what I was trying to achieve. I want my fucking girl back and no one is going to get in my way. You ended things with her and are already hurting her by spending time with my cousin, so get the fuck out of here before I decide it's time to teach you a fucking lesson. You're through with her."

Spencer's jaw remains clenched, but I feel the fight leave his body and I let up on him. He spins around and gets in my face. "You fucking hurt her again and I'm coming for you."

"Same goes with Lacey. She's my blood. One fucking foot wrong and I'll take you out." Spencer's eyes flick down to the box and I step in front of it. "Just go."

With one final look towards her door, Spencer slinks away and I'm left standing in the hallway wondering what the fuck just happened. All I know is that I don't want to leave her alone.

I grab the box and make my way back inside her apartment while making sure to lock the door behind me. I dump it on her dining table, making a point of not looking deeper than the leather jacket and giving myself a glimpse of her life with him. I'm not interested. All that matters now is moving forward.

Needing to feel her back in my arms, I make my way down to her room, step out of my shoes, and peel my shirt over my head.

I slip back under the covers and as if sensing me, she instantly rolls back into my arms which is exactly where she stays.

CHAPTER 12

TULLY

Sun streams through my bedroom window and I wake squinting into the early morning light What the hell? Usually, I close the blinds before going to bed.

It takes all of two seconds for it to hit me. Rivers.

Not only was he here last night, but there's a strong arm curled around my waist and my back is pressed against what feels like the comfiest brick wall I've ever had the pleasure of being up against.

He's all man. He always was, but after four years in the military, his body has been sculptured to absolute perfection. He's simply delicious. One day…not today, probably not tomorrow and most likely not this week, but one day I'm going to explore every inch of him and rediscover this new Rivers. How could I not? It'd be a crime against womankind if I didn't eventually take him for a test drive.

Shit…

Just last night I vowed that I'd never go back to him and here I am considering all the different ways I'd let him take me. I wouldn't mind letting him bend me like a pretzel and fucking me to within an inch of my life, but then, I also want to see his face. I want to watch him, watch the way he works my body, watch how he touches me.

A shiver runs down my spine as the softest groan pulls from within me. I can count the times I've been with Rivers on one hand. We had a brief moment back in high school, back when I thought the best of him. I thought we'd finally broken that barrier and everything was going to be perfect between us. That night with him was incredible.

People always say that when you're in love with someone, sex means so much more and being eighteen and naïve about the world, I thought it was all bullshit...that was until I was with Rivers.

It was more than I could have expected. I still think about that night. In fact, it surfaces into my brain more often than it should. The very next day, he broke my heart and that's the day that I realized that I could never fully trust him again despite how terribly in love with him I was.

Following that, I wasn't with him again until he had returned from his first part of training with the military. Just like the first time, it was amazing. He has this way of making me feel things that I've never felt with other men. Either it's because of our history and the way we love each other, or he has some wicked tricks in the bedroom that other men need to be reading up on.

I realize way too late that my ass has been pushing back into his incredibly hard junk and my hips fly forward before he wakes up and assumes I was trying to get lucky. After all, that train of thought in his mind can only mean failure for me. If he comes at me like that, I won't be able to resist him. Tasting his lips on mine last night was almost enough to kill me. I don't know what I'd do if it was anything else I was tasting.

Get a grip, Tully!

Looking back over my shoulder, I take in his sharp jaw

and trail my eyes up to his. He's still fast asleep, but after his time in the Military, I don't doubt that even the softest whisper from me would have him on his feet, standing at attention...you know, the other kind of standing at attention. He's already got the first kind mastered and damn, it certainly felt bigger than what I remember.

I slip out from under his arm and creep out of bed, trying not to wake him. I'm sure the past four years have been hard for him and after what he's been through, he deserves all the sleep he can get.

To be honest, I'm not entirely surprised to find him in my bed. When I asked him to stay until I fell asleep, I knew there was a good chance that he wouldn't leave and I think last night, a piece of me wanted him to stay. All I could think about was the story he told me of growing up with his father and I needed nothing more than to be held in his strong arms.

I didn't consider what this morning would be like waking up with him, I didn't consider anything. All I wanted was to be close with him and I knew he'd give me that, no questions asked.

A piece of my soul died when he told me of the horrors he'd been through growing up and something tells me that's only the beginning. I haven't worked out if I'm better not knowing or if I need to get it all out of him. Telling me seemed like the hardest thing he's ever done, that he'd have preferred to be out fighting a war than sitting in my car spilling all the details from his past, but afterward, it was as though he was a new person. The weight of those horrors lifted off his shoulders and it felt incredible to be the one to help him do that. But the question is if I can handle hearing more. It nearly killed me last night, but I liked what it did for him.

I stand at the end of my bed, slipping my feet into my slippers as I watch him sleep. He agreed to stay until I fell asleep and I have a feeling that he truly meant it, so why is he still here?

Samuel Rivers is not a patient man and I'd bet my last cent that he tried to leave. Just as he tried to give me my space, but ended up bombarding me at work. I don't think it's physically possible for him to stay away, but the fact that he's trying until his patience runs out speaks volumes.

Next time he tells me 'The ball is in your court, I'll leave it to you to make the next move' I'll know better and realize that what he's actually telling me is, 'I'll hover close by until I think you've had enough time to think it over and when I deem myself just about to go insane, then I'll come and make the decision for you.'

Some things never change but for some reason, I've always found his over the top, domineering, alpha douchebaggery the biggest fucking turn on and to be honest, I absolutely love it.

When he stormed into my store with that look of defiance in his eye, tight jaw, and stalkerish tendencies, I nearly jumped him. He's so fucking sexy, he's the whole fucking world to me and it tears me apart that I have to break his heart time and time again to keep him at arm's length.

With my stomach grumbling, I remember that we never got around to eating last night and I leave him sleeping in my bed.

First things first, If I'm going to be spending my day thinking about a little eight-year-old boy wielding a knife and being forced to end someone's life, then I'm going to need coffee…and lots of it.

I get busy with my brand new coffee machine. I've been saving for this bad boy for weeks now. I could have gotten one a while ago, but when it comes to coffee, I wanted the best and unfortunately for me and the rest of the world, having the best usually comes with an expensive price tag.

I fire her up and as I watch her make magic as my mind wanders back to that little boy. Rivers said he didn't know what happened to the children of that family, but I have a bad feeling in my gut. Anton is all about making money and he's not above selling orphaned children.

I wonder what kind of information I could find on the internet. I just need to do a little math and work out which year it would have happened and search through all the unsolved murders in the area. There will be names in there and then I'll add a little Facebook stalking. Everyone is on Facebook now, but it's a long shot. Those kids would have changed their names or moved away. They'd be lucky if they even remembered who their mother and father were. Hell, their names were probably never disclosed for privacy and child protection laws.

My coffee machines beeps, signaling that the yummy goodness is ready and just as I reach for it, two strong arms come down on either side of me, caging me against the kitchen counter.

I instinctively relax into him and curse my traitorous body for its ho-ish behavior. His arm moves and I expect it to curl around my body, but when he reaches for my coffee and takes a sip, I don't even find myself getting mad. I'm currently living in bliss, but if anyone else was to touch my coffee, they'd lose their fucking head. There's just something about Samuel Rivers that makes everything right in the world even when he's in the middle of performing the most criminal acts against me.

My head falls into his chest and I force my eyes open, trying not to allow myself to get distracted by his manly goodness which is when I realize there's a huge cardboard box sitting on my dining table. My brows pull down as I take it in. "What's that?" I question. "Did you put it there?"

"Mmm," he grumbles. "It's nothing. I had an interesting night is all."

I'm two seconds from digging for more information when he nuzzles his face into my neck and I lose all train of thought. Hell, I lose all sanity and find myself tilting my head to give him more access.

What the hell am I doing? I'm supposed to be kicking him out and taking a stand. I'm supposed to be letting him know that I no longer trust him and reminding him where my door is, but let's face it; I'm a horny bitch who hasn't got off properly in four years.

Rivers' lips roam over my neck and a groan slips out of me as he nibbles gently on my ear lobe. I feel his smile against my neck and once again, I find my ass pressing back into him.

A warm hand travels from my waist down my body until it cups firmly between my legs only briefly dealing with the ache that pulses there. "Correct me if I'm wrong," he murmurs in the deepest voice I've ever heard, "but you were having a dirty dream this morning."

I suck in a breath as my eyes close, trying to figure out what he's talking about when he presses that hard column against my ass, instantly reminding me of my morning. I was thinking about the few times we'd been together and in doing so, I'd pressed myself against him, just like I'm doing now.

Shit. He must have been awake, just laying there enjoying me rubbing myself against him. I should be mortified, but it's Rivers and it'll take a lot for me to feel embarrassed when it comes to him.

"I don't know what you're talking about," I tell him.

"Uh-huh," he breathes as he returns his lips to my neck.

Another groan is pulled from within me and I find my arm sliding up until it's curled around the back of his neck. "I think you should go," I say though it comes out way too breathy and needy, letting him know exactly how badly I'm affected.

"I'll go," he tells me as his hand starts rubbing over the top of my pajama shorts. "Just as soon as I'm finished here."

I grind down against his hand, needing more as a squeak is pulled from me. There's no fighting it. I want it so bad.

His lips continue their sensual assault against my neck as one hand works between my legs and the other works my body, sending me into sexual bliss.

SHERIDAN ANNE

Rivers grows harder by the second and I want nothing more than to spin around and take hold of him, to feel his velvety skin beneath my fingers once again, to watch how my touch affects him just as he does to me. But I can't. The hold Rivers has on my body forbids me from moving even an inch and what's more, I wouldn't have it any other way.

Rivers' hand slips under the fabric of both my shorts and underwear and the second his fingers come into contact with my clit and begin rubbing circles, I'm a fucking goner. A breathy gasp sails out of me as my knees buckle, making me grip onto my counter to avoid falling into it.

His foot is at mine and he kicks it open, leaving me wide open and soaking wet, desperately craving and needing so much more.

He doesn't disappoint. When it comes down to this, Rivers never disappoints.

Two thick fingers find my entrance and he pushes them in deep as my head falls back onto his shoulder. I clutch onto the counter as though it's the only thing keeping me grounded and find my face turning towards his.

His lips meet mine seconds before he uses his thumb to continue those torturous little circles against my clit.

In. Out. In. Out. OH, FUCK! This is good.

My body is forced to the edge, but I find myself holding on for more. "I need...more."

"I got you," he whispers, picking up his pace as his thumb adds a little pressure.

A groan tears from my throat and I scream out his name. He works my body like a fucking pro and I want nothing more than to strip off naked, climb up on this fucking counter, and bend myself over, offering myself up to him like a Thanksgiving turkey.

I need him to fuck me and I need it to be messy.

I need my ass spanked.

I need him to claim me.

I need him to pound into me, giving it all he's got.

I want bruises left on my skin.

I want to be left red fucking raw and utterly spent when he deems that he's through with me.

Fuck…

What I need is Jesus.

Rivers' hand slips inside my tank and under my bra that I failed to take off before bed and cups my breast as I grind my ass against him. He squeezes my breast before running his fingers over my nipple and sending an electric shock right down to my pussy. Feeling my reaction, he does it again and again being just as rough as I need.

With one last circle rubbed over my clit, my world explodes. I detonate around his fingers and scream out his name once again. His lips catch mine and his fingers never let up, not until I've finished riding out my orgasm.

I gasp, trying to catch my breath. What the fuck was that? It was as though the devil came and possessed my body because it has never reacted so strongly to a man's touch. I was on fire.

I sag against him and he catches me with ease. "You're fucking beautiful when you come," he murmurs against my neck.

I feel my cheeks flame, but for the most part I like his words. I like how they make me feel like the sexiest woman who ever lived. I turn in his arms and look up into his eyes that don't seem so haunted anymore.

"I know," he murmurs, reaching down between us and adjusting himself in his pants. "I'm leaving now."

A wicked grin spreads across my face as I slide my hand up his shirt. "You don't need to leave," I tell him, loving the deep ridges of his abs beneath my fingers. I slide my hands up to his chest and splay them out, wanting to touch as much of him as possible.

"Yeah, I do," he says, slowly nodding his head as he takes my hips and pulls me into him so I can feel exactly what he's got going on down there. "I want to fuck you until you can't

SHERIDAN ANNE

walk, Tully, and if I stay then that's exactly what I'm going to do."

"Maybe that's exactly what I need you to do."

"I know, baby," he says as he slides his knee between my legs, rubbing it over my pussy. "You're dripping wet for me. You need me to slam you down on this counter, open you up wide and fuck you just as bad as I need to be between your fucking legs with your taste on my tongue."

My knees go weak again and I find myself ready for round two. I clutch onto his forearms, holding him to me, terrified that he's about to walk out that door leaving me with an ache that I couldn't possibly deal with myself.

I shake my head before reaching for the front of his pants. "Don't go. Not yet."

Rivers catches my hand in his and gently returns my hand to his chest. "If you touch me, I won't be able to stop, and as much as you need it, you're not ready for it. If I was to fuck you exactly like you wanted me too, you'd hate me for it afterward and that's not a risk I'm willing to take."

I search his eyes, absolutely sure that he's wrong. How could I regret something so good?

He leans into me, resting his forehead against mine. "The ball is in your court, Tully. You come to me when you're ready in here," he murmurs, pressing his hand to my chest, "and I'll give you everything you could possibly need."

With that, he presses his lips softly against mine and lingers there for a brief moment before pulling away. He steps back, keeping his eyes on mine. "Remember, Tully. I plan on loving you for the rest of my fucking life and no matter how long it takes, I'll be there, but you know me, babe. I'm not a fucking patient man." He winks. "Don't make me wait long."

He steps up to my front door and in a heartbeat, he's on the other side, pulling the door closed between us, leaving me staring after him wondering what the hell I just allowed to happen in the middle of my kitchen.

All I know is that was incredible.

Rivers made me feel something I haven't felt in so long. Hell, he made me explode and has left me needing so much more. It's only seven in the morning and my coffee is cold, I've got drenched panties, and all I can focus on is hurrying down to my room to dig out my vibrator and hope that I can somehow cure this ache that's continuing to build within me.

CHAPTER 13

TULLY

I sit squished up next to Henley, flicking through the pictures she took on her phone of her honeymoon in Italy and Paris and I've never been so jealous. Looking through all these pictures reminds me that I haven't taken a break since leaving high school and I could really use some time off, but I couldn't bear the thought of leaving my store.

Don't get me wrong, Candice is great, but she's not ready to take control and I couldn't trust anyone else to do it. While Henley and Noah are both supportive of what I do, they wouldn't know a damn thing about flowers. Mom and dad are also pretty useless when it comes to that as well so it's just me. I'm all I have, but I knew that when I first opened 'Read My Tulips' and I was more than ok with it then so I should be ok with it now.

Maybe I could just close for a long weekend during a bad season to give myself a few days…but on second thought, maybe not. I don't like the idea of the store being closed. I've made a reputation of being the best, and the best isn't someone who closes up for a few days. It's just unheard of when it comes to 'Read My Tulips.'

Noah hovers behind the couch watching us going through the photos and correcting everything that Henley has to say. Apparently, she's remembering it all wrong when in fact, something tells me that Noah's the one who's got it all wrong.

We both tune him out and send him away to make us some cocktails as we finish going through her honeymoon in peace.

They got back yesterday and I decided to give them the day to unwind and catch up on a little sleep as something tells me that not a lot of that has been happening over the past three weeks.

As soon as we're done with the pictures, Henley turns the tables on me and demands to know exactly what's been going on here. Noah returns with our cocktails and just when I think I'm off the hook, he sits down with an expectant look, wanting in on the conversation, so I roll my eyes and get on with it.

"Well, I got pretty messed up at your wedding and somehow ended up at mom and dad's place."

Noah scoffs. "Don't act as though you don't know how you got there. We already know Rivers was the one to take you home."

"Yeah," Henley laughs. "You were pretty fucked up. I can't believe you passed out."

"It wasn't that bad."

"Yeah, it was," Noah grins. "Do you need to see the pictures from the reception? You looked as though you couldn't even stand and then you had an argument with your boyfriend and got drunk with the guy who fucked you up in the first place."

I wince. "I'm sorry. I hope I didn't ruin it for you guys."

"Are you fucking kidding me?" Henley howls with laughter. "Watching you write yourself off was the highlight

147

of my night."

"Gee, thanks," Noah grumbles, turning on his wife with an unimpressed glare. "Are you forgetting the part where we got married and when I fucked you behind that big oak tree while everyone was having photos taken?"

"Oh, yeah," she chuckles as a flush creeps into her cheeks. "That was pretty good."

I try my best not to throw up. These two have always been so in your face about their sex life, never sparing any gruesome details despite how much I beg. Henley simply can't help but share while Noah does it just to gross me out because apparently, that shit is funny. If the shoe was on the other foot though, he'd probably go searching for the guy and knock him the fuck out for touching his sister. I swear, the guy thinks he was put on this earth just to be my over-protective security detail He should know that I can take care of myself.

Got to love double standards!

"So, what else has been going on?" Henley asks, taking a long sip of her cocktail in an attempt to cover her smirk.

I look away, focusing on my drink. "Nothing. Just been working."

"Right," she grins. "You mean to tell me that Rivers has been home for three weeks and all you've been doing is working?"

A shiver runs through my body at the mention of his name. Images of him touching me and setting my body on fire flare through me and if I'm not careful, Henley and Noah will know exactly what's been going on with just one look at my face. I school my features and reach for my drink. "Yep."

"No," Noah throws out in that 'I'm the fucking king, I know better' tone of his. He narrows his eyes on me as he watches me carefully. "It's more than that."

I roll my eyes. "I don't know what you guys were expecting. Yes, Rivers is home, but he's been giving me space just like he should."

"Uh-huh. So, when he called the day we left and promised that he was going to win you back, he didn't show up and force his way through your door? Come on, Tullz. We know Rivers better than that. He would have been wherever you were every fucking chance he got."

I shake my head as I glare at my rotten twin brother. "I freaking knew it was you who gave him my address."

Noah just grins like a job well done. "So, he has been coming around?"

"Yes…and no."

"Eh?" Henley grunts.

"It's complicated. I mean, there's Spencer to think about."

Henley's eyes bug out of her head before she throws herself at me. "That's right. I totally forgot that you broke up with him. I hope you let him down easy."

"Wait. You knew we broke up?" A sheepish look crosses her features and I clench my jaw, realizing exactly how they would have known. "That freaking bastard. He has such a big fucking mouth."

"To be fair," Noah grumbles. "We didn't know for sure. It was just an inkling."

I shake my head. "I didn't want you guys to find out on your honeymoon and then spend your time worrying about me."

Noah shrugs and gives me a devilish grin. "Nah. I wasn't worried. In fact, I don't think the thought even entered my mind."

Henley throws a cushion at him and it smacks him right in the face. "Shut up, you dork. You spent every single night panicking about her. I had to take your phone off you so you wouldn't flood her with calls and texts."

Noah's glare turns on me. "I couldn't have flooded her phone even if I want to because someone blocked my number."

I shrug my shoulders unapologetically. "What can I say?

You were calling me four times a day to check-in. Do you even talk to Henley that much?"

Noah rolls his eyes. "It wasn't four times a day."

"Yeah," Henley grumbles with an eye roll of her own. "It was." She looks at me. "So, what's happening with Spencer? You guys are actually done? Like three years, four proposals, and an unfulfilled promise to move in all finished?"

I press my lips into a tight line. "Yep."

"So…?"

"So…nothing. There's nothing to say. It's over and now he's hanging out with your cousin," I explain, hoping the sting in my heart isn't showing on my face. It still hurts to think about and sucked even more when I got around to unpacking the box on my dining room table.

I had the great idea of packing up his things to help me find a little closure and ended up dropping it off at his place to find her car sitting in the driveway, right where mine would usually be.

It fucking sucked, but what can I say? I've spent every day of our relationship thinking about another man. I guess in this situation, I'm the dick. I have to keep reminding myself that Spencer deserves to be happy.

Noah flies off the couch and looks down at me in rage as Henley's mouth drops. "WHAT?" he roars. "He's fucking Lacey?"

I shrug my shoulders. "Maybe. Maybe not. I'm not too sure actually. All I know is that they're hanging out a lot."

"Already?" Henley gasps. "It's too soon for him to be moving on. What the hell is he thinking?"

Noah scoffs. "Probably thinking about getting his dick wet. I can't fucking believe him. How dare he do this to you? Does he have no fucking respect for the shit you two have gone through? Three fucking years and he's already fucking someone else. I could kill him."

The door flies open and Rivers strides in with a proud grin and opens his arms wide as though we should all be honoured to be within his presence. "Who the fuck are we killing?"

Noah spins around and his fury instantly leaves him. "Hey. How the fuck are you?" he beams, throwing himself over the back of the couch to get to the front door. He meets Rivers in the middle and the two of them throw their arms around each other like long lost friends. Though, I guess that's exactly what they are. "Where have you been? I was expecting you to storm through the door hours ago."

Rivers peers up over Noah's shoulder and his eyes bore right into mine, sending a pink flush over my cheeks. After all, the last time I saw him, his thick fingers were buried deep inside me. I try to control myself, but Henley's eyes are already on me with a knowing smirk on her face. "I wanted to give you guys some time to unpack," Rivers explains, never once taking his eye off me.

The boys separate as Henley gets up and welcomes her brother. "Unpack?" she scoffs, giving him a quick hug. "I probably won't get around to unpacking for a few weeks, hell maybe even a few months."

Rivers gives her a funny stare. "A few months?" he questions. "Why? Have you got shit going on?"

"Nope. Just can't be fucked to do it."

Every eye in the room rolls. "I'm not surprised."

Henley gives him a bright smile before sucking in a sharp gasp as her eyes bug out of her head. "You've never been here before. Come in. Let me show you around." She grabs hold of him and pulls him through the living room in her desperation to show off her home to her big brother.

As Rivers passes across the back of the couch, he looks down at me and runs his fingers over the back of my shoulders. A satisfying shiver takes over me and my eyes close for the briefest moment. "How are you, Tullz?" he murmurs in that deep voice that seems to send me insane, but what makes it worse is knowing without a doubt that there's one hell of a sexy smirk playing on his lips.

A wide smile crosses my face and I try my best to rein it in. "No complaints."

A sparkle hits his eye and something tells me he's thinking about the very same thing that's been occupying my mind for the last few days. "Uh-huh," he murmurs just a second before Henley grabs hold of his wrist and pulls him into her kitchen.

I turn back to Noah and realize that he's been staring. "Bullshit all you want," he tells me with a knowing grin. "Something went down between you two."

I shake my head, but I'm unable to control my smile. "Don't know what you're talking about."

"Right."

It's clear as day that Noah knows something has been going on and despite the fact that I actually have no idea what that is, I'd expect my brother to be losing his mind, except he's grinning at me as though he couldn't be happier. In fact, despite being friends with Spencer, he never once greeted him at the door the way he just did with Rivers. Though, that could very well have something to do with the fact that they're long lost best friend finally reunited after four years apart, except when they saw each other at the wedding three weeks ago, but it's not like they could fuck around and be boys at the wedding. Here, in the privacy of Noah's home, they get to be their complete idiotic selves.

"You know that I'm cool with you guys being together, right?" Noah murmurs, for our ears only.

"First of all, that's bullshit. You've never been cool with the idea of me and Rivers together. And second...just no. Too much has happened. Spencer and I only just broke up and...I don't know. I can't let him break me like that again."

"Tullz," he says looking me right in the eye "You love him and you always will. It's as simple as that. And for the record, I've watched you barely living over the past four years. The sparkle in your eyes has dulled and while Spencer helped keep you together, he didn't make you feel the way that Rivers does. I mean, fuck. He just walked through the door and you look more alive than you have in years."

"Would you keep your voice down?" I demand.

He raises a cocky brow. "It's true though."

"What's true?" Rivers asks, striding back into the room and dropping down on the couch right beside me. Though judging from the look in his eye, he already knows exactly what's being discussed here.

I look across at him and find myself unable to stop the flirtatious smile that has the apple of my cheeks raising and squishing right up into my eyes. "Do you have to make everything your business?"

Rivers' finger snakes across the couch until it's pressed right up against mine. He winks and something stirs within me. "Consider it a weakness."

Henley drops down onto Noah's lap and just like that, she launches into her recap of her honeymoon all over again so Rivers can hear all the gruesome details. She gets about five minutes in before the boys somehow manage to change the topic in a way that has Henley thinking it was probably her idea.

We cover everything from what we've each been up to, not just over the past few weeks, but over the past four years, filling Rivers in on everything that been going on in our lives.

Noah explains how he got into firefighting and how his current chief is getting close to stepping down. He's been encouraged by everyone he knows to apply for the role, but he's hesitant as he's not one for paperwork, so who knows what's going to happen there.

Henley tells Rivers about her four years in college and how she managed to find an incredible job researching DNA just as she always wanted. Though to be honest, when she talks about that stuff, I tend to zone out. It's way too complicated for me to understand. She attempted to explain it all one night and I ended up with a headache. Once she's done with that, she explains everything that's been going on with her mom, knowing that deep down, Rivers would want to hear all about it.

The topic has me watching him carefully. I've never really known anything about his relationship with his mom and it has me intrigued. Even more so when he tells us that he visited her when he first got home and signed the house back over to her name. Though, that's about as much as he was willing to say on the topic and quickly shuffles the attention over to me.

I skip straight over myself, not wanting to share the past four years of my life. Besides, he knows the important stuff; I opened my business, it's successful, and I bought myself a kickass apartment.

As Rivers shares the details of his past four years, I can't help but think about what Noah said. I love him and it's as simple as that. But is it? He hurt me when he left, but after hearing what his life was like growing up, I have a better understanding of why he needed to get away from it and why he was so desperate to keep it from not just me but the world.

His years in the military have very clearly changed him. It's as clear as day that he's not the same closed of boy that he used to be. He's a man and he's come home telling me that he's finally ready. He's defeated all his demons yet I'm still here trying to hold it against him.

What the hell is wrong with me? He's wanting to hand me everything I've ever wanted on a silver platter. He's ready to give me the world and I'm holding on to pain from years ago for something that was out of his control. Yes, he left without saying goodbye, but he was desperate and we've all done things we regret out of desperation.

Noah's right, I do love him and that's something that will never change. I glance across to Rivers only to find his eyes already on mine with concern deep within their depths, and it hits me. I'm looking at my future, but I'll never be able to grasp it because I'm too busy punishing him for the past which was something completely out of his control.

I shouldn't be concerned about hurting Spencer because we all know he's not concerned about hurting me. So, what the hell am I holding back for?

He's here and he's ready to make it work while I'm busy being a fool. I should be grabbing hold of him with both hands and never letting him go.

'Are you ok?' Rivers mouths, reaching across the couch to place his hand on my knee.

I nod as I slip my hand under his and weave my fingers between his. 'More than ok.'

Rivers' eyes narrow in curiosity and I see the questions piling up in his mind. He's clearly very intrigued by this sudden change of heart, but he's not about to do anything to push me and risk ruining this moment.

I'm about to tug on his hand and ask him if we can go and talk when Henley gets up and steals my attention. "Where's Aiden and Barker? I thought they'd be showing up at some point," she yells over her shoulder as she heads into the kitchen to grab everybody another round of cocktails.

I spin around on the couch and look through to the kitchen as Rivers' thumb runs back and forth over my skin, making it nearly impossible to concentrate. "They're probably halfway to Vegas by now."

"What? What the hell for?"

I shrug my shoulders while trying to remember what Aiden had told me the other day, only it's harder than I thought because it was right after Rivers had left my apartment and my mind was otherwise occupied. "Umm...I think he said something about his little sister's 21st."

"Oh, yeah. That's right. Now you mention it, I think I recall him saying something about a Vegas trip. Did Barker go too?"

I scrunch up my face, feeling like an awful friend for not knowing all this. "Maybe. I don't know to be honest. I think they're in the middle of being off in their on-again/off-again relationship."

"Shit. Really? I hope he's got someone there with him. Aiden loose in Vegas is not a good mix. He'll probably get a taste for glitter and become a showgirl."

"Actually, I picture him as more of a burlesque dancer," I laugh. "But don't worry. I'm sure Spencer is probably there to keep an eye on him."

Rivers scoffs. "Really? First, the dickhead is shacking up with my cousin and now he's out partying in Vegas?"

"Give Spencer a break," Henley tells him. "The poor guy just had his heartbroken by the love of his life."

"What the fuck are you talking about? He broke up with Tully. She's the one who should be out partying and living it up, not him."

Henley's head comes shooting out of the kitchen, leaving her body hidden behind the wall. "WHAT" she gasps, staring at me as though I've committed the ultimate betrayal.

I wince before scowling at Rivers. "Really? You just had to go and open your big mouth."

He grins down at me before tugging on my hand and pulling me into his chest. "Sorry," he laughs, kissing my temple. "But I'm done letting you play games. No more holding anything back because it's not been doing you any favors. Besides, there's nothing better than watching you squirm."

I shake my head and rest into his chest. "You know, despite what everyone keeps telling me, I kind of hate you."

"Yeah," he laughs. "I hate you too."

CHAPTER 14

RIVERS

There's nothing better than sitting amongst my pack. The original four. It's as though we've come full circle. We started strong, then I fucked it all up and after four years, we're finally able to get back to where we started. Though, things have changed and we've all grown in our own ways, it will never change the fact that these are my people.

Tully sits curled under my arm as Noah and Henley argue about the finer details of their honeymoon. It's as though neither of them was actually there and they're making it up as they go. Either that or they each went on separate honeymoons because the way they're both recapping it is as though they're telling me two completely different stories.

"So…" Henley says slowly, turning her gaze on Tully after Noah gave in and let her tell her story the way she wanted. After all, she's drunk a little too much to bother arguing with. When Henley's like this, sometimes it's just better to admit defeat. "Who's up for a game of 'Ultimate Truth or Dare?"

A grin spreads wide over my face. I'd recognize that look in her eye anywhere and from the way Tully's head is shaking against my chest, I'd dare say she knows exactly what Henley's up to. "I'm in," I declare.

Noah laughs as he grins at his twin sister. "Count me in, too."

"No," Tully says. "No way."

"Don't tell me you've forgotten how to have fun," Noah questions. "Or maybe you're just a pussy now."

Tully grabs a cushion and launches across the room at her brother only she misses and it smacks Henley fair and square in the face, though she doesn't seem to care. "I'm no pussy, Noah Cage. I'm the furthest thing from it. I just don't feel like having you three fuckers gang up on me. Don't act as though I haven't worked out your little game. You idiots are so predictable."

"Sorry, sis, but being scared that we're going to gang up on you is something a pussy would do."

Tully's eyes narrow and she sits up off my chest to glare at her brother. She sits forward, resting her elbows on her knees and gives her brother a look that I haven't seen since high school. It's the one that would have all the girls running scared and the boys dropping at her feet, and I don't doubt that she hasn't used it over the past four years. "You're so fucking on, but you better be warned. I'm not holding back. I promise you, if you three make me do or say something that I don't want to, you're all going to pay."

My dick practically jumps out of my jeans to say hello. How is it one fucking speech about taking me down gets me so hard?

Henley grins excitedly across the room at Tully as I slide down on the couch and adjust myself. Fuck, what I wouldn't give to be sliding into my girl right now. Hell, I don't even care if she's pissed off. She can scratch those nails up and down my back for all I care, as long as I get a taste of that warm pussy again. I just had to go and tell her that the ball was in her court. She's probably going have me waiting for years just to prove some kind of point. Even if she did though, I'd wait and I'd do it with a fucking smile on my face because she's worth it.

Though, something tells me I won't be waiting much longer, judging by the way she looked at me earlier. It's as though she had figured something out or resolved something within herself because she went from cowering in the corner of the couch to holding my hand and allowing me to wrap my arms around her.

I've never been so fucking content.

I'm going to marry this girl one day and it's going to be the best decision I'll ever make. In fact, I've already made it. There's no 'umming' and 'ahhing' over this one. She'll be my wife just as I know that one day she'll bare my children.

"Alright," I grin across the room to Henley. "Who's starting?"

"Fuck that. She's not choosing. I'm first," Tully declares, keeping her glare on her twin brother. "Noah. Truth or Dare?"

His eyes narrow right back on hers as they fight for the claim of who gets to be the superior twin. Noah will never stop until he claims the title and I'm pretty damn sure he only gets it because Tully usually grows bored of this game and gives in too quickly, and I have to say, I'm happy to see that some things never change.

Noah raises a brow. "Dare."

There's a slight lift in the corner of Tully's lip that tells me Noah just played right into her hands. "I dare you to take your wife down to Kitty Kat's Play House and have her pick out five different things of various siz-"

"Whoa. Hold it right there," I say as my mouth drops. "How the hell do you know about Kitty Kat's Play House?"

Tully turns to look at me with a sparkle in her eye. "Wouldn't you like to know," she says with a wink.

Well, shit. I didn't think it was possible, but somehow my

dick is even harder. "Yeah, actually. I would."

Tully rolls her eyes. "Kat comes and gets fresh flowers for her store nearly every day. Quit stressing. I haven't turned into some wild, kinky nympho while you've been gone."

"Can we get back on track here?" Henley says. "I'm intrigued by this dare."

Tully grins. "Right. So, you need to go down to the Play House, find five different things. Could be handcuffs, a vibrator, it could be a twenty-inch, bright pink rubber dildo for all I care, but all five things need to be bought, tried, and tested."

Noah grins. "Hell yeah. I'm down for this."

"I'm not finished yet, brother dearest." His face falls. "Henley will be choosing all five things and all five things need to be used on you in the one...how should I put it? Session?" She smirks devilishly at her brother with a cocked brow, letting him know that he chose today to fuck with the wrong girl. "Simply put, you're going to let wifey go all '50 Shades' on your ass."

He shakes his head looking slightly horrified, but slightly intrigued. "No. Who knows what kind of shit she'll choose."

"I guess that's the risk you have to take. I mean, you wouldn't want to back out and have everyone know that deep down, you're really just an insecure little pussy."

"Screw you. You better hope that you don't get me when your turn comes," he warns, standing up and taking his wife with him. "We'll be back, and when we are, you fuckers better be long gone because I'm not about to let my wife defile me while you two are sitting in the next fucking room."

With that, Noah storms out the door with Henley trailing behind him. She spins around to look at Tully with a grin the size of Texas on her face. "Remind me to thank you after this," she laughs excitedly before winking and having Noah tug on her arm, making her fall out the door.

"Oh! For the record," Tully calls after them. "I don't want to hear about this tomorrow."

The door is closed and I'm left gaping at my girl. "What the hell was that? You realize you'll have absolutely no way of knowing if they actually go through with this dare. I taught you better than that."

A flush takes over her cheeks as she reaches out and takes my hand once again. "I, um…actually did it on purpose."

My brows dip low. "What are you talking about?"

Tully winces. "I wanted to get rid of them for a while so we could talk and I figured that sex was the only thing that would keep them distracted long enough. Besides, if they actually go through with it, I'll be set up with decent blackmail for the rest of my life."

"You realize that he's going to get you back so much worse."

"Let him try," she laughs. "The old Tully is back and I'm betting there's not a lot he can do to take me down."

"That's my fucking girl," I grin, pulling on her hand and hauling her up onto my lap until she straddles me.

Tully looks down at me and something morphs within her. The cocky attitude that she was using with her brother dissipates into nothing and all that's left behind is fear. I can't help but reach up and tuck a stray lock of hair behind her ear in my need to touch her. Tully's head falls into my hand and I look up into her big green eyes. "What is it?" I murmur, needing to know what's going on in her mind.

"I've been making the past three weeks a living hell for you when I should have been inviting you in."

"Babe," I sigh, not wanting her to feel guilt over the past three weeks.

"No, just…listen, ok?" I nod and she takes a deep breath before slowly letting it out. "Every time I've seen you since being home, I've done nothing but push you away. You scare me, Rivers. You hold the power to destroy me and you very well nearly did. I've been terrified of letting you back in knowing that if you were to leave again, I…I wouldn't be able to make it. Not again." Tears start filling her eyes and

I'm wiping them away before they even have the chance to fall. "I've kept you at arm's length, but every time you come near me, it's even harder to keep you away. You make me feel things that no other man has ever made me feel. Over the past few years, I've felt weak because I haven't been able to move on from the one guy who broke me. I've felt like a fraud allowing Spencer to get so close, and I've felt like a liar telling everyone that I've been fine when in reality, I've been anything but."

I pull her in closer and wrap my arms around her. "I never intended to hurt you."

"It's taken me until the other night to truly understand that," she tells me. "When you told me about your life with your father, I realized how selfish I'd been begging you to tell me all those years. I should have just let you go."

"No, you shouldn't. You cared enough to want to know the real me. No one else has ever cared like that and I was wrong. I should have opened up to you while I had the chance, but I was scared that you weren't going to love me when you realize what I'd done."

"How could I have not loved you?" she cries as her eyes fill with love. "You're everything to me. You always have been. You're the strongest man I know and for the first time in four years, I feel alive. I'm done holding back, Rivers. I want you back in my life. I miss you every fucking day, I just don't know how to do it without keeping myself guarded. I want to trust you and I don't want to be scared that one day you're just going to take off, but I can't. It's always in the back of my head and I don't know how to get past that."

Tully's forehead falls to mine. "I promise you, Tullz. I'm not going anywhere. I'm in this for the long haul, but I get it. I've shut you out one too many times and pushed you away and now you need to learn how to trust me again and that's ok. I'll give you all the time in the world."

I raise my head and press a kiss to her forehead. "I told you right from the start that I'm going to make this right.

You're my life and my future and I'm not going to do anything to screw that up again." I press a hand over her heart. "This is where I belong now. My past is buried in the past and I've got you to thank for that. You, Noah, and Henley, you all fought for me when I'd given up. I should have had more faith, but I was scared. You all did what I couldn't do and because of that, you've given me a chance to open myself up and move on."

"I don't want to push you away anymore," she whispers.

"You're ready for this?"

"How could I not be? I've been in love with you since I was eleven years old. Having you in my life is what makes me happy."

Relief settles into me. I've heard her say those words over and over again, but hearing them while knowing that she's finally letting me back is the best fucking feeling in the world. I've got my girl back and after four long years of pain, she's finally letting me come home.

My hand curls around the back of her neck and I hold her close while looking into those eyes that have always lived in my dreams. "I love you, Tully."

Her eyes close and then finally, her lips are on mine. Tully's arms curl around my neck as she pulls herself impossibly closer. Her tears continue falling down her face as she kisses me, but they quickly begin to dry up.

Tully pulls back ever so slightly before looking me in the eye and slowly peeling her shirt up over her toned body. My hands instantly take her waist and the second my fingers brush against her bear skin, warmth spreads through me like wildfire.

Tully reaches around herself and unclasps her bra before allowing the red fabric to slide down her arms. She bares herself to me as she silently watches me and I've never seen anything so fucking beautiful.

I pull her back in and my lips find the sensitive skin of her neck as her fingers weave into my hair. I trail my lips down over her collarbone and down to the curve of her breast. Her skin is so soft, just as I've always remembered.

My lips run over her nipple before I suck it into my mouth and tease my tongue over it. Tully's back arches and her head falls back as a breath escapes her. Her fingers fist into my hair and I find my own digging into the skin of her waist, holding her tight as she rocks her hips forward, grinding herself over me.

How did I get so lucky?

My head is telling me to slow things down and make this moment last all night long, but my body is desperate for her touch. I've been starved of her for way too long and if I don't get a taste soon, I might not make it.

I find her lips and pull her body harder against mine, loving the feel of her bare tits pressed up against me which is when I realize that it can't happen like this. This is the moment that's going to kickstart the rest of our lives together and something tells me that starting it on my best friend's couch where he naps during the day probably isn't the way to go about it.

My hands curl under her ass and I lift us both up before walking down the hallway. "What are you doing?" Tully questions, tightening her legs around my waist.

"You're not some cheap screw, Tullz. If we're doing this, then we're doing it right."

She melts into me as I push my way through the door of the spare bedroom and before I've even finished placing her down on the dresser, her hands are already pulling at my shirt.

My shirt is tossed across the room and she grabs the front of my jeans and yanks me forward, holding me close while locking her legs around me. I kiss her as she releases the button on my jeans and pushes them down my hips.

My erection springs free and she doesn't waste a second wrapping her tight fist around me, pumping up and down while running her thumb over the tip.

I'm seeing fucking stars.

I can't physically go any longer without touching her.

Making quick work of her jeans, she pushes up off the dresser and I tear them down her legs, dropping them to the ground somewhere near the rest of our clothes. Tully's legs instantly wrap around my waist, pulling me in once again while taking hold of what's hers and getting back to work.

My fingers trail up her thigh and I grin as I leave a wake of goosebumps behind. I cup her pussy before sliding my fingers between her folds and running my fingers over her clit.

Tully's whole body flinches with the touch and she groans, needing more. Not one to disappoint, I press down on her clit and start rubbing slow circles before sliding two fingers deep inside her.

Tully's head falls to my shoulder and despite how badly we both want to make this last, I doubt neither of us has what it takes to hold back. Besides, I have the rest of my life to make her feel all kinds of incredible, right now, I just need to be inside her, claiming her, and showing her exactly what she means to me.

Using my free hand, I slide her forward on the dresser until she's right at the edge and as if reading my mind, she pulls her legs in tighter, dragging me along with it. I slide my fingers out as she lines me up with her entrance and with one slow thrust into her, everything is finally fucking perfect in the world.

Tully bites down on her lip and curls her arms around me until her hands are at the back of my shoulders and her nails are digging in while I slip an arm around her back, holding her close as the other claims her hip.

I begin moving and despite being deep inside of her, it's still not enough, so with her lips on my neck, I lift her off the dresser and take her to the bed where I continue to make love to the woman I've been craving for more than half of my life.

I give her exactly what she needs and in doing that, she does the same for me.

I kiss her until she can't breathe, touch her until her back is arching high off the bed, and fuck her until she's screaming out my name and forgetting the world around her.

And just when she falls to the bed, utterly spent, we start all over again.

An hour passes before we see the headlights pull up outside the spare bedroom window and realize it's probably best we get out of here. After all, Tully set Noah and Henley a dare that nobody should be unlucky enough to overhear. But seeing as though they've been gone for so long, I'd dare say that the bet has already been completed.

Tully and I roll out of bed and do our best to dress before Noah and Henley make their way inside, but luck seems to be on our side tonight as they're taking their sweet time.

Remembering Tully's shirt and bra is on the living room floor, I dash out and grab them as I finish doing my jeans. Tully practically rips her bra from my fingers and I smirk as she rushes to put it on while listening to Henley's laughing from outside.

We emerge from the spare bedroom just as the front door is opened and we meet in the living room to find a bag hanging from Henley's fingers and an anxious look marring Noah's face.

Tully laughs as she throws herself towards the bag and plucks it from Henley's fingers. "Did you get five things?" she questions as she goes to look inside the bag.

Noah snatches it right back. "Yes, there are five things and that's all your messed up little self needs to know."

"Come on," Tully laughs. "Stop being such a chicken. What's in the bag."

"None of your goddamn business."

Tully rolls her eyes and looks to Henley with a raised, questioning brow. "Well?"

Henley grins right back at her while nudging her husband

with her elbow. "I swear, if he makes it through the night, I'll tell you all about it tomorrow."

Noah throws his arms over Henley's shoulder and pulls her into his side. "You'll do no such thing," he warns before looking to me and Tully. "What are you guys still doing here anyway? I thought you'd have left ages ago."

I can't help but look down at my girl to find her eyes already sparkling with joy before I glance back at Noah. "We had some things to talk about."

"And?" Henley prompts, not missing the look in her best friend's eyes.

Tully leans back into me and without even thinking about it, my hand circles her waist, holding her that bit closer. "And...we're working things out," Tully explains.

Henley's eyes bulge out of her head and she starts jumping up and down while an ear-shattering squeal rips out of her. Noah though, looks as though he could be sick. "You screwed my twin sister in my spare bed, didn't you?"

My hand clenches on Tully's waist and she places her hand over it, lacing her fingers through mine. "Just be thankful it wasn't on the couch," I tell him, for the first time admitting something like that without the fear of getting knocked out.

Tully grins wide as a soft chuckle slips from between her lips. "Well...it nearly was."

Noah hangs his head. "Fuck. Now I have to buy a new one."

"Calm down," Tully laughs. "We didn't have sex on your couch."

"I know, but now I won't be able to sit on it without thinking about the fact that you 'nearly' did."

"Yeah," she says, stepping out of my arms and grabbing her phone and keys off the coffee table and then dragging me towards the door. "I'm not even going to pretend to be sorry about it. It was fucking incredible and I plan to take him home and do it all over again."

I can't help the wide grin that spreads across my face as my girl looks back up at me. I know she's only trying to stir her brother, but something tells me that she means every fucking word and I can't wait. Hell, she has a whole apartment full of furniture that I intend to bend her over.

Tully pushes through the door and comes to a stop as she takes in the black dodge RAM sitting right behind her car, making it look like some sort of clown car. "What the hell is that?" she questions, scrunching up her face.

"It's my new truck," I explain, looking over it with pride as Tully begins to gawk. "What?"

"That's yours?"

"Yep."

"It's huge."

"Uh-huh."

She shakes her head as Henley's phone screeches to life behind us. "Speaking of huge things," Tully murmurs looking up at me with a sparkle in her eye. "We need to discuss your piercing."

"What piercing?" I laugh as the screeching phone is finally answered. "I had to get rid of it when I joined the Military."

She nods. "Exactly my problem."

With my hand in hers, Tully starts leading me out to my new truck, bypassing her little black car so she can check out my new ride. I start digging for my keys when Henley's voice has me spinning back around. "Rivers," she calls out. "That was Mom."

"What?" I demand with wide eyes. "Is she alright?"

"Yeah," she says as a smile slowly spreads across her face. "More than alright. All the paperwork went through and the judge signed everything off. She's free. Mom's coming home."

CHAPTER 15

TULLY

The past two weeks with Rivers have been incredible. It's so much more than I could have imagined. With Spencer, I was barely getting by, but this…this is as though I'm finally alive for the first time in my life.

He lifts me up, he makes me feel things no other man has ever made me feel, and the sex…well, that's on another whole playing field. It's simply mind-blowing.

Though I always knew it would be, it's part of the reason I fell in love with him in the first place. But I'm not going to lie, despite how incredible it's been, I can't help that nagging feeling that one day he's going to leave.

I have to learn to trust him again and that's going to be one of the hardest battles I'll ever face. I want to trust him so damn bad. I want to believe that this is what it's going to be like until the end of time, but I'm terrified of allowing myself to believe it. If I'm right and he does leave, I don't know how I'll ever survive.

I hate being that weak girl who revolves my life around

a man's decisions. I should be stronger. I should be able to stand on my own two feet and tell him exactly how it's going to be, but when it comes to Rivers, I'm putty in his hands. And what's more; I like it that way.

Over the past two weeks, he's let me take things slow despite the fact that we already know exactly where this relationship is heading. I don't want to rush this. I want to rediscover him in the way that I didn't get the chance to do the first time around.

He's been my guy since I was eleven, but the past two weeks it's as though he's completely new. He's my same old Rivers, but now with so much more to give and I wouldn't have it any other way. He encourages me, he supports me, he lifts me up, and lets me believe that the world is in my hands, and I absolutely adore him for it.

How did I go four years without him in my life? I feel as though we've missed all this time together, but had we not, would it still be the same? If Rivers didn't join the military and learn to forgive himself, would he be the man he is today? Would he have ever found the courage to open up to me and share his world? Something tells me that the answer is 'no' and that the past four years were a necessity that I need to move on from.

Those four years are what brought Rivers back to me and I need to learn to be grateful for them rather than hating it for how I fell apart while he was gone.

Is it selfish for me not to trust him now? Apart from leaving without telling me, he has never done a thing that wasn't in my best interest.

Shit. Why does this have to be so hard?

I kick my jeans off and pull my shirt over my head before I feel Rivers hands at my back, helping me to unhook my bra before his arms circle my waist and he pulls me in hard against his bare chest.

My head falls against him and I raise my chin to kiss his jaw. "How are you feeling?" I question as his thumb trails back and forth over my hip.

"Alright," he murmurs. "I don't know. I keep feeling as though I've forgotten something."

"You haven't," I promise him. "Your mom has everything she could possibly need at home. You made sure of that."

His face scrunches up as he gently shakes his head. "Maybe I should go back. I don't think she should be alone tonight."

I turn in his arms and look up into those dark, intense eyes that have completely captured me. "Your mom has gone eleven years without a shred of privacy. Trust me, she probably needs to be alone more than you could possibly know."

"Yeah, but…"

"No," I tell him. "She has your number if she needs anything and something tells me Henley is going to be stalking her for the next few weeks. You've done everything you could have possibly done to make sure she's comfortable. She has somewhere nice to sleep, she has food, and electricity, and you even made sure she has a car and a job. She has the world at her feet and now it's time for you to step back and let her live her life the way she wants."

Rivers lets out a deep breath. "I just worry about her. I have so much to make up for."

"I know," I tell him, resting my hands against his chest. "And you will, but it's not going to happen overnight. You've already spent all day with her. We can go back in the morning, cook her a nice breakfast, then take her shopping for a new wardrobe. Trust me, with you as a son, she's never going to go without, but she needs tonight to just…take it all in."

Rivers' head falls to mine as he let out a deep breath. "I really hate it when you're right."

"You better get used to it," I laugh. "Something tells me you're going to spend the rest of your life hating on me for being right."

He rolls his eyes as a devilish grin rips across his face. "You wish. If anything, I'm just telling you that you're right because I've got a lot to make up for, and from the looks of it," he says, running his fingers down my waist and watching as goosebumps rise on my skin, "my plan is working."

"You're an ass," I laugh, pulling myself out of his arms and finding my sleep shirt. I pull it over my head before trudging to my bed and sliding in between the sheets.

It's been a huge day. We were up at the crack of dawn. I had to go into 'Read my Tulips' this morning to complete a huge order and had all hands on deck. Henley and Rivers both came along to help Candice and I get it done so we could all be there when Gina was released at 9 am. Since then, it's been all about helping her settle in.

We took her grocery shopping to get the things she liked in the house and took her to find some home décor so she could make her space her own.

It's just past eight at night and we've been with Gina all day. It's been such a long road getting to this point. Four years ago when Henley first put her mind to getting Gina out, I thought it was a lost cause, but she stuck to her guns, and we finally made it. Though we wouldn't have gotten where we are without Anton's confession.

Apparently, he's all about righting his wrongs now, but I can guarantee that there's no way in hell he'd be able to right them all. After all, he's murdered countless of people in cold blood. I think Rivers has done the right thing by avoiding that trainwreck. I won't allow him to get caught up in his webs ever again. We've all come so far since high school and it'd be a tragedy to end up there again.

Rivers walks over to his side of the bed and digs his keys, phone, and wallet out of his jeans before letting the weight of his undone belt buckle pull his jeans to the floor. The buckle clatters against my floorboards and he steps out of his jeans before sliding in beside me.

I'm instantly pulled into his side as a deep yawn takes over me. I try to keep my yawn classy, but sometimes those fuckers just overtake your body and possess you until the moment finally passes.

I snuggle into his chest as I turn on Netflix and go through my nightly ritual of deciding what to watch while Rivers grabs hold of his phone and begins doing whatever the hell it is that boys do on their phones.

Not finding anything that holds my attention, I drop the remote to the bed and look over at Rivers' screen. "What are you looking at?" I murmur as another yawn rips through me.

"House listings," he grumbles, turning his phone slightly to give me a better view of the screen.

My brow raises in curiosity. "What the hell for?"

"Well, I highly doubt mom wants her grown-ass son crashing with her, especially now that she only just got her freedom back."

"Good point," I say, reaching over and scrolling back up as he passes a nice little cottage style home. "This looks alright. The house could use some upgrades, maybe a little paint, and a bit of love, but there's a huge yard."

"Nah," he grumbles, clicking out of the listing and continuing to scroll. "Too small. It only has two bedrooms."

I scoff. "Two bedrooms? How many were you looking for? There's only one of you."

His only response is a wide grin that has my mind spinning with untold mysteries. Could he possibly be thinking about filling those rooms with…I don't know, children?

My brows furrow and I find myself watching him as he scrolls through the listings, absolutely complexed by the realization that I'm not terrified by that train of thought. Had that been Spencer, I would have been running for the hills, but the idea of building a life with Rivers, sharing our home, and having children running around a big, open yard with two dogs and a bunny rabbit has warmth spreading within my heart.

The second the thought goes through my mind, I realize that I want it more than I've wanted anything in my life, and I want it all with this incredible man sitting right beside me.

Why the hell isn't this scaring the shit out of me?

I was so hesitant when it came to Spencer asking me to move in with him, I put it off and off, and off. Every time the topic came up, I found a way to change it, yet here with Rivers, he hasn't even suggested it and I'm already making a mental list of all the things I want to take with me.

I shouldn't be thinking about it though. We've been together for all of two weeks. It's way too soon. We have so many hurdles to get through before we can discuss moving in together.

Though, it does have me wondering what was holding me back with Spencer. Was it the apartment I wasn't willing to let go of or was it because I knew deep down that I was with the wrong guy? Because right now, I couldn't give a crap about leaving my apartment despite how much I love it.

Damn it. I really need to stop reminding myself how much of a bitch I was to Spencer.

My eyes fall back to his phone and watch as he opens one of the listings for a home in the middle of Haven Falls, right near where Henley grew up. The first picture is of the front of the home, showing off a double garage, a fenced yard which is outlined by beautifully cared for hedges.

The home is similar to my childhood home. A typical Haven Falls, three bedroom, brick home. There's a backyard with space for a pool, a deck, and a huge tree that casts a perfect shadow over the lawn. Absolutely perfect for a little boy to be running around playing soccer while his little sister splashes in the pool which could be built in.

I can picture our lives in this home. I can picture

walking around the kitchen while I nurse my pregnant belly, I picture Rivers crashing down onto a couch in that living room or working away on his Firebird in the garage.

I see it all.

Shit. I'm getting way ahead of myself here.

"I like this one," Rivers says. "It's got potential."

"Potential for what?" I question.

Again, all he does is grin and this time, I know for sure that he's thinking exactly the same thing that's running through my mind.

"When were you planning on moving out and actually buying a place?"

"As soon as possible. I don't want to overstep it with mom. We've only just started working on mending our relationship."

"Yeah, I get it," I tell him, looking back up at him. "You know you can stay here until you find your own place. There's no need for you to crash with your mom if you don't want to."

Rivers' phone gets dropped to the bed as he grabs hold of me and rolls us until he's hovering above me and looking down at me with a smile so wide that it lights up his eyes. "Are you asking me to move in with you?"

"I, um…no. That's not what I was saying, but…I mean, I guess so. I'm just suggesting that there's no rush to buy a place. We have here to live and I want to be where you are, though, it's just a small apartment and not exactly great for…"

"Having a family?" he questions with a teasing grin.

"Yeah."

Rivers' lips come down on mine and he kisses me with everything that he's got before slowly rising back up and gazing deep into my eyes. "You want to have a family with me?"

"Well, I mean, not right this very second, but one day…definitely."

He smiles. "I'm going to give you the whole fucking world, babe. Anything you want, I'm going to make it happen."

"I know," I tell him. "I…"

Rivers' phone ringing on the bed cuts me off and he groans, hating that this moment is getting interrupted. "Sorry, babe," he sighs, reaching across the bed for his phone to silence it, only as he flips it over to see the screen, his brows dip down low. "Shit. I should take this," he says, rolling off me.

"It's fine," I tell him, watching on in concern as he sits up in bed and hits the accept button.

Rivers brings the phone to his ear. "Hello," he says. There's a slight pause before he continues. "Yes, Sir. This is Samuel Rivers."

His tone tells me exactly what I need to know; the man on the other end is someone of importance within the military. Worry grips me and I find myself latching onto Rivers' arm as I listen to the barely audible, muffled voice on the other end. It's too quiet for me to figure out what's being said, but the way Rivers' eyes flick back to mine with nothing but regret has my heart racing in my chest.

"Yes, Sir. I understand. I'll be there." There's another short silence. "Thank you, Sir. Goodbye."

With that, Rivers ends the call with his hands falling into his lap. "What?" I demand as the regret in his eyes shine brighter and brighter by the second. "What is it?"

Rivers shakes his head as he watches me and I've never seen someone look quite so defeated. My heart starts to sprint as the dread begins to weigh on me. He reaches for my hand, lacing his fingers through mine before closing his eyes and pulling me into his chest. "I'm so sorry," he says, completely broken. "My presence is required on another mission. I'll be deployed tomorrow afternoon. They need me on the next flight."

A long breath comes sailing out of me. "What?" I say

as tears instantly begin to fill my eyes. "How...why? You...you just go home."

Rivers squeezes me. "I know."

"How long?"

He shakes his head and I feel the movement of his chin skimming across the top of my hair. "I don't know, Tullz. It could be a few months or it could be more. It depends on the mission."

"No," I cry. "This isn't fair. I only just got you back."

Rivers hand soothes up and down my back before he lays us down and holds me in his arms. "I don't know what to tell you," he murmurs. "I've just spent the last few weeks promising you that I'm home for good and that I'm not going anywhere and just when I get you back, I have to leave."

Tears stream down my face. "Why you? Surely, there must be someone else they can get."

Rivers lets out a deep breath and is silent for a moment before giving me a gentle squeeze. "I'm a sniper, Tullz, and a really fucking good one at that. Only a few can shoot as accurately as I can. I have a set of skills with guns and a certain talent for going into battle and being able to leave my emotions out of it. I guess I have my father to thank for that." He lets out a sigh. "I'm going to be debriefed in full tomorrow, but there have been some major casualties in a deployed unit that require emergency back-up. They're in a tight position and require me to help complete their mission."

My head whirls with that information. He's a snipper, and a fucking good one, and now that skill has him being deployed into a dangerous situation. Where are all the other snippers at? Why couldn't they have chosen one of them? Surely, Rivers isn't the only one available right now.

But the bigger question is, how did the sniper they were already using become a casualty?

Rivers wipes the tears off the side of my face.

"Tullz…are you alright?"

I shake my head into his chest. "I…I don't know. I just…I can't."

"I know," he says, curling his arms around to get a better hold on my body. "It's going to be ok. It's just a little setback. I'm going to be fine. I'll go, do the mission and get it over and done with, and then be back here in no time."

"You make it sound so easy," I cry. "All this time, I've gotten by from telling myself that you were just at the base. I never knew if you were deployed or what kind of situations you were facing, but this…how am I supposed to breathe every day knowing that you're out on a mission where anything could happen to you? How am I supposed to know that you're safe or if I'll ever see you again?"

"Hey," he says, cutting me off. "You can't think like that. It's going to be fine. I'm going to be fine, Tully. Do you hear me? I am coming home to you and when I do, I'm going to make it right."

"I don't want you to go," I tell him. "Please, don't go."

"Trust me, babe, I'd give anything to be able to stay here with you. I love you so fucking much. The idea of leaving you is killing me."

I hold onto him a little tighter as his lips press down on my forehead.

There's absolutely nothing I can do about it. Whether I like it or not, Rivers is leaving tomorrow to go and fight a war and this right now is the last time I'm going to get to spend with him. Hell, who knows, this could be the last time I'll ever spend with him.

The thought brings on a wave of tears and I do my best to control it. If this is the last chance I'll get to spend time with the man I love for who knows how long, then I'm not going to spend it crying. I'm going to suck it up and make the most of a bad situation.

I can cry once he steps onto that plane and not a second before. I don't want to send him off with the image of me being broken. I need to be strong for him. I need to let him know that no matter what, when he gets back, I'll be right here waiting.

Samuel Rivers is it for me and no matter how long the Military insists on stealing him away, I will always be right here waiting. Besides, when it comes to forever, what's a few extra months?

With that resolved in my mind, I will pull it together for the next twenty-four hours. I need to make the most of my time with him even if that means spending the next twenty-four hours between the sheets.

I raise my chin and as he wipes away my final tear, and with that, Rivers' lips come down on mine which is exactly where they stay until we're both falling asleep, dreading what's yet to come.

CHAPTER 16

RIVERS

Dread sits heavy in my gut as we pull up at the airport. I have loved my time in the military. I've never felt bad about leaving and have always been ready and willing to do what I need to do, until now.

I never expected that I'd be leaving quite so soon, right after getting my girl back at that.

This isn't how this was supposed to go down.

I knew that at some point, it was likely that I'd be deployed again, especially after the skills that I've gained over the past four years, but to be here only a few months after getting home? It's unreal, but I get it. In a perfect world, I would have been home for at least twelve months before being called to serve again. Hell, most marines on reserve get four years, but this is the life I signed up for and when my country needs me to stand tall, that's exactly what I'm going to do.

Only this time, I have someone to come back to that's going to make leaving harder than it's ever been before.

Missions for me always used to be about finding myself. They were hard and dangerous, and sometimes downright terrifying, but a part of me looked at them as my way of giving back after the disgusting things that I've done. Missions were the jail sentence I so desperately deserved, but now that's all behind me, and truth be told, I feel as though this one is going to be different.

Being on a mission gave me a sense of purpose and helped set my mind to something to make not thinking about her easier, but now that's all changed. There won't be a second where I'm not thinking about her and my gut is telling me that this mission is going to be the hardest one to get through.

I'm fucking lucky that it's only going to be a few months; at least, I hope it's only a few months. Truth be told, I could be out there for six months or longer, it's all details that I'll find out when I get debriefed. But hell, sometimes shit happens and quite often, it never goes to plan.

I stayed up all fucking night, watching as Tully slept in my arms. She was trying to be strong, she was trying to show me that she's going to be alright, but I saw her breaking inside. It's like the past coming back to haunt her, only this time, I have every intention of coming back to my girl.

Nothing will stand in my way when it comes to getting back here and picking up where we left off. I mean, fuck. It was only twelve hours ago that I was looking at house listings and picturing Tully and I truly starting our lives together and now we have this set back to deal with.

We're going to be ok. We have to be ok.

I don't know if I could handle coming home again to find my girl with another man, but I know she'll wait. I feel it in my gut and from the way she's allowed herself to open up to me over the past few weeks, she knows this is the real deal. She knows I'm coming home to her and she knows that not a damn thing will stop me.

I don't care what happens to me over there or what kind

SHERIDAN ANNE

of mission they're sending me on, as long as I know that I have Tully's heart, I'm going to be just fine. The military can't put me through anything worse than what I've already suffered at my father's hands. I'm going to be ok.

I've trained for this and I've been on many missions over the past few years, each one drastically different from the last. I'm ready to face down anything, especially with the wallet-sized photo I have on my girl that will remain in my chest pocket day in and day out until I'm standing before her again.

I look down at Tully as we stand at my boarding gate, surrounded by friends and family, yet all I see is her.

I hear my flight being called and watch as all the people around me begin to get up and start making their way over to get their boarding passes checked, but there's still time. There has to be. I don't care if I'm the very last person to get on that plane. I'm not wasting a single second.

I draw Tully into my arms and she nuzzles her face into my chest, willing herself not to cry, but I see the pain etched on her face. It's been there since the second I received that phone call.

Henley steps into my side, wrapping her arms around both me and Tully. "Be safe, big brother. I only just got you back. I'm going to be pissed if I don't see you again for ages."

"Oh, I'll be back," I tell her with a wide grin, tightening my hold on Tully. "I can't possibly leave you guys to look after my girl. Last time you threw her into the arms of another man. I can't let that happen again."

Henley rolls her eyes. "Blame us all you want, jackass, but you know just as well as we do that all that Spencer bullshit is on you. Do I need to remind you that you're the dickhead who never came back in the first place?"

Gina shakes her head. "All these years I was devastated that you two never got the chance to develop a close sibling relationship. You know, the one where you can't possibly go two minutes without getting on the other's nerves? But it seems I had nothing to worry about."

"I can't help it," Henley grins. "Someone has to help deflate his ego every now and then, otherwise he'll be strutting around here thinking he's king shit when we all know that role has already been claimed by Noah."

"Hey. How did I get dragged into this?" Noah grunts, pulling Henley out of his way to step into my side. Noah wraps an arm around my back and claps me between my shoulder blades. "Don't be a fucking hero, alright? Henley's right. We're going to be fucking pissed if you don't come home."

Tully scoffs into my chest. "He's coming home even if it means that I have to go over there and drag his ass back."

"Damn straight, babe," I laugh, running my hand down the back of her hair before looking to her brother. "You have my word. I'm coming home. I've already wasted so much time and I don't intend on fucking things up like that again." I pull against her. "This girl is my fucking world and the second I get back, I'm going to make all her dreams come true. Just keep an eye on her until I get back."

"You know I will," Noah murmurs before glancing down at his sister and studying her face, "though, something tells me she's going to be just fine."

I couldn't agree more. While she's going to be hurting and missing me, just as I will be pining for her, she knows deep down in her heart that I couldn't possibly stay away again. I've been able to see a clear path to the future I want with her and I won't let it slip through my fingers this time.

The line at the boarding gate begins to dwindle down and my heart continues to sink. I say goodbye to everyone while keeping an eye on the tears that Tully keeps forcing herself to hold back.

I hate that she's forcing herself to be strong. She's spent the last few years holding back her true feelings and I won't stand for that shit anymore.

With a final hug to everyone in our group, I pick up my bag from the floor and lace Tully's hands through mine.

Together we join the end of the line so we can have just a slither of privacy as I try to find the words to say goodbye. I turn into her and look down at her beautiful face as she lets out a heavy breath and kills me inside.

I take hold of her shoulders with both hands and hate the way they seem to have been slumped in defeat since the second I received that call. I pull her shoulders back, forcing her to stand tall. "Look at me, Tully."

Her head rises slowly and I find the same red-rimmed eyes that have been watching me all day long. "I was up all night, trying to figure out what I can possibly say to you that will make this all ok, but I don't think such words exist."

"I don't think they do," she agrees, her eyes growing more and more watery by the second.

"This is the life I signed up for. I never thought I'd be able to reach this point where I'd have you standing by my side, but I have and for the first time in four years, I don't want to go."

"Then stay," she whispers, her voice breaking with the turmoil she's feeling within.

Fuck. Why does this have to be so goddamn hard?

I pull her into my arms and press a kiss to her forehead. "You know that I can't," I tell her. "I'd give anything to be able to stay here with you and start building our lives together, but know that the second I can, I'll be coming home to you. I fucking love you so goddamn much, Tully Cage."

Her tears spill over and run down her cheeks before dropping and splashing onto my arm as I step up in the line. She raises her chin, flashing those broken eyes while looking into mine. "I love you too," she cries. "Don't be gone for too long because I don't want to wait to start my life with you."

I take her face in my hands and look her in the eyes, feeling myself breaking inside. "I won't," I promise her. "I swear to you, Tullz. The second I get home, it's you and me. I'm going to give you the whole fucking world. You're my queen and don't you ever forget that, ok? I know it's going to be hard and you're going to curse me out because you miss me, but just know that no matter what, every time you find yourself thinking about me, I'll already be thinking about you. You're the sun in my sky, Tullz, and when you're not there, it's only darkness for me. I don't exist without you. I have no choice but to come back to you because, without you, I'm not living."

Tully pushes up onto her tippy toes, pressing her forehead against mine. "Why does it have to be so hard?"

"Because that's what happens when you love someone."

Her eyes close and I can't help but press my lips against hers. I wrap my arms around her waist and crush her body against mine as I kiss her with every last piece of me. I give her everything she needs to get through the next few months and in return, she does exactly the same for me.

As Tully pulls back and looks up at me, she places her hand against my chest. "Don't look back, ok?" she begs. "When you step through that gate, don't turn around. I need you to be the one to walk away because I'm not strong enough to do it."

"Babe," I breathe, not knowing if I'll be strong enough either.

"Please. I just…if you look back, I'm going to run for you and I'll never be able to let go. Please, just do this one thing for me."

"Ok," I tell her as the lady at the gate clears her throat. I glance over to her to find her hand outstretched, waiting to check my boarding pass. I reluctantly hand it over while looking down at Tully. "Be good, ok? Don't you go falling in love with somebody else."

She smiles up at me and that one little smile is all I need to get me through the next few months. "It's not possible," she whispers, pressing up to her tippy toes once again and gently brushing her lips over mine. "I love you, Rivers."

My boarding pass is returned and the woman indicates

for me to pass, but I find myself hesitating, not ready to let go of my girl. "I love you too, Tullz. Just think of it as a vacation. I'm not at war, I'm not facing down the enemy, I'm on a tropical beach, living it up, and deep down, you're just pissed and jealous because I didn't take you with me, alright?"

"You're an idiot," she laughs.

I shrug my shoulders. "I try, but promise me, ok? I don't want you thinking about the bad stuff."

"I promise."

With a smile, I look up over her shoulder and take in my friends and family all standing back and giving us the time we need to say goodbye. I give them all a wave and most wave back apart from Henley who wipes a tear and falls into Noah's arms, right where she belongs.

I look back down at my girl, trying to convince myself to let her go. "I'll miss you, Tullz."

"I'll miss you, too."

With that, I lean in and press a lingering kiss to her lips. "Goodbye."

As I pull away, I let her hand fall to her side and I take a step back. She goes to walk forward with me but Noah steps in behind her, holding her to him as she struggle to free herself from his grasp.

Everything inside of me shatters, but I suck it up knowing that she'll be ok and with every last bit of willpower that I possess, I turn around and walk through the gate, not once looking back.

CHAPTER 17

<u>One Week Deployed</u>

Rivers,

I don't know how I've managed to survive this past week. It's honestly been the hardest thing I've ever suffered through. The second I got home from the airport, I sat down to start writing this letter, but I forced myself to put it off and wait, otherwise, the time is going to pass so slowly.

I don't know where you are or what kind of things you're facing. I don't even know if you're going to get this, but just know that I haven't stopped thinking about you. I miss you so much already and I'm scared because it could only get worse from here. I promise you, the second you get home I'm probably going to attach myself to you, but that's the risk you take when you play games with my heart.

I've spent the last week thinking about what I actually want to put in this letter and to be honest, I can't figure it out, so I'm winging it. But it has had me thinking about the differences between you going away now and when you went before.

I think the first time you left; I wasn't sure where I stood with you. There was still that question of if you were truly mine or if you were just with me because you knew it was your last chance. I hated you when you left because I didn't know if I was ever going to see you again.

But this time it's different. I know you're coming home to me and for some reason that makes it so much harder. I'm not sad despite feeling empty, yet my heart is so damn full knowing that you're coming home to me. I don't know how to separate my emotions and understand them, but I'm sure as the time passes, I'm going to figure it out.

I guess all that matters is that I'm not broken. When you came home, you healed something inside of me. I was so stupid to give so much of myself to you before. You took my heart with you and I wasn't able to heal without it, but things are different now. You gave it back to me and fixed it while making it so much stronger in the process. And now, I think I've learned to love you in a much healthier way.

I've never been so happy despite wanting to hate you for going to a tropical beach without me. I hope you're getting sunburned!

I really hope you get this letter despite the fact that I was just rambling on about complete bullshit the whole time. I know you hate writing and I know how much you would have hated writing the last few letters you sent, but if you get this, put me out of my misery and write back.

And just know, that if you do get this and don't write back...well, that just makes you an ass and I'll make you pay. Maybe I'll find a voodoo doll or something like that!

I love you so freaking much!

I can't wait until you come home so I can screw your brains out!

Tully
Xxx

One Month Deployed

Tully,

Really? You're going to get a voodoo doll to make me pay for being an ass? I'd like to see you figure out how to do that shit. Though I better not push my luck and just write back because a scorned Tully is someone to be very afraid of!

I fucking miss you, babe. I got your letter late last night and I swear, seeing that little envelope with your handwriting on the front was enough to make everything right in the world.

I don't really know what to tell you. This tropical beach sucks. The sand is hot and the waves are reckless. Your wish came true! I actually am getting sunburned! But don't stress, babe, we have plenty of shit here to handle it. I should have been better about protecting myself. The sun is pretty unforgiving over here!

I haven't stopped thinking about you. Every chance I get, you're on my mind. It's actually kind of annoying. That squawky voice of yours that's usually yelling at me about something, but then, I've always kind of liked it when you put me in my place. I love that fire within you. It's hot as hell.

It's never long before I start picturing your smile, and fuck me, Tullz, it's enough to keep me going. That is until I start thinking about the night you pulled out that can of whipped cream, and I end up walking around a bunch of dudes with a fucking hard-on.

You have to know how sorry I am for putting you through all that pain for the last four years. I hate that I did that to you and that your heart was hurting so damn bad. I swear to you, Tullz, I'm going to do whatever it takes to make it up to you. Hell, I'll make this time away up to you as well.

You're right, I hate writing, but if it means having some sort of communication with you, then I'll do it.

When will you learn that I'll do absolutely anything to make you smile?

You're my fucking world, babe.

Rivers.
P.S - Send nudes!

Two and a Half Months Deployed

Send nudes? What do you think this is?

You know, just because of your crass behavior, I'm not even going to address this letter to you properly so you can spend the rest of your time away wondering if this letter was actually meant for you. Who knows, maybe I'm writing to some other poor soul who needs a little of my shining personality and squawky voice in his life!

But…because my man asked and I'd do anything he needs, then he better check the pictures stapled to the back of this letter.

Do you like my new lingerie? I bought it just for you.

How is it already two and a half months? It seems like the postal system is purposely taking their time just to fuck with me. I miss you so much and I don't think you'll ever truly understand just how happy it made me when I saw your letter in my mailbox. To be honest with you, I cried like a baby! I had a shitty day at the store and getting your letter made everything better again.

I can't wait until it's your warm arms I get to come home to and not a letter with the nastiest handwriting I've ever seen. I mean, damn boy! You need to see someone about that or at least take some classes.

You know, you're so damn lucky to have me. I must be the funniest person you know!

So…I don't mean to bring up a touchy topic, but I wanted to let you know that Spencer and Lacey have officially started dating and she's already moving in. I know you probably don't give a shit about what's going on in their lives…or well, maybe you do for Lacey's sake, but the reason I'm bringing this up is to let you know that I'm doing perfectly fine.

I met up with him last week and talked it all though and I think he gave me what I needed to be able to forgive myself for holding onto him the way I did, especially when I've always known that you're the only man I'll ever love. I never should have done that to him, but seeing that he's happy with Lacey just makes it all better. I'm truly happy for them and I hope that one day you'll be able to build some sort of friendship with him. He really is a good guy.

I had Henley pop over yesterday thinking I needed some cheering up and to be honest, I didn't need it. If anything, it's her sorry ass that needs the cheering up for being married to my jackass brother!

You wouldn't believe how annoying he's being, constantly checking up on me as though I'm about to go insane without you. That stupid boy. Next time he spontaneously pops on over here, I'm going to give him something to worry about and trust me, it's not going to be me! Though, something tells me that I have you to thank for that bullshit.

Anyway, I better go. The delivery man just arrived with tonight's feast and I don't want my food to get cold. You know how I get when I don't get what I want!

I love you to the freaking moon and back. I hope you're being safe and not being an asshole to your unit. I know you can get a bit…cranky when you're missing me.

Tully
Xxx
P.S – I have a pretty epic surprise for you!!!

Four Months Deployed

Babe,

You certainly are the funniest person I know, but unfortunately for you, it's not in the 'haha' kind of way!

I don't know this other guy that you're supposedly sending your last letter to, but just know, I'm already fucking jealous of him.

Good thing I was able to intercept the letter and hide that picture away before he was able to see what's mine, otherwise I'd be more than just jealous of him, the fucker would be dead! Actually, did you delete those pictures off your phone? I don't want anyone else getting their slimy hands on that! That sexy body is all mine.

Wait…don't tell me you went to the store to get it printed? Please tell me you printed it at home? Shit. I shouldn't even ask. I already know the answer to this and trust me, you'll be getting a piece of my mind on the matter when I get home.

In other news; I fucking love your new lingerie. I can't wait to get home and rip it off your body. These pictures have me getting around like a walking hard-on and there's nothing I can do to get rid of it, and before you say the one thing I know you're going to say, I've fucking tried, but there's nothing quite like the real thing.

That photo, though! Fuck me, babe! I can't wait to get home and taste that sweet pussy of yours. I'm going to give it to you until you're screaming my name and neither of us remembers what fucking day it is!

I feel as though I should be returning the favor in some kind of way, but I don't exactly have a camera to be capturing anything, so in the meantime, you're going to have to make do with a drawing. Flip over the letter and check it out! Does it do me justice?

What am I doing? I'm opening myself up to some kind of cheap shot from you. Besides, you can't lie. It does me incredible justice!

I'm happy for you that you seem to be able to put Spencer behind you. I was worried about you. I knew after first hearing that they were getting close that it could hurt you, but you've overcome it like some kind of goddess. Besides, together, we've got so much more than anything you could have possibly had with him, even being apart from each other now.

What's this surprise you're talking about? You know I don't like surprises. I can never handle them very well. I like to know what's going on at all fucking times. I expect an explanation in your response, otherwise there's going to be big fucking trouble!

I love you, Tullz.

Rivers.

(I really hope these letters aren't checked before getting sent out, otherwise I'm really going to come across as a fucking perve!)

Five Months Deployed

Rivers,

My eyes!!!!! How dare you send me such drawings! Though, don't you think you're being just a little too kind to yourself? That drawing, though. I don't think I've ever seen a stick figure with such a big dick before, and don't for one second think that I didn't miss the fact that the stick figure version of yourself was doing unspeakable things to himself!

But seeing as though you asked, it does you more than enough justice.

In fact, a little too much justice. I wouldn't be surprised if you turned into one of those guys who lives by the motto 'It's not the size that counts, but how you use it.'

It's ok, Rivers. Don't be hard on yourself. We all have our downfalls!

Speaking of your nether regions...we really need to book you an appointment to reinstate that mighty piercing of yours. I NEED it back!!!!!!

You know, I didn't think you could have me blushing while you're so far away, but what can I say? I love your dirty talk...or well, dirty writing? I've been thinking about you every night and damn it, I try to resist, but thinking about all the things you're going to do to me when you get home has me so damn desperate.

I heard that you can get molds of your partner's junk made into dildos for when they're not around...I think we're going to have to look into that for the next time you decide to get deployed and leave me behind all wanting and needy.

Moving on from my horn dog desires and onto this surprise, It's a fucking good one. At least, I hope you think it's a good surprise. Otherwise...tough shit! I think you're going to love it. I'm so excited about it!

How much longer are you going to be gone? This whole waiting to get you home thing is getting annoying. At the start, I was coping pretty well, but now it's like playing a game of monopoly when you're losing against Noah – It sucks and I want it to end, but no matter what I do, nothing will change. I just have to wait it out.

I've been spending some time with your mom. She's wasn't settling in with her job and apparently, her boss was an ass, so Noah went in and dealt with him while Henley and I got her a new job in a clothing store. She seems much happier now. She's doing really well. You should be proud of her. She tells me every day how much she misses you. You probably should have told her about the tropical beach thing too!

I miss you. These past five months have been driving me crazy but every day that passes means one less day until I get to see you again...whenever that might be.

I love you so much.

Do unspeakable things to yourself tonight while you think about me, and I promise, I'll do the same!

Tully
Xxx
PS I'm getting cushion covers made with your drawing on them to replace all the ones in my apartment. Maybe I'll get some pillowcases and some tanks made up too!!

Six and a Half Months Deployed

Tullz,

I'm fucking coming home, baby!!!!!!!
I don't know when you're going to get this letter. It could be days or it could be weeks, but just know, that when I get home, I expect to find you as naked as the day you were born, ready and waiting for me. Hell, you better warm up my side of the bed because I have no intention of leaving it.

This is finally it, babe! I'm coming home and now it's our time to shine. We're going to make this happen. You and me; this is the start of the rest of our lives and I get to spend every day of forever showing you just how much you mean to me.

I've told you a million times before that you're my world and that feeling hasn't changed since the day I first fell in love with you.

I miss you and I can't wait to see you.

I love you so fucking much that I don't even care if you decorate your whole damn apartment with that stick figure drawing, as long as I have you in my arms, I'm a happy man.

I'll see you soon,
Rivers.

CHAPTER 18

TULLY

I stand in the middle of my kitchen, smiling like a fool as I read his words to me. He's coming home. I can't fucking believe it. It's been the longest seven months of my life, but it's nearly over.

The second he walks through my door, the rest of our lives can finally begin and I can't fucking wait. Rivers is my guy and I've gone far too long without him. Don't get me wrong, receiving his letters over the past seven months have been incredible, but it's nothing compared to the real thing. Not even close.

Unable to stop myself, I read the letter again and then twice more just to make sure I read every single word correctly. His excitement in his words shines through and has me bubbling with joy.

The only downfall is that this is the military we're talking about, meaning I have absolutely no way of knowing when he sent this letter, because the guy is incapable of writing the date at the top of the page, and I have absolutely no idea of knowing when he's actually going to get home.

Rivers could have received the news he was going home weeks ago and he could nearly be here or it could still be another few weeks wait. Judging by our other letters, I'd say he probably sent this out nearly a month ago, but there's no real way to be sure. Sometimes I'd be waiting only a few weeks before his letter would come and other times, it'd be nearly two months, so I won't be getting my hopes up, not just yet.

I start looking around my apartment. I have so many little surprises for him and if he barges his way in here, I don't want any of them to be ruined, though, he knows about my new cushion covers. I couldn't believe my eyes when I first saw that drawing of a little stick figure getting himself off, but I don't know why I was so surprised. That's so typically Rivers that I should have been expecting it. Especially after the photo's I sent to him.

I was nervous about sending them. I wasn't sure if mail got looked at before being sent to the soldiers so it was definitely a risk, but I knew that once they landed in Rivers' hands, they were safe. There's no way he would have let them out of his sight, even in the middle of a war zone. Protecting the people he loves has always been his goal and he'd die before betraying that or letting anyone down.

Me? I was different. In order to protect me, he needed to hurt me and that's something we'll both struggle with for the rest of our lives. Though 'struggle' might be the wrong word. I certainly struggled for the past four years but I've been learning to put it behind me. I understand his reasoning now and with that came forgiveness, and that forgiveness sure makes life a hell of a lot easier.

I go about my living room on a Thursday afternoon cleaning up after myself. It's been a huge day with orders at the store, a check-up at the clinic, and then stopping by the store to pick up some fresh groceries for the new healthy diet I've been forcing myself to stay on for the last few months, and to be honest, it doesn't suck. It's just time consuming. Rather than calling for take out, I actually have to cook, which at first I hated, but I've been learning a lot of new tricks and Henley has been adamant about teaching me a thing or two. But let's face it, it'll be years before I can reach her skill level in the kitchen.

With the living room now in order and my feet beginning to ache after such a big day, I grab Rivers' letter off the kitchen counter and drop down onto my couch. I absolutely adore reading, but tonight, I'll be content just reading his few paragraphs over and over again as no book could ever bring me more joy.

I squish myself into my stick figure cushion and pull the stick figure blanket over my lower half and get comfortable. I mean, my home is currently covered in Rivers' little horny stick figure man. I have mugs, a pajama set, blankets, and cushions. I even had one printed and framed up on my wall. I just hope Rivers doesn't do the same with the picture I sent him.

The thought has a cheesy as fuck grin ripping across my face and I find my eyes dropping down to the paper to take it all in again.

I'm fucking coming home, baby!!!!!!!!

Since the second I found his letter sitting in my mailbox, I've been kicking myself. Who knows how long it was sitting there? I haven't checked my mailbox for three days, but I guess, seeing as though he's not here with me right now, it really doesn't matter. But I would have loved to be fawning over the letter for longer if I could.

His letters have been more than I could have imagined. When I wrote him that first letter, I was expecting a response of maybe three or four words, in true Rivers fashion, but he gave me so much more than that, and although I've missed him like never before, his letters were my saving grace that helped pull me through.

Screw Noah and Henley's endless checking on me. that

did nothing to help me get by. I mean, I guess that's a little unfair. I love them both so much, but there's a difference between coming to see me to spend time together and checking on me to make sure I haven't turned into the crazy cat lady.

There's a knock on my door that has me groaning.

Speaking of Noah being an overprotective asshat, that would be him showing up for his daily check-in. Without fail, I have seen my douchebag, twin brother every single day since Rivers got on that plane. Whether it's here at home, at my store, while I'm visiting mom and dad, or hell, he even crashed my girls' night with Henley and Aiden. It's getting a bit much, but from this letter in my hand, it seems I won't have to deal with it for much longer.

My eyes snap up to the massive clock on my wall. 8 pm. Right on time. That tells me Noah has just finished his shift and he's popping in here for two seconds before going home to spend his night with his lovely wife.

I roll my eyes and set a scowl onto my face so he gets the full effect as he walks in. "Come in," I groan, loud enough for him to catch the annoyance in my tone.

There's an amused scoff on the other side of the door before I hear the familiar sound of the handle turning. I drop my eyes back to the letter, ready and prepared to tell Noah all about it, but it's going to have to wait because Noah has set himself a routine.

First, he's going to walk into the center of my living room and his eyes are going to roam over my face with concern. The second he realizes that I'm fine, his expression is going to soften and warmth is going to spread into his smile. Then, he's going to ignore my ranting as he raids my fridge and eats everything I own, and just when I think he's good to leave, he'll hurry down to my bathroom to chuck a shit. I mean, I love him and all but why does he have to do that in my bathroom? He has a perfectly good one at home.

He'll swiftly stink out my home and then drop down on

the couch beside me before telling me all about his day. I'll never actually admit to him, but hearing him talk so animatedly about his job and the adventures he gets to go on is what I look forward to most. You know, apart from receiving these letters.

The door opens and I expect Noah to walk across the room as he's done every other day, but then I feel his heavy gaze trained on me by the door and I can't help but raise my chin to figure out what the hell he wants.

My eyes snap up and the second they do; my whole fucking world is rocked.

Rivers.

It's not Noah at all.

I suck in a deep breath as a smile spreads wide across my face. Rivers just stands there, staring at me as though he can't believe what's right in front of his eyes. "Fuck, you're beautiful," he whispers into the silent room, shaking his head in disbelief.

With his letter clutched firmly in one hand, I throw the horny stick figure blanket off me and fly to my feet as best I can before rushing towards him, but in my excitement, I miss one very important thing – his surprise. His very fucking big surprise.

Only it seems it's not something that I have to remember as he does all the work for me.

Rivers' brows drop down in confusion as he throws his hands out and gestures down my body. His eyes bug out of his head and despite his confusion, I can't help the overwhelming joy pulsing through me. "What the fuck is this?" he demands. "Did I miss something?"

I come to a stop just a few feet in front of him and glance down at the seven-month baby bump protruding from my stomach before looking back up at the shocked man in front of me. I bite my lip as a sheepish expression crosses my face. "I told you I had a surprise for you, didn't I?"

His mouth drops open before he closes it only for it to

drop right back open once again. His eyes rake up and down my body, staring at me in disbelief. "You're pregnant," he whispers, still trying to make sense of what's right in front of him.

My arms circle my stomach as I give him an encouraging smile and slowly take another step towards him. "I am," I murmur, starting to get a little nervous. I mean, we had only just gotten back together before he had to leave and now I'm springing a baby on him. "I found out about two weeks after you left."

"I...baby?"

"Yeah," I smile. "We're having a baby."

"This is real? You're not pulling some sick prank on me? There's really a baby inside that sexy body of yours?"

"Yes, you dork," I laugh, taking another step and allowing him to slowly come to terms with the fact that we're two months out for having a child. "I'm sorry I didn't tell you in our letters, but I couldn't stand the thought of not telling you this in person."

Rivers shakes his head in wonder as a smile slowly spreads across his face and suddenly, he's standing right in front of me, pulling me into his arms and crushing me against his chest. "I fucking love you, Tullz," he says with a laugh. "We're going to be parents. We're having a fucking baby."

I pull back with tears of joy pooling in my eyes as I look up into his intense, stormy eyes. "You're ok with this? You don't hate me?"

"How could I ever hate the woman bringing our child into this world? I'll admit it, I'm a little confused and...shocked maybe, but babe, I'm fucking ecstatic. I knew I wanted this with you since I was eighteen years old and for so long I thought I'd never get it." His hands gently come to rest against my stomach as he stares at it in wonder. "This is a fucking gift, Tullz. You're a fucking gift. I'm just sorry that I haven't been here to help you with it."

"Don't be sorry," I whisper. "As long as I knew that you

were coming home, I could handle just about anything this baby threw my way."

"You're my fucking queen, Tully Cage."

I can't resist him any longer.

I push myself up onto my tippy toes and throw my arms around his neck while pulling him down to meet mine. My lips press against his and for the first time in seven months, I'm finally home.

I've been terrified of telling him about this baby. Most guys would have freaked out. They need time to comprehend this kind of shit and I was scared that he was going to run…well, not permanently, but at least for a few days trying to wrap his head around it, but he didn't. He accepted this baby just as easily as he accepted me back into his life seven months ago.

I knew he wouldn't hold it against me for not saying anything as we have a pretty unordinary situation, but I couldn't stop that feeling that told me that he'd be upset. That he'd think I was hiding this baby from him and that I was purposefully keeping him in the dark, but truth be told, I wanted him focused.

I didn't want him worrying about me throwing up in the middle of the night or suffering from cramps and heartburn. I needed him to concentrate on the mission. I needed his head in the game because being out on the field like the way he has been is life or death. He's not playing out there and because of that, I knew it was safer to ask for forgiveness and let him come to terms with the fact that he was going to be a daddy when he returned.

Besides, there's nothing quite like seeing the look on his face that still hasn't disappeared. He's absolutely elated and I realize that I had nothing to fear. He trusts me completely and knows that no matter what, I would have made the right decision for our child.

His hands circle my waist and he holds me tightly, not for one second letting me slip even an inch away. When he releases my lips and pulls back, my body wants to scream out for more. "How are you feeling?" he questions, studying my face.

"I've never been better."

He grins wide and gently skims his lips over mine. "That's not what I meant and you know it."

I laugh as I watch him still coming to terms with it. "I've been fine. There have been a few rough moments, but nothing that I haven't been able to handle. I didn't want you missing out on anything so I've been taking lots of photos as my belly grew and documenting everything that the doctor has been telling me. I've been really good, Rivers. Eating healthy and exercising as much as I'm allowed."

"I don't doubt that," he murmurs, dropping his gaze down to my stomach once again. "You're going to make an incredible mother."

My eyes fill with tears and I curse the stupid hormones coursing through my body that have turned me into this constant state of unstable emotions. "You really think so?"

"I fucking know so," he tells me before grabbing the hem of my shirt and slowly sliding it up over my stomach. "Let me get a good look at you."

I raise my hands so he can slip the shirt over my head and not a moment later, it's dropped to the floor and his hands are instantly cradling my stomach. "Fuck, Tullz," he says, taking me in with my protruding stomach and swelling breasts. "Pregnancy suits you."

I smile as he drops to his knees before me, placing him directly in line with my stomach. He leans in and presses a kiss to our baby before looking up at me with nothing but pride. "This is really happening."

"It is."

His hands roam over my stomach, caressing it with the utmost care and despite feeling like a cow for the past few months, I've never felt so beautiful. "Have you found out the sex yet?"

I shake my head. "No, the doctor asked, but it didn't feel right without you. I wanted to wait until you were back. I thought we should do that together or maybe wait until I give birth."

"I think we should wait," he agrees. "But what's your gut telling you? Boy or girl?"

I scrunch up my face, thinking about it for the millionth time. "Up until last week, I was thinking it was a little girl, but now I can't help this feeling that's telling me it's a little boy just like his daddy."

Rivers pushes back up to his feet and cradles my face. "No, I think you were right. It's definitely a little girl. Stubborn like her mommy, but when it comes down to it, as long as the baby is healthy and has two parents who love it unconditionally, then it really doesn't matter."

My bottom lip pouts out and I instantly turn into a blubbering mess. "Stop it. You're making me cry," I tell him, fanning my face to try and control the tears. "I've been an emotional wreck."

"Oh, geez," he laughs, taking my hand and leading me back towards the couch. "How many buckets of ice cream have you gone through?"

"None," I snap. "I've been healthy, remember."

Rivers' eyes bulge out of his head. "Shit. I don't know which is more surprising. The fact that you're seven months pregnant or that you haven't been binging on ice cream."

"Shut up," I laugh, swatting his arm.

He falls into the couch, pulling me down beside him while being as gentle as can be. Rivers curls an arm around me, drawing me into his chest when he notices the design on the blanket and the cushion covers. He picks one up and studies it with a fond smile. "Shit. I can't believe you actually did this."

"Yeah, the second the idea popped into my mind; I couldn't resist. I got us matching pajamas too."

"Fuck me," he groans. "I'm assuming you're going to

force me to actually wear them?"

"You're damn right, I am."

Rivers rolls his eyes as I relax deeper into him. "You're fucking lucky that I love you," he murmurs making a wicked grin spread across my face.

"Just you wait until you discover all the other things I've been doing to keep myself busy over these past few months."

A horrified expression cuts across his handsome face before he shakes it off and begins on the questions that I have no doubt have been plaguing his mind over the last seven months. We talk about everything. I tell him step by step how the pregnancy has been, I fill him in on the Spencer and Lacey situation, give him an update on his mom, and share all the juicy gossip on Henley and Noah, though, there really hasn't been much.

He tells me about his mission and while some of it seems downright terrifying, all he manages to do is get me hot. I mean, I'm a woman with needs and after thinking about my badass, soldier boyfriend absolutely killing it out there, I seem to be unable to control myself.

"Come on," I tell him, lacing my fingers through his before pulling myself up off the couch and dragging Rivers along with me "It's getting late. We should go to bed and then we can see everyone in the morning. Candice can cover me, Noah's on a late shift, and I'm sure Henley can go in late. It'd be great to have just the four of us together again."

"Whatever you want, you got, Tullz," he tells me as he follows me down to my bedroom. "But you're right. I should probably head over and see mom after that. I'm sure she's been worried this whole time.

I roll my eyes, thinking about just how understated that comment was. "You have no freaking idea."

"Oh, no," he groans. "I hope she hasn't been bugging you."

"No, not in the least," I tell him. "She's been great. She's so excited about being a grandmother."

A fondness creeps onto his face as his eyes fill with love. "Yeah," he says. "She's going to absolutely love it."

I push open the door of my bedroom and the conversation takes a dive, making me wonder what the hell is going on. I turn back to Rivers and take in his face, only to find it staring at my bedspread with a strange look that has his raging, jealous, alpha side coming out.

Rivers shakes his head before dropping my hand and muttering to himself. "You've got to be fucking kidding me." Not a second later, Rivers storms straight back up the hallway and into the kitchen while I hear him opening and closing drawers until he's striding back down with a pair of scissors.

I realize what his intentions are way too late and before I know it, he's cutting up my Jason Momoa bedspread until there's nothing left and looking down at it with a proud grin for a job well done.

Not a second later, he takes my hand and tugs me towards my bed, being careful not to let me fall. "From now on, I'm the only man you'll ever need in your bed. Got it?"

Well, damn.

Heat floods me. What can I say? There's something incredibly sexy about this man's possessiveness over me. I crawl across the bed until I'm straddled in his lap with his hands at my waist. "You know, I think you might just need to remind me why you're the only man I'll ever need. I seem to have forgotten."

"It would be my fucking pleasure."

With that, he curls his hand up my back until it's circles the back of my neck and he slowly lays me down on the bed. His lips move to my neck and he doesn't stop until the neighbors know his name.

CHAPTER 19

RIVERS

Tully grins down at me from where she straddles my morning wood, though morning probably isn't the right word for it. I've slept half the day away out of pure exhaustion from the past seven months.

Tully rocks her hips forward and briefly closes her eyes at the contact of my hard dick against her pussy, but it's the handcuffs dangling from her fingers that makes me groan.

I don't know about other chicks during pregnancy, but Tully was on fire all night. It's as though she physically couldn't get enough. She was a she-devil and I fucking loved it. But it could also have something to do with the fact that we haven't seen each other in seven months.

Most men would think it's that, but truth be told, it's most likely the hormones making her want it more than usual. But damn, the handcuffs? I mean, if she's down for a little wildness this morning, then I'm right there with her. Whatever she wants, my girl gets. Hell, I don't even care about Henley and Noah coming over shortly, this is a much better way to start to my day.

Tully's hand runs over the top of her baby bump and I can't help but lower my gaze. I still can't fucking believe it.

It almost seems surreal. The last time I saw Tully, she was perfect in every way, and then BAM, she's seven months pregnant. I guess when you're so far away, it's hard to keep track of time, especially when it comes to things like pregnancy. In my head, I was expecting to walk in and see her just the way I left her, but apparently, I left her with a little more than just my heart.

I've never been so happy though.

All my adult life, I've had this fear of finding out that I've knocked up some chick and have to father some woman's baby, but it's Tully and the thought of starting our family now instead of later has me more excited than I've ever been.

We're bringing a child into this world and to be honest, I'm a little scared of fucking it up, but I know with Tully by my side, we're going to be ok. I wasn't lying when I told her that she's going to make an incredible mom. Hell, one day she's also going to make an incredible wife, but one thing at a time, right?

All I know is that she's fucking radiant. She has this beaming glow about her which makes me lose my breath every time I look her way, even in the dark of night, that glow was still radiating out of her. She's beautiful and knowing that my child is growing inside of her is an even better feeling.

I'm going to be a daddy and what's more, I'm going to do everything in my power to make sure that I'm nothing like my father. I'm going to give my child a great life and he or she is going to be the happiest kid in the world.

Tully rocks forward once again and draws me out of my mind. I can't help but reach around and take her perfectly plump ass in my hands. "Do you want to play a game?" she grins, letting the handcuffs swing back and forth on her finger.

I can't resist running my fingers down her side and fall in

love with the way goosebumps rise on her skin. "You fucking bet I do."

"Ok," she says with overwhelming enjoyment in her eyes. "You need to sit up."

I raise a brow, wondering where the hell this is going but if I'm about to have crazy, wild sex with my pregnant girl, then there's no way in hell I'm about to stop to ask questions.

She's running the game and quite frankly, I absolutely love it when she takes charge like this. It's sexy as hell, especially with her breasts that seem to be spilling out of her too small bra.

Have I mentioned how fucking good pregnancy looks on her?

I sit up and watch as her eyes darken with excitement. She holds out a hand, indicating for me to place mine in hers and without a second thought, I play along. She grins wickedly and my morning wood becomes morning fucking steel.

This is going to be fun.

Tully cuffs my wrists and I watch her with intrigued excitement, wondering where she's going with this and how it's going to play out. "Alright," she says, scooting off my lap until I'm sitting alone in her bed. "Now, I need you to step your feet over the top of your hands."

My brows crease as I look up at her. "What?"

"Just do it," she pleads, giving me those big puppy dog eyes that I can't seem to resist.

I let out a confused huff and do what she says. After all, I've heard the stories about what could come from disappointing a pregnant woman and that's something I'm not so inclined to do.

I watch her, as she kneels forward and pushes me back. "I need you to lay down."

Again, like a good little boy; I follow orders.

With my hands cuffed under the back of my legs, I start to wonder what's actually going on, but all trace of thought leaves me as she slides off the bed and looks down at me like a hungry lioness, ready to pounce.

I mean, I can't say that I've ever been handcuffed before, but in my head, my hands would be cuffed to the bedposts or something like that, not cuffed together where I can still move around.

Her grin widens. "Put your feet up."

"I'm sorry…what?"

"Just do it."

I think this through…if my feet are up in the air and I'm handcuffed, then that leaves my ass extremely vulnerable and I know Tully likes to get a little wild in the bedroom, but I'm not quite sure I'm down for that. "You're not planning on sticking something in my ass, are you?"

"What?" she balks out laughing. "No. I mean, not unless you want me to?"

"No thanks."

"I'm glad we got that sorted, now put your feet up in the air."

"Why though?"

"Just do it already," she laughs.

I let out a groan as I quickly realize that maybe I've been a little misled. I don't think she's in here to get down and dirty and something tells me that maybe I've been playing right into her game, but hell, I'm curious and I'm certainly not one to disappoint.

With a groan, I lift my feet off the bed and watch her carefully, trying to work out her plan. She dips down beside the bed until I can't see her and emerges a second later with a bucket of water. "What the hell are you doing?"

"You'll see," she says with that mischievous sparkle in her eye that I love so damn much.

"You better not be about to pour that on me."

She gasps, feigning horror as she steps up to the end of the bed. "Would I do that?"

"Yeah, actually. You would."

Her response is a devilish smirk that has me wanting

nothing more than to jump off this bed and run the fuck away, but in this position, it won't be that easy. Tully raises the bucket and places it on the bottom of my feet. "Make it balance," she instructs me as I shake my head.

"Don't tell me that you're leaving that fucking bucket there."

"You know," she says, slowly stepping away from me while making sure the bucket is safely balanced above me. "I've spent the last seven months picturing you on a tropical beach, having the time of your life while I've been at home missing you, and you know what? I think a little payback is in order."

With that, she pulls the keys for the handcuffs out of the side of her bra, drops them in the bucket and walks over to me. "Don't you dare leave," I warn her.

Tully kneels on the side of the bed and dips her face before pressing a feather-soft kiss on my lips. "I love you," she murmurs. "Don't spill any of that water on my bed."

With that, she walks out of the room, laughing the whole way down the hallway.

"Tully?" I yell. "Get that fine ass back here and take this damn bucket off me."

"Sorry," she calls back with laughter strong in her voice. "I can't hear you."

That little…

I find myself laughing. If anyone walked in here right now, what they'd see…fuck. I look like a fool, which is exactly what I am. I should have known she was going to hold me accountable for the past seven months, which I deserve. I just didn't know it was going to be in the form of playing pranks.

But…she should know me better than that and after the training I've had over the past four years, this isn't exactly a situation that I'm unable to get myself out.

I mean, it's not exactly going to be easy. I'm not the most flexible mother fucker around, but I can make it work without spilling even a drop of water because I plan to turn this game right around. No one, not even Tully Cage, will get the best of me.

I pull my knees right down to my chest and shimmy my cuffed hands up the back of my legs, watching the bucket in fear as one wrong move will have that bastard falling on my face and that's not exactly how I plan on waking up.

I get my hands over my feet and catch the bucket as I go, feeling so fucking proud of myself. I get up off the bed and place the bucket down on Tully's bedside table before fishing through the freezing water for the key and freeing my wrists.

I do it as quickly and as quietly as I can before taking the handcuffs and the bucket before sneaking out of the room with the kind of stealth that I'd use on one of my missions.

I stop at the end of the hallway and listen out. She must be in the kitchen.

Peeking around the corner, I find Tully with her back to me and way too much of a skip in her step. She's proud of herself and that has me the happiest mother fucker who ever lived. She thinks I'm still lying in bed with my feet in the air and a bucket of water dangling dangerously over my face.

If only she knew that I have her cornered.

With the bucket under my arm, I step into the kitchen behind her and place the bucket down before creeping into her back. The moment she realizes that I'm free, her back stiffens, but with her bump in front and me at her back, she's got nowhere to go.

I take her wrists and she sucks in a breath as I cuff her hands behind her back. "Oh…" she laughs. "You're free."

"Mmhmm," I grumble, leaning forward and pressing my lips to her neck. "That wasn't a very nice game. I think you need to be punished."

She sucks in another breath. "Really, now?"

"Uh-huh."

I grin to myself as I pull her a step away from the counter before leaning her over it and making sure the bump is as safe as can be. I run my fingers up the inside of her thigh, loving the way a groan slips from between her lips and with my hand remaining on her back, I reach across and grab hold of the bucket.

I step in behind her, letting her feel my erection against her ass and hold back a groan of my own as she pushes back into me, wanting more, but that's going to have to wait.

I place the bucket on the top of her ass and watch as her body stiffens. "What are you doing?" she demands with her hands flailing around, trying to grab hold of the bucket that's just out of her reach.

"You didn't think I was really going to let you get away with that, did you?"

"You're an ass."

"Damn straight, babe," I tell her grabbing hold of her ass and squeezing it, loving how despite the bucket on her back and the fury radiating out of her eyes, she's still incredibly turned on.

As soon as she gets herself free of this mess, I'm going to have to do something about that. After all, I can't have my pregnant girlfriend running around with an itch that needs to be scratched.

I stand back and watch the show as she huffs and grumbles all sorts of curses under her breath before she waddles towards the sink and somehow manages to throw the bucket off while making it tip towards the sink. Water goes everywhere, but for the most part, it heads for the drain. The kitchen is going to need a few towels though.

Tully straightens herself out and turns on me with a ferocious glare as she pulls on her cuffed wrists. "You're dead, you know that, right?"

"Whatever you've got for me, babe, just remember that I'll outdo you every single time." With the water on the floor, pooling at her feet, I step into her with the key and turn her around to free her wrist. I lean into her and nuzzle into her neck. "Bring it on, Tullz. I'm ready for you."

Her body sags into mine and my arm curls around her waist. Her ass is pushed back into me and not a moment later, I bend her over the counter and give her exactly what we've both been needing.

I scoot around the kitchen with a towel beneath my feet as Tully works on cleaning all the spilled water off the counter. She did a fucking good job of making sure that it went everywhere.

I finish off on the floor and throw the wet towels into the laundry room before going and helping Tully with the counter. Naturally, I can't keep my hands off her or her bump. Every time I look at her, she takes my fucking breath away. I can't believe this is happening, but more so, I can't wait to show her the surprise that I have for her.

Tully's surprise was fucking huge, so there's no way I'll be able to outdo a child, but I've got something up my sleeve that I'm hoping was the right move. Otherwise...I don't know. I hope I don't screw things up before we've even had a real chance of getting started.

Just as we finish putting the kitchen back together and get some proper clothes on, there's a knock at the door that has a wide smile spreading across my face.

My fucking pack is here.

Tully skips out of the bedroom while pulling a shirt over her head and makes her way to the door as I trail behind her, keeping my eyes on her perfect ass.

We get to the door to find Henley and Noah standing before us. Henley is barely able to control her excitement and barges past her best friend before throwing her arms around me. "You're home," she squeals.

"Damn straight, I'm home," I grin, spinning her around before helping her find her feet.

She moves aside as Noah comes in and takes her place,

pulling me into his arms and clapping his hand against my back. "It's good to see you," he chimes. "How the fuck have you been?"

"Who cares about that?" Henley laughs, looking up at me. "You're having a baby. I'm going to be an aunt!"

I look across to Tully who can't wipe the grin off her face as she pushes her brother and me out of the doorway so she can close the door. "Would you all stop crowding my door?" she says. "The neighbors are bound to complain about the noise."

"What are you talking about?" Henley says, scrunching her face at Tully. "You have great neighbors."

Tully's face flames. "Yeah, that was until Rivers and I kind of kept them up all night."

Noah shakes his head and walks towards Tully's couch, dropping down and pulling a stick figure cushion out from behind his back. "I can't unhear that," he says. "I liked it better when you were with Spencer and kept all that shit to yourself."

"What can I say?" Tully laughs, practically skipping towards her brother and dropping down beside him. "I'm happy and when I'm happy the whole fucking world needs to hear about it."

"Shit," he groans, sliding down on the couch. "I can't even pretend to be upset about that. This is only the beginning, isn't it?"

Tully looks across at me with a beaming smile. "It sure is."

I drop down on the opposite couch and my pack instantly falls into mindless chatter. I can't help but feel that I've finally come full circle. My group is together again and this time, nothing is standing in the way of us being the incredible four that we used to be.

I never thought I'd be so happy to have normal back, except this is a much better version of normal. I have my girl by my side with my child growing in her stomach. I no longer have to worry about where I'm going to sleep at night, if I'm going to accidentally run into my father on the streets, or who's keeping Tully warm at night. No, I'll never have to worry about that shit ever again. This new version of normal is more than I could ever ask for. It's fucking perfect and for the first time in my life, I'm content.

I have a home now, well sort of. My father is in prison and my mother is right where she should be. And Tully; the most important one of all, is finally standing by my side, willing to live the rest of her life with me, willing to bare my children, and love me until our dying days.

How could I want more in life?

There's only a slight chance that over next few years that I could be deployed again, but I've done my time. I've served my four years and now I have another four years of reserve, but if Tully wanted me to, I'd leave the military. I hope she doesn't, though. I know going away sucks and will be hard, especially with a child to think about, but the Military is my home, just as much as Tully is.

The Military offered me the freedom that I couldn't find anywhere else and no matter what, I'm always going to be grateful for that.

"So," Henley says, stealing my attention. "Has Tully shown you all the progress photos of her bump growing?"

I grin as I look to Tully before glancing down at the bump she's currently cradling. "No, we've, uh...been a little preoccupied."

Noah groans again as Tully shoots to her feet and grabs a folder off her dining table. Not a second later, she comes to sit down on my lap and I can't help but rest my hands against her thighs as she opens the folders and starts showing me every tiny little detail.

She starts right from the beginning where she first discovered her pregnancy. She was at work and the smell of the flowers was overbearing and making her nauseous. She came home early, laid down in bed and after watching a movie on Netflix, she realized that her period was late. She instantly took a test, and the very next page has a picture of the positive piss stick.

I flip through each page, learning about her doctor visits, and taking in the ultrasound pictures. I watch with emotions that I can't quite make sense of as I see her bump steadily growing.

I focus on a photo of Tully at four months. She stands in Noah and Henley's living room, but I can't shake the feeling that something looks different than the last time I was in that room and then it clicks. I look up at Noah. "You got a new couch."

"Yeah," he chuckles. "I had to get rid of the last one after what you two did on it."

"What?" I laugh as Tully rolls her eyes. "But we didn't fuck on it. I thought you knew that."

"I do, but now that Tully's pregnant, I didn't think I'd ever be able to look at my niece or nephew without thinking about the fact that it all started on my couch. So, yeah. I got rid of it. Some dude living in his mother's basement owns it now."

I shake my head. "You're a fucking idiot, man," I laugh. "What's going on with you? Last I heard you were thinking about applying for a promotion. Was it the fire chief or something like that?"

He nods. "Yeah, that's right. I was offered the position, but after a bit of thinking, I turned it down. Maybe in another ten years or so I'd be happy to push papers around my desk, but not yet. I like what I do too much and why fix something that isn't broke?"

"Good call. Though, something tells me it's because you like playing hero too much."

Noah scoffs. "Like you're one to talk. Do I need to remind you where the fuck you've been for the past five years?"

"Four and a half," I correct.

Tully scoffs and rams her elbow back into me. "Trust me.

It's closer to five."

I grab hold of her, wrapping my arm more firmly around her only to feel our baby inside of her, kicking at my arm. Tully grins down at me. "Do you feel that?"

"Fuck yeah, I do. That's incredible."

"Yeah, just wait until I have to push it out."

"Fuck me," I gasp, sucking in a breath. I hadn't thought about that. It's going to be horrifying. Not the actual birth, but Tully. She's going to be a fucking monster and I'll have no choice but to stand by her side and let her tear me limb from limb, but then I wouldn't have it any other way.

The door opens and not a moment later, Aiden comes strolling in with Barker, actually looking happy for a change and announces to the world that they've finally decided to make it work.

Tully shoots up off my lap with Henley and the four of them do some sort of happy dance while Noah and I just stare on, wondering what the fuck is going on.

It turns into a party. Tully calls Candice and tells her that she's not coming in and warns her that if she burns down her store, she'll hunt her down and kill her. Henley calls in sick while Noah just goes with the flow as his shift doesn't start until tonight.

Spencer comes over with Lacey and for the first time, I don't feel like kicking his ass. Maybe Tully was onto something this whole time about him not being such a bad guy. Though, he's dating my cousin now so it's not as though I'm going to take my eyes off him.

By the time night falls and everyone leaves, I'm left watching my girl and realize that I don't want to wait another minute. I walk up behind her in the kitchen and reach around her to turn off the taps; the dishes can wait. "Will you come somewhere with me?" I murmur, kissing her cheek. "I've got a surprise of my own."

Tully turns in my arms, looking up at me with her big eyes. "What kind of surprise?"

"You're just going to have to wait and see."

CHAPTER 20

TULLY

Where the hell is he taking me? When he asked me to come with him for a surprise, I figured he wanted me to go to the bedroom with him again. After all, he only got back last night and he hasn't left my apartment. It's not as though he's gone anywhere to organize a surprise. Yet here I am, sitting in the passenger side of his shiny Dodge RAM wondering where the hell he's taking me.

Rivers looks across at me with the same sparkle in his eyes that hasn't gone away since we left my apartment. "Would you quit thinking so hard?"

"I can't help it," I complain. "I'm confused. I don't know what the hell is going on or where you're taking me? I mean, I declared a freaking prank war on you this morning. Who knows what's about to go down? You know," I continue, realizing that I need to stop, but finding that an impossible task. "Stress isn't good for the baby."

"Just two more minutes and we'll be there."

"Two more minutes?" I grunt, looking out the window,

but not really seeing much as it's after nightfall and I have only the street lights to go by. "We're in the middle of residential streets. Where could you be taking me? There's nothing out here but houses."

Rivers grins, taking pleasure in my confusion. "You'll see," he promises me, reaching out and taking my hand in his before lacing our fingers together just as they should be.

I groan and fall back into the seat. Have I ever mentioned that I don't handle surprises very well? I'm more than happy to make other people suffer through the knowledge of a surprise, but when it comes to me? Hard pass.

The Dodge RAM comes to a stop on the curb in a road filled with residential homes and I look around, trying to find some sort of clue as to why the hell we're here. There are no stores around, no cafes or restaurants, no parks. It's clear as day that Rivers has just lost his mind...unless there's someone in one of these houses that he's taking me to meet? Hmm, I wonder who it could be? Maybe someone from his past.

I start looking around at the few homes we could possibly be visiting and decide to settle on the one to my right as something about it is...I don't know, familiar. I just can't work out why.

Rivers jumps down from his truck before racing around to help me down. I mean, any other time I'd be jumping from this thing like a pro, but with this baby growing inside of me, I'm taking every precaution to be careful.

Rivers leads me towards the house and I take it all in. There's a pathway that's dividing a beautiful yard, a fence around the perimeter, and beautiful hedges the whole way around.

I look a little harder, confused as all hell while trying to place it. Why can't I figure this out?

As we step up to the front door and Rivers raises his hand, I find myself pulling back on him. "Where are we?" I whisper yell as to not embarrass myself in case the person we're visiting inside can hear.

Rivers looks down at me, watching me as the sparkle in his eyes seems to shine so much brighter. A sheepish expression crosses his features and he looks back out at the yard with pride. "So, I sort of did something."

My eyes narrow on him. "What are you talking about?"

"Do you remember the night before I was deployed?"

"Yeah," I say as my eyes narrow further. "We were looking at home listings."

He nods slowly as if waiting for me to understand something and as I look back out at the property and rake my eyes over the brick home, it finally dawns on me. "This is the house you were looking at."

"Yeah," he smiles. "When I left, I couldn't stop thinking about that night and what I was feeling while we were looking at this listing."

"What do you mean?"

"That look in your eyes," he tells me. "When we were looking at it, it was as though you could see our future here. You could see us being together and raising our family, and the second that happened, I couldn't let this home slip through my fingers."

"You're losing me again," I tell him.

"I bought it."

"What? How? You've been away."

"Don't you worry about that," he tells me. "Just know that I bought this home and I know we've hardly begun, but nothing would make me happier than having you move in here with me where we can raise our baby together. Hell, maybe have another and a few dogs like I know you've always wanted."

Tears well in my eyes as I look up at him. "I've always wanted a bunny rabbit too."

"I'll get you a fucking tribe of bunny rabbits if that's what you want."

I look back at the house. "You really bought this?"

"I sure did, Tullz. I want to build a life with you. I was

planning on waiting to ask you to move in with me, but the second I laid eyes on you, I knew that was never going to happen. I need you with me now." Rivers rests his hands against my bump. "You're my everything, Tully, and you've made my world so much bigger with this child. I want to do this right and I don't want to wait."

"You're crazy," I tell him as the tears fall from my eyes. "I can't believe you did this."

"What do you say?" he questions slowly, making me realize that he's actually a little nervous about this.

I push up onto my tippy toes and throw my arms around his neck before drawing him in and kissing him with everything that I've got. "There isn't even a question in my mind. Nothing in this world could possibly make me happier," I tell him. "Of course, I'll move in with you."

Rivers straightens as he looks down at me, searching my eyes. "Are you serious? This isn't another prank and you're about to pull the rug out from under me?"

"No," I laugh. "I'm serious. I want to be here with you. I want to start our family in the right way and I want to give you everything you've ever wanted. I love you so much, Rivers. I've never been so damn happy."

He grins like a thirteen-year-old boy watching his first porn before pulling me in hard and crushing his lips against mine. He kisses me until my knees go weak and when he finally finds the strength to pull back, he takes my hand and practically rushes through the door.

As we walk around our new home, we take it in with wide eyes. This is the first time Rivers has walked through it too, so really, he took a bit of a risk buying the place without checking it out, but the risk paid off. This home is beautiful.

There are three bedrooms and the second I peek my head into the smaller one, I instantly see the nursery and joy overtakes me. We have two months before this baby comes so we have a lot of work to do to make this place perfect for this baby, but we can do it. I don't care about the other rooms, as long as my baby has a beautiful room to sleep in each night, I'll be happy.

The rest of the house gives me 'the feels' just as it had when I was looking at the listing all those months ago.

There's space for a pool out the back with that beautiful tree that creates just enough shade over the yard. I can picture our summers playing out there, splashing around while soccer balls go flying. Maybe we could even build a cubby house for the kids in the tree. There's a double garage with room for Rivers' to finally start working on his Freebird and space for me to have my own little reading nook.

Nothing has ever been so perfect.

As we finish walking around, I realize that there wasn't a hint of hesitation within me. I knew the second he asked that this is what I wanted. In fact, I've always known, but fuck, I'm not going to lie. This is one hell of a surprise. I wasn't expecting this though I had a feeling that over the next few months we'd talk about it, but we'd never get around to it and keep living in my apartment because we'd be busy with the baby.

Fuck me. He just blew my freaking mind.

Once we finish taking it all in, we find ourselves sitting out on the back deck, though without any furniture out here, we're left to sit on the floor, but I don't mind.

Rivers' arm circles my waist as he pulls me into him and rests his other hand against the baby that's been using my rib cage for target practice. "This is the beginning of our future, Tullz," he tells me. "We're going to be happy here."

I lean my head into his shoulder. "We are," I sigh. "But I'm already happy."

"I know," he tells me before looking down at me with a seriousness that's enough to have anyone pulling back in concern. "How do you feel about all this if I were to be deployed again?"

I press my lips together before looking out at the to-be pool once again. I consider my answer for a moment, trying to picture how I'd handle it. "You once told me that this is the life you signed up for and it's because of that life that I get to now have you in mine. If you were to get deployed again, I'm not going to lie, I don't know how I'd handle it. It would be hard and I'd have to learn how to single parent for a while, but I can see how much you love that part of your life and I'd never take that away from you. So, yeah, I'll adapt, but let's just hope that they let you stay home for a while."

He nods and draws me back into him. "Thank you," he murmurs. "You're right. I do love being in the military, but if you wanted me to or if it was too hard, you know I'd leave. In a fucking heartbeat. I'd do anything for you."

"I know you would, but you need to remember that I'd do anything for you too and being in the Military is a part of who you are, and I'd never force you to make that choice. I went into this knowing that deployment is a possibility and if and when it happens, we'll work it out, but for now, let's just focus on starting our lives together."

"I fucking love you so much," he tells me.

I press my lips together, unsure how to tell him what I need to say, but feel that while we're discussing our future, now's probably the right time to get it off my chest.

"What's wrong?" he asks me.

I shake my head, looking up at him. "Nothing's wrong," I tell him. "It's just…I kind of did something while you were gone too." His brows pull down and concern begins to flood his eyes. I hurry in to ease his worry, but truth be told, I really don't know how he's going to take this. "It's not bad," I promise. "It's just that…I'm not entirely sure that it's something you're ready to discuss."

Relief has his shoulder lowering as he relaxes back into me. "What is it, babe?"

I swallow back my fear and decide to just get it over and done with. "Do you remember that day we were sitting in my car outside 'Read My Tulips' and you were telling me about…"

He nods, finishing my sentence. "About my past."

"Yeah…well, you had told me there were two children that day and that…"

"I never knew what happened to them."

"I found them," I tell him, rushing out the words to get it over and done with. "I had this need to check up on them and make sure they were doing alright. Your story hit something within me and…I'm sorry, I should have talked to you about this first, but you were gone and I…"

"You found them?"

I nod, looking up into his eyes that seem so far away. "I did and they're doing ok."

"Are…" his words fall short and I realize that he's not sure of what he wants to know or if he's really ready to know, but in order for him to heal and move forward, sometimes hearing a bit of good news can help heal wounds that you didn't realize were still gaping wide open.

"Their names are Skylah and Blake. And you were right, after they lost their parents, life really sucked. I haven't worked out exactly what Anton had done with them, but they popped up on the radar last year. They must have been able to get away from wherever it was they were as there's nothing on them before that. It looks like they're living in Aston Creek now with family."

"Aston Creek?" Rivers questions. "That's only a few hours from here."

"Yeah, I know. I looked that up too."

"How did you find all this stuff out?"

I shrug my shoulders. "I mean, I had to do some pretty epic investigating and searching to try and figure out their names, but once I did, it all pretty much came out on Facebook."

"So, you think they looked happy?"

"I'm not sure, to be honest. They looked as though they've seen way too much for their age, but they also look like fighters. They're ok, Rivers. They made it through the other end just like you did."

He takes my hand and laces his fingers through mine. "Thank you, Tully," he murmurs. "Those two pop up in my dreams every now and then. It's good to know that they're doing better."

I nod as my head falls to his shoulder. "Maybe one day we could go and visit them."

"I don't know, Tullz. I'm the monster in their story just as Anton was the monster in mine. A visit would probably do me good, but this is about them and I don't want to cause them any more pain than what I've already done. Let's leave them be and hope that one day, they can find their own happiness."

I take hold of his chin and draw his face to mine before brushing my lips over his. "You really are the most selfless, incredible man I've ever met," I tell him. "I'm the luckiest girl in the world to have you loving me the way you do."

"No," he says, shaking his head. "I'm the lucky one. Now, what do you say we christen this place?"

"You don't want to wait until we have a bit of furniture?" I grin as his lips come down against mine.

"No way," he laughs, falling to the deck and bringing me down with him. "What can I say? I'm a friendly guy and it would only be polite if we let the neighbors know exactly who we are."

I shake my head, grinning down at the man who has made me feel every tiny emotion humanly possible since the day I first met him.

This next part of my life is going to be the biggest adventure that I'll ever live through and I can't wait.

EPILOGUE

TULLY

I pass my little Lily Rivers off to my mom as I work on shoving my tits back inside my shirt. This whole breastfeeding thing is really not as beautiful as all the books suggest. I mean, there's a human being sucking on my tits most hours of the day. It was hard enough with just Rivers insisting on having them in his mouth, but now I have this tiny little human who insists on squeezing my nipple between her little toothless gums. I mean, fuck, give a woman a break. That shit actually hurts, but I wouldn't change it for anything.

The past two months since her birth have flown by. I can't believe just how quickly it's gone. It feels like only yesterday that Rivers and I were in that hospital room cursing each other out. Though, if you asked him, he'd say that I was the one doing the cursing. But here we are, two months in and absolutely in love with this beautiful little creature that we've brought into this world.

I'm not going to lie, it's been incredibly hard and I don't know how I would have done it without Rivers, but something tells me that it's only going to get worse from here. I mean, mom keeps telling me these horror stories about teething and poo explosions that go right up their backs, and honestly, I'm a little freaked out.

So far, we've suffered through the sleepless nights, the torturous days where she wouldn't feed properly, and of course, the dreaded sore tummy.

Rivers has been great with everything and has been there every step of the way, making sure I have everything I need. He had told me that he feels a little useless at the moment as it's always me having to get up in the night to do the feeds with her, but he couldn't be more wrong. He's always the first to get up to change her diapers and always the one rushing in and taking her away when it's time for her sleep.

He loves being a daddy just as much as I love being her mommy.

If I'm completely honest with myself. I feel like a hot mess. My hair hasn't been brushed in two months, I'm still wearing my maternity pants, and I accidentally poured breast milk into my cereal instead of the full cream milk I'd only gotten out of the fridge two seconds before.

But I feel myself slowly coming back. The more confident we become with this little girl, the easier it is for me to make it through each day, and really, I shouldn't be complaining; she's an excellent sleeper. In fact, she downright loves her sleep. She must get that from me.

I get my boob situation sorted and make sure I'm not about to start leaking everywhere like I did while I was out at dinner two nights ago and completely embarrass myself. Once everything is where it needs to be, I look up at mom to find her propping Lily up over her shoulder and helping her to burp to avoid those damn tummy aches, and just like her father, she does it loud and proud.

I've been trying to focus on myself a little more over the past two days and finally convinced myself to start walking in the hopes of finding my previous sexy body, so that's exactly what I've been doing.

I got the stroller set up, got Lily dressed and ready for an outing, and pulled on my runners before packing every tiny item in my house that lily could possibly need in the hour or so that we'll be out. I kissed Rivers and he spanked my ass before helping me out the door with the stroller.

It started great. I walked for about fifteen minutes, humming to a little '5 Seconds of Summer' when I turned down Noah and Henley's road. I had all intentions of walking straight past, but when I saw mom's car parked out front, I found myself taking a little detour.

And that's exactly where I've been for the past three hours.

Poor Rivers, he's probably worried sick about me, either that or he has fallen asleep on the couch and completely lost track of time.

I stand up from Noah's back deck and hold my hands out for Lily when mom scoffs at me and adjusts her in her arms to put her off to sleep. "Get your own baby," she tells me in a baby voice as she looks down at my little angel. "This one is mine."

I roll my eyes. I guess I won't be seeing Lily for a few hours. She'll end up sleeping in mom's arms and that's exactly where she'll stay until I physically have to steal her back.

Not wanting to miss the opportunity to have this rare time to myself, I slip in through the backdoor and find my way to Noah and Henley's kitchen, knowing they have all sorts of goodies hiding in here.

I mean, screw the diet. I was careful during my pregnancy, I deserve to treat myself. After all, I did push a watermelon out of my lady bits and it wasn't pretty. I can cry about my weight tomorrow while Rivers holds me and reminds me that I'm still the most beautiful woman he knows.

God, my man is such a suck-up, but it works every damn time.

As I rummage through the freezer and find the emergency tub of ice cream that Henley always keeps in here for me, I hear the familiar sounds of Noah and Rivers' hushed conversation coming from just outside the open front door.

I grin to myself. I should have known he'd come looking for me.

I grab myself a spoon and flop down onto the couch which Rivers and I are yet to christen and dig in as I try to find a little peace and quiet. Only the boys' stupid conversation is a little too hard to tune out. Do they realize just how far their voices carry? They're not discreet at all.

I groan to myself and jump up. If I intend to have any quiet, then that front door needs to be closed.

As I make my way across the living room, their conversation has me slowing down. "Dude, check this out," Rivers murmurs, trying to be quiet.

There's a short pause before Noah booms out. "Holy fuck. You bought it."

Bought it? Bought what?

"Yeah, man. I hope she fucking likes it. I've been staring at these goddamn rings for weeks trying to figure out which is the best one for her."

Wait...did he just say rings? As in...

"She's going to love it," Noah murmurs proudly. "When are you going to pop the question?"

"As soon as I fucking can," Rivers says.

My mouth drops open as I listen to what must be one of those bro, black clap things. "Fuck, yeah," Noah hollers. "She's going to be so fucking pissed that I knew about this before her."

I can't stop my feet from moving.

I throw myself out the door and stare at Rivers who looks like a fucking deer caught in headlights. "We're getting married?" I squeal, my heart racing a million miles an hour.

Rivers' mouth drops open and I watch as he struggles to

find what the hell to say when he's saved by an ear-shattering squeal coming from inside the house.

Noah, Rivers, and I glance around at each other before making a break for it. The only person it could have been is Henley and a scream like that tells me something is incredibly wrong.

The three of us barge down the hallway, searching her out until we're practically breaking down the bathroom door. "What's wrong?" I demand as I rush in to find Henley slumped on the ground with none other than a pregnancy test clutched between her fingers.

Her head whips around as she singles out my brother. "YOU," she yells, flying to her feet and pointing him out. "YOU IMPREGNATED ME WITH YOUR DEVIL SPAWN."

My mouth drops open as I look back at Noah. "I, umm. What?"

Henley starts flailing around as elation fills me. "How could you?" she cries, throwing her hands up before tossing the pregnancy test at Noah. "I don't want to be pregnant. I'm not finished being a Rockstar yet."

"You're...?"

"I'm not even a grown-up yet," she continues, ignoring Noah's freak out, though come to think of it, he hasn't moved a muscle. "And now I have to be someone's mom? I can't be a mom! I'm just a kid."

"You're nearly twenty-three," I cut in, finding her meltdown a little too amusing.

Henley shoots a sharp glare my way. "Shut up, you."

I zip my lips.

"What am I going to do?"

Rivers elbows Noah in the ribs and when he gets no response, he takes over. He walks straight into the bathroom and collects Henley in his big arms. "You're not wrong," he tells her. "You're not finished being a Rockstar, but look at Tully, having a child and absolutely rocking it. It makes you stronger. You're ready for this, and despite Noah's inability to form a sentence right now, he's ready for this too. Besides, you practically raised your little sister. You already know what to do. You two are going to make incredible parents, you know, right behind me and Tully, of course."

Henley's brows dip down as she pulls out of Rivers' arms. "Excuse me?" she demands. "That's bullshit. Me and Noah are going to kick your asses at parenting."

"No," I shake my head. "Me and Rivers have this mommy/daddy thing down."

"Really?" she laughs as tears spring to her eyes. "Do I need to remind you that you were putting Lily's diaper on backward for the first week of her life? Noah and I are going to whip your asses."

"Uhh…" Noah grumbles, seeming to swallow back fear. "Yeah, we've got this."

He steps into the bathroom and walks right up to Henley before taking her shoulders and looking down at her, but there's no mistaking the excitement in his eyes. "Are you sure that you're really pregnant?"

She nods. "Yeah. At least, that's what the test says. I checked it a few times just to be sure."

"And…you want this?"

"I mean, it wasn't exactly part of my plan. I wanted to wait another three, maybe four years, but if these idiots can make it work, then I don't see why we can't too."

"FUCK, YEAH!" Noah booms, grabbing his wife and crushing her body against his. "WE'RE HAVING A FUCKING BABY. This is the best goddamn day of my life. First Tully and Rivers are getting married and now this. YES!"

Henley grabs Noah's arms and rips herself out of his hold and she looks to me and Rivers. "Wait. What do you mean they're getting married?"

I grin. "I just busted Rivers showing Noah the ring."

"WHAT?" she screeches as she starts jumping up and

down. "You're getting married?"

I shrug before turning and looking up at Rivers with a cringe. "I mean…are we?"

A beaming smile overtakes his handsome face as he curls his hand around my waist. "I was planning on giving you the big proposal like I know you want, but I guess that's kind of ruined now. But, baby, it's in your hands. If you say yes then you better fucking believe it, we're getting married because I can't go another day not knowing that you'll be my wife."

I throw myself up into his arms and lock my legs around his waist. "Yes, of course. I want to marry you so freaking bad."

"You'll be my wife?" he questions, his lips hovering just above mine with a wide, proud grin.

"Yes, I'll be your wife." Rivers' lips come down on mine and he kisses me greedily while Henley squeals in excitement behind us.

I find myself pulling back as I ignore the high-pitched screeching coming from my best friend. I look up into the eyes of the man who will soon become my husband. "Just so you know, I'm not getting around and telling people that I got engaged in a bathroom. That's not the kind of standards I want to set for our little girl, so I'm still going to need the big, over-the-top proposal."

Rivers shakes his head as the amusement shines brightly in his eyes. "Why am I not surprised?"

I can't help but laugh. "Does being husband and wife truly mean that there are no secrets between us?"

"Sure does," he says, narrowing his eyes.

I look across to my brother and give him a tight smile. "Sorry, Noah. I guess this means that I have no choice but to tell Rivers what those five items were that you guys bought from Kitty Kat's Play House."

Noah's face falls and the rest of ours light up with a sick enjoyment. "No," he gasps before turning on his wife accusingly. "You told her?"

"Ahh, shit. I knew that was going to come back and bite me in the ass," Henley cringes. "But now that Rivers is back, technically we can pick up where we left off. Whose turn is it?"

"Mine," Noah rushes in before turning his devilish gaze on me. "Truth or fucking dare, Tully Cage?"

Well, shit!

ABOUT THE AUTHOR

Sheridan Anne is a wife to a smart-ass husband, Mumma to two beautiful girls, twin sister, daughter, and friend who lives in beautiful Australia. Sheridan writes both romance and young adult fantasy books on a variety of topics and can be found on most days with her family or writing during naptime. To find out more or to simply say 'hello', connect with her on Facebook.

www.facebook.com/SheridanAnneAuthor/

SERIES BY SHERIDAN ANNE

The Guard Trilogy

Kings of Denver

Denver Royalty

Rebels Advocate

Broken Hill High

Haven Falls

SHERIDAN ANNE

Made in the USA
Middletown, DE
24 December 2019